SPIRITS AND SMOKE

Also by Mary Miley

Roaring Twenties mysteries

THE IMPERSONATOR
SILENT MURDERS
RENTING SILENCE *
MURDER IN DISGUISE *

The Mystic's Accomplice mysteries

THE MYSTIC'S ACCOMPLICE *

* *available from Severn House*

SPIRITS AND SMOKE

Mary Miley

First world edition published in Great Britain in 2021 and the USA in 2022
by Severn House, an imprint of Canongate Books Ltd,
14 High Street, Edinburgh EH1 1TE.

Trade paperback edition first published in Great Britain and the USA in 2022
by Severn House, an imprint of Canongate Books Ltd.

severnhouse.com

British Library Cataloguing-in-Publication Data
A CIP catalogue record for this title is available from the British Library.

ISBN-13: 978-0-7278-5043-0 (cased)
ISBN-13: 978-1-4483-0633-6 (trade paper)
ISBN-13: 978-1-4483-0632-9 (e-book)

Typeset by Palimpsest Book Production Ltd.,
Falkirk, Stirlingshire.

ONE

Officer Kevin O'Rourke's eyebrows shot up when he saw me answer Madame Carlotta's front door. I was shocked to see him too, but I'm better at concealing my reactions.

'Mrs Pastore? I-I wasn't expecting – that is . . . I thought you . . .' O'Rourke looked up and down our quiet residential street as if he'd lost his dog.

'Good day to you, officer. You were thinking I lived at Mrs Jones's boarding house,' I said helpfully, 'and you were right, at least until last week when I moved here.'

Clearly he'd not come to see me. I waited for him to state his business, but he seemed reluctant to spill the beans. Some people are like that when it comes to dealing with mystics. They're nervous or embarrassed or suspicious or afraid of looking foolish.

'I've come to talk to Madame Carlotta Romany, if you please. She lives here, doesn't she? I was given this address.'

'She does indeed. Madame Carlotta stepped out to market, but that was over an hour ago, so I expect her back at any moment. Would you like to come into the parlor, out of the cold, and wait for her?'

He gave a grateful nod, so I opened the door wider to admit him. An unwelcome blast of frigid air came with him. Today the gusts off Lake Michigan were blowing sharp enough to cut through the thickest wool a lamb could grow, skimming some of the fallen snow off the drifts and driving it sideways, making it hard to see the row houses across the street. Lots of people think this is why they call Chicago 'the windy city', but the truth is, the nickname came about because of our windy politicians who never stop speechifying.

'Yes, ma'am, much appreciated,' he said, brushing the snow-flakes off his broad shoulders and removing his cap before crossing the threshold. He was a big Irishman with ruddy cheeks, blue eyes, an unruly mass of sandy hair dented where his cap had pressed, and an accent that showed no trace of the old country, meaning he had probably grown up here in Chicago's large Irish community.

'You can wait in here,' I said, as he stamped the snow off his galoshes onto the hall rug. Madame Carlotta, convinced she was the reincarnation of a gypsy queen, had furnished the parlor to reinforce her dubious ancestral claims: blood-red velvet upholstery throughout, a bold Turkish carpet, marble-top tables cluttered with statuettes of angels and the Virgin Mary, a set of brass scales symbolizing the archangel Michael, and an étagère laden with crystals, fortune-telling globes, charms, ashtrays, and whimsies. The three narrow windows were hung alike with purple damask that puddled on the floor. As I started to offer him some coffee, a plaintive cry wafted down from my bedroom on the second floor. 'Excuse me. My baby . . . I'll be right back.' And I left the policeman standing there, glancing uneasily around the room like something was going to jump out and bite him.

I'd fed Baby Tommy not half an hour ago, so he wasn't hungry, nor was he wet or stuck by a diaper pin. His was the cry of a lonely boy who just wanted to be held, so I brought him down to the parlor and settled him on my lap across from Officer O'Rourke. I knew the man. I had helped him a few weeks ago with information concerning an elderly gent who had been poisoned by his nephew with arsenic – affectionately known in the murder business as 'inheritance powder'. I'd turned over what proof I had and waited for the slow gears of the law to grind to a satisfactory conclusion. Last I'd heard, some judge had ordered the gent's body exhumed. Finding evidence of arsenic would provide ample reason to arrest the nephew for murder . . . except that the nephew had died under mysterious circumstances immediately after leaving one of Madame Carlotta's séances. I figured the police were investigating the nephew's suspicious death. Since I'd been involved – some would say I'd caused the whole thing – I needed to step carefully here.

'Is Madame Carlotta your landlady, then?' O'Rourke asked.

'Indeed she is. I'm lucky to be here. Mrs Jones's boarding house wasn't terrible, but living here is more like being in a home.'

In truth, Mrs Jones's place was gruesome, but since she was the only landlady who would take in a boarder who was a young widow with a new baby – and only then because Miss Jane Addams at Hull House pressed her – I didn't dare complain. The purpose of Miss Addams's famous settlement house was to help poverty-stricken immigrants and I was Chicago born and bred, so it was my great good fortune that she let me stay there for the few weeks before and after the birth of Baby Tommy. I'd had nowhere else to go.

'And how old is the little one?' he asked politely. Baby Tommy was always a good conversation starter.

'Five and a half months. He got his teeth early, and he's been sitting up ever since he was five months old. I put him on the grocer's scales last Monday, and he weighed almost seventeen pounds. Mrs Jones said that was more than most his age.' It was obvious to me that Tommy was an advanced baby in every way measurable.

'A healthy boy,' O'Rourke added in a nervous, awkward manner that made me think he was not a father. Then, clearing his throat, he launched his mission. It was just as I'd suspected. 'I've come about the death of Noah Bristow. He attended a séance here the night he died. The tests came back from his uncle's body, by the way. They discovered arsenic – you were right about that, Mrs Pastore. It would seem the lad had poisoned his uncle and was trying to poison his aunt as well.'

Old news. I merely nodded, pressing my lips together real tight so I wouldn't burst out with one of those unwelcome I-told-you-so's. Gloating never advances your cause. And my cause was to keep on this cop's good side.

'Were you at the séance that night?' he asked.

I was wary about saying too much when it came to Madame Carlotta's séances and my role as her investigator and shill in order to protect both her and myself. Neither occupation was particularly admirable: as her investigator, I dug up facts about the departed souls her clients were trying to reach so she could make uncannily accurate pronouncements during the séances. As her shill, I acted the part of a bereaved widow to convince others at the table that Madame Carlotta was a genuine mystic with real clairvoyant powers.

Shills were common in the olden days. Traveling snake-oil salesmen planted one or two in their crowds to drink some of the elixir and boast of their miraculous cure. Magicians relied on shills in the audience to help certain tricks, and auctioneers used them to bid up the price of the item on the block. After I was widowed and Tommy was born, I had tried to find honest work, but no one would hire a nursing mother with a baby. I had no way to support myself, no family to take us in, and no luck in finding a wet nurse who'd look after Tommy while I was on the job. Working for Madame Carlotta beat begging on the church steps or selling myself on the street corner. I wasn't exactly proud of what I did, but I was proud of how well I did it.

I'd known Madame Carlotta when I was growing up in our old neighborhood on Chicago's Near West Side, back when she was plain old Mrs Myrtle Burkholtzer and her daughter Alice and I were school friends. When I ran into her again ten years after I'd left my parents' house, she'd found a new home, a new name, and a new life as a mystic who connected people with the spirits of their deceased friends or relatives. What she did wasn't illegal. There was no law against holding séances or telling fortunes. There were laws about bilking people out of their money, though, so Madame Carlotta made sure she never charged for her services. She accepted donations.

When I attended her séances in the guise of a grieving widow, it was in no way a fake since I was still mourning the loss of my husband, Tommy, who'd been driving trucks for Johnny Torrio and Al Capone, delivering booze to speak-easies, when he was shot in the forehead by rival bootleggers from Dean O'Banion's North Side Gang. My job was to help séance clients get in the proper frame of mind, to improve Carlotta's reputation by showing success in connecting with my own husband's spirit, and to lead the group in placing money in the donation basket after the séance. If I wasn't needed during a particular séance, I often helped Freddy, Carlotta's invisible teenage assistant, with what she called her 'spiritual enhancements'.

O'Rourke was a decent policeman who had played straight with me in the past when I'd gotten into a little trouble during a speakeasy raid. I trusted him pretty far, but I hadn't told him about my relationship with Madame Carlotta. And I didn't plan to start today. Better he think I was just a boarder in her house. I was saved from answering his question by the slamming of the back door as Carlotta and Freddy entered the kitchen, stomping their cold feet on the linoleum and calling, 'Maddie? We're home!'

'I'm in the parlor,' I warned in a clear, loud voice, 'with Officer O'Rourke from the police.'

There was a brief silence, followed by the creak of the back door opening quietly and closing again, telling me that Freddy had turned around and slipped out. I could almost hear him thinking, *Cheesit, the cops!* The orphan boy's fear of the police stemmed from the years he'd lived on Chicago's rough streets, and no amount of convincing would persuade him that not all cops were mean.

Carlotta's peculiar blend of innocence, ignorance, and faith in her psychic ability made her immune from fear. She probably thought O'Rourke was a potential client, come to make an appointment. Simpering a bit, she swanned into the room with one hand outstretched, as if she expected her fingers to be kissed. The gesture confused O'Rourke, who rose to his feet with a furrowed brow. After a second's hesitation, he took her hand in his and made a short, awkward bow. 'If you please, Madame Carlotta, I'd like to talk with you about your séance the night Noah Bristow died.'

'Excuse me,' I said, 'I'll just take Tommy upstairs—'

'Do stay, Maddie,' said Carlotta. 'I am always happy to help the police, and you might be able to fill in the gaps when my poor memory fails me. Now, sit down, Officer . . . O'Rourke, is it? A good Irish name. Some of my father's people were Irish. County Clare. Tell me how I can help you.'

'I'd like to know about the séance you held that night. What happened to make the young man rush off and disappear? What happened to cause him such concern that he would flee?'

'Well,' she began dramatically, smoothing her skirt, 'it was like this – oh Maddie, how about bringing us some cider, dear? And some of this morning's gingerbread from the pantry?'

Leaving Tommy propped on the sofa where he could show

off his new sitting skills, I slipped into the kitchen to rustle up the cider and cake. I could hear their conversation.

'That young man became agitated when the spirit of his uncle descended from the heavens and accused him of murder, and when, on top of that, other spirits appeared and made the same charge, and all of them warned his aunt, Mrs Weidemann – she's my client, or she was then – to throw the wicked murderer out of the house before he killed her too. We were hoping for a confession that would give the police reason to arrest him, but our chief aspiration was to warn Mrs Weidemann about her dreadful nephew.'

Carlotta's clear voice carried the distance. Her outrage was genuine. She had a big heart and a kind nature that didn't need to put others down to boost herself. The nephew's treachery had shocked her to the core.

'We? Who is "we"?' O'Rourke's deep voice was soft but penetrating.

'The archangel Michael and me – and the spirits of the deceased, of course.'

'Archangel Michael?'

'My spiritual guide. It was he who originally convinced me of my gift of clairvoyance.'

'When was this?'

She frowned. 'Oh, about three or four years back. It came to me gradually, although I'd long felt something otherworldly calling me. It started during the night. Dreams. When it spilled over into daylight, I was forced to take him seriously.'

'So you claim to be a genuine spiritual medium?'

'I don't need to make claims, officer. My record speaks for me.'

'And what is that record?'

'I am no charlatan, sir. No money-grubbing trickster who traffics in the pain of others. I have been in business for over a year now, providing a valuable service to grieving people by connecting them with their loved ones in the Great Beyond. I'm an ordinary woman who happens to have a gift that enables me to breach the boundary between the living and the dead. And I am pleased to say that I have had some success. Admittedly not as much as I would like, but my powers are becoming stronger as time passes, like a muscle grows stronger with weight-lifting exercise. You know of the Weidemann affair. There have been others. I dare not name names. It would violate the sanctity of my clients' private lives.'

'You are not violating any confidences here, Madame Carlotta. I spoke with Mrs Weidemann not long ago, and she related the details of her séance, assuring me that the messages and signs from her husband contained information no one else could possibly have known. She said you never once asked for money.'

Ahhh . . . so he already knew the answers to his questions. I was glad I hadn't lied when he asked me if I'd attended the Weidemann séance. I would need to tread carefully with this man. He was no fool.

'Some clients insist on making a small donation, but Mrs Weidemann is correct. My gift comes from God. It cannot be bought or sold like a sack of potatoes. Oh, there you are, Maddie.'

I set the tray on the table and poured a glass of fresh cider for O'Rourke and another for Carlotta. She took her time as she sipped it and urged slices of gingerbread on both of us. I waited, wondering why, if O'Rourke had already gleaned the details about the séance from Mrs Weidemann, he needed to hear them again from Carlotta. Was he checking on one of them? Both of them? Did their stories agree? I watched O'Rourke out of the corner of my eye as I dropped crumbs of gingerbread into Tommy's baby-birdlike mouth.

'Some of us have been talking down at the precinct. Some of us are believers in Spiritualism. Some are skeptics. Others just don't know. But most of us agree that something happened here that night, something that scared a murderer to death, to say it plain and simple. We were wondering if you would be willing to work with us in the future. I mean, if we should come to a situation where we were stumped, maybe someone in your spirit world could give us some information, as they did with Mrs Weidemann.'

Carlotta preened. 'Why, bless my soul, I would be honored to help the police in any way I can,' she said, shooting me a guilty glance. I knew why. It was my investigations that provided her with the details she needed to stage a successful séance. I gave her an imperceptible nod, which she interpreted correctly.

'We can't pay you,' O'Rourke added.

Carlotta stiffened her spine. 'I wouldn't accept payment if it were offered, young man. I consider it my duty as a responsible citizen of the great state of Illinois to help the police.' No doubt the possibilities were not lost on her: working with the police would bolster her reputation in the Spiritualist community, if an occasional slip of the tongue let it be known that she had been asked to assist them.

Time to impress the cop with my forthright honesty. 'Excuse me, Officer O'Rourke, but I'm afraid we were interrupted before I could reply to your question about whether I had attended the Weidemann séance. I was at the table that night. But I have nothing to add to what Carlotta has already told you.'

'Did you reach your own husband's spirit that night?'

'I'm afraid the nephew turned violent and disrupted the session before my turn came. The spiritual connections were broken. But I have done so often in the past.'

He looked from me to Carlotta and back again, as if weighing his next question. 'Are you two ladies related?'

Because I wasn't sure what he was driving at, I couldn't decide how to respond. The truth was, we were no kin, but I'd once told O'Rourke that Freddy was my cousin – which he wasn't – so perhaps he was chasing something there. A long silence would have been suspicious, though, and fortunately Carlotta spoke up with an answer that blended yes and no.

'Distantly.' She smiled fondly and reached over to squeeze my hand. 'Maddie has been a precious part of my life since she was a little girl.'

'I see. Well, ladies,' he said, rising from the sofa, 'I thank you for your time and for your willingness to help the police with spiritual matters in the future.' He fixed his cap firmly on his head, took his farewell, and strode out into the bleak December day.

Carlotta, watching him from the window as he disappeared down the street, gave a deep sigh. 'Well, well, well. Who would've thought it possible? You and me, working with the Chicago police!'

I wasn't sure it was such a nifty idea.

TWO

Carlotta had given me three new names to investigate for an upcoming séance, so the following day, I bundled up Baby Tommy and set out to earn my keep.

I braided my dark hair into two plaits and wound them around my ears, like the actress Pauline Frederick does in the pictures. Sometimes I wished I had enough gumption to bob my hair like Louise Brooks with all her lovely bangs, but each time I'd pass a barbershop, I'd remember how Tommy loved my long hair, and I couldn't do it. I wrapped a scarf around my head and put on my fine blue wool coat that Tommy bought me two years ago at Marshall Field's. To match my eyes, he said. How I missed that man!

'Hurry up, Freddy,' I called to the second-floor room that served as the 'enhancement' center during séances. It was indisputably Freddy's room – he spent most of his time in there, even took some of his meals there and slept there too, on a pallet in the corner, like he was guarding the mysteries of his trade from harm or discovery. We kept our filing cabinet in there with my notes on clients so if they should ever come back – and many did – we could refresh our memories. In her infinite capacity for self-delusion, Carlotta paid little attention to these goings-on. She believed she was psychic and clients believed she was psychic. Freddy and I played along. Who were we to spoil the soup?

The freckle-faced boy came clattering down the stairs, dressed in the second-hand suit I'd bought him last summer so he could help me at the courthouse by posing as an errand boy for a law office. The trouser legs hovered above his ankles, but we couldn't afford a new pair and he didn't care anyway. Taking his cap and coat from the rack, he lifted the corner of the shawl that covered little Tommy's face and said, more to Tommy than to me, 'Ready or not, here we go!'

Getting to the Cook County Courthouse required two streetcar rides and a short walk – not an easy jaunt for a woman on a wintry morning with a baby in her arms. Back when Tommy was smaller and the weather was warmer, I'd carried him in a basket, but he'd outgrown that. These days, I wrapped him up tight in an old shawl that I tied around my neck and back and carried a satchel with a clean diaper, my notepaper, and pencil on my other shoulder. He was getting heavier every week, but I was strong. And there was no alternative. I couldn't begin to afford a baby buggy.

Yesterday's fierce wind had died down but the morning temperature was surely below freezing. One of Chicago's new snow loaders chugged its way along our street, devouring snowdrifts with its giant scoop, lifting and dumping the snow onto a conveyor belt that dropped the endless mess into a dump truck. As soon as one truck was full and the driver had chugged away, another took its place.

'Where do you suppose they take all that snow?' I asked idly, not really expecting an answer. But Freddy was wise to life in the street. 'To the river,' he replied. 'They dump it in there.'

I should have known. Chicagoans dump everything into the river. It's an old habit. Raw sewage, slaughterhouse waste, factory sludge, unwanted chemicals . . . The Chicago River had long flowed like an open sewer into Lake Michigan where all our drinking water comes from. Finally, about thirty years ago when things became unbearable, city fathers realized that something had to be done before dysentery, typhoid, and cholera strangled America's second largest city. So they used a canal and gravity to force the river to flow in the opposite direction, joining it to the Des Plaines River to the Illinois River to the great Mississippi River and out the Gulf of Mexico. Naturally that didn't thrill the folks living in the cities alongside those rivers, but the courts ruled for Chicago and the engineering feat of the century was completed some eight years later. Ever since, Lake Michigan's water has been drinkable.

Freddy's thoughts must have followed my own, because he asked, 'Were you there when they reversed the river?'

'I was just a little tyke, but I remember going with my brothers to the edge of the river the week they opened up the dams so we could see if the river really did flow in the opposite direction.

And it did. The cold water from Lake Michigan flowed through the city and washed the filth south.'

'That must have been something to see.'

'Well, water flowing south isn't that exciting to watch, at least not for a child, but all the boats and barges that sailed past were.'

We trudged carefully along the shoveled paths toward the first electric streetcar stop, marked by a black pole with a white stripe. We dodged pedestrians right and left as our shoes crunched on the cinders and sand that city workers threw down. Normal conversation became impossible over the grinding engine noises and constant honking from the crush of black automobiles and delivery trucks jostling for position in the street. 'I'll carry your bag,' said Freddy, his breath making clouds in the air.

We'd done this many times since that first day last summer when I'd gone by myself to the courthouse to look up a will. A will is a wonderful tool for a medium. It gives specifics that can be used in the séance, details such as the names of relatives and particular items they'll inherit. Sometimes the will mentions burial instructions and a cemetery, which leads to another goldmine of useful dates and names and relationships on adjoining gravestones. And wills are public record, which means anyone can look at them just for the asking. Anyone, that is, except an unaccompanied young woman, as I learned on my first visit.

Last summer, I'd walked into the crowded room with Tommy in his baby basket and asked one of the clerks behind the counter how a person could see a will. The clerk looked me up and down like I'd crawled up from the sewer before pointing to a table against the wall where a stack of request forms sat waiting for me. Fill one out, take a number, hand it to the clerk . . . seemed simple. Except I was the only woman in the place and these clerks weren't the sort who believed in ladies first. Skipping past my number, they waited on every man in the room until I had to leave to nurse Tommy. When I returned, they said I'd lost my spot and would have to begin again. Determined to outlast them – I *had* to see that will – I sat on a bench to wait until they acknowledged me. I never found out who would have won this standoff, because just then an elderly alderman hobbled by. Spotting me and the empty room, he asked, 'Are you waiting for someone, young lady?'

'No, sir. I'm waiting to have my request filled. I've been here for more than three hours.'

Aghast, he glared at the clerks who had buried their noses in paperwork so they wouldn't have to meet his eyes. Finally, one of them, a big-bellied man with coke-bottle spectacles and a face red as raw meat barreled up to the counter and stuck out his hand to take my request form. No apology, no comment, but in no time I had the will I was looking for. It was a matter of twenty minutes to extract the information Madame Carlotta could use. I left the courthouse knowing I could not count on a friendly alderman strolling by every time I came in, so I concocted a plan to use Freddy as my agent. He requested the will while I waited for him at a table around the corner. It worked.

And months later, it continued to work. Today I had three names from Madame Carlotta. Three new people who had called for appointments. The new style dial telephone she'd installed recently was proving well worth its five-dollar-a-month fee. Nowadays, only a few of her clients – older widows more comfortable with the old social conventions – wrote for appointments. Modern folks preferred the telephone. Her business was increasing. Word-of-mouth referrals came in almost daily. I reviewed today's names with Freddy.

'One is Janusz Manikowski. His widow made the appointment. He died last summer. No other details. Wonder what she wants . . . Her appointment isn't until next week, so we'll just check for a will today and leave the rest of the investigation for later. Another is Mrs Frederick B. Horde, whose son and his wife wish to contact her. They're coming this Thursday night. The third is the brother of Herman C. Quillen, who died recently. Not sure when exactly, but maybe a week or so ago.'

Freddy nodded. I knew the names were burned into his brain. He couldn't read and he couldn't write, but he was miles away from stupid. He could remember anything he wanted to, better than any actor on the stage. Better than me – I had to write things down.

At the courthouse, I filled out the request forms, handed them to Freddy, and sat at a worktable in an alcove to wait. It wasn't long before he joined me. 'Here you are,' he said. 'There are only two. Mrs Horde didn't have a will. I'll play with Tommy while you take notes.'

That didn't surprise me. Many women died without a will because everything they owned legally belonged to their husbands anyway. It just made my job harder.

By this time I was used to reading wills, so I skimmed quickly through the legal blather until I reached the parts that mattered. Janusz Manikowski's will had been written by lawyers so it wasn't until page three that I broke through all the highfalutin words and found the specifics. 'Seems Mr Manikowski was a shopkeeper of some sort,' I said, sharing details with Freddy as I wrote, 'with a store near Lincoln Park. He leaves the store and its contents to his son John Manning – likely the son was born here and the father was the immigrant. Probably spoke with an accent. I'll make sure, though.' That would matter if Freddy was called on to provide some spooky dialogue from the deceased.

I set aside the Manikowski will and picked up Herman C. Quillen's. Someone – probably Herman himself – had written it out by hand in a spidery script that made me think he'd had palsy when he wrote it. I checked the second page and yes, the signature was in the same hand. Mr Quillen had written out his own will quite recently. It was dated March twenty-first, 1924.

'Herman Quillen doesn't seem to have been married,' I began, 'or he was a widower without children. In any case, he leaves his worldly estate to his two sisters, one living in Lincoln, Nebraska, the other here in Chicago, but no addresses for them. Odd, there's no mention of his brother. That's who's coming to the séance.'

'Maybe they didn't get along and that's why his brother is trying to contact him, to make amends,' offered Freddy. 'Or maybe his sisters need jack and the brother doesn't.'

'Or maybe the client isn't who he says he is.' That happened more often than you'd think. Sometimes it was because people didn't want to use their real names when dealing with a mystic. Other times it was because they were involved in some sort of swindle. Which was it this time? 'All he told Carlotta was that he wanted to get some information about a bequest. In any case, there's not much here – no addresses and not many specific details, but never mind, I'll hope for better luck with the obituary. Maybe it will mention a cemetery and I can find a tombstone – oh no, it's too soon for the tombstone to have been installed. Drat.'

Carlotta had three kinds of clients. There were the thrill-seekers, usually young flappers out for a night's adventure. They came in pairs or groups and erupted into nervous giggles or frightened screams during our eerie enhancements. They required little research, lucky for me because there's not much anyone could turn up on the backgrounds of young, unmarried girls. Most of Carlotta's clients were grieving relatives in search of comfort: widows and widowers seeking to connect with their deceased spouses, adult children wanting to reach their departed parents, or relatives trying to contact a loved one lost to the Spanish flu or the Great War. Of those, men were easiest to investigate because they left the greatest amount of evidence: newspaper articles, wills, obituaries, business addresses, professional associations, military service, and the like. Since women seldom had professional jobs and few wrote wills, my only hope was a sentimental obituary that listed survivors and a couple of random bits of useful information about their lives. Occasionally we got the dregs, cheats and pikers who wanted Carlotta to look into the future to tell them how to bet at the horse races or what to buy on the Chicago Stock Exchange. Few of them actually made it to a séance – Carlotta had become adept at sniffing them out and refusing them admittance.

After Freddy had returned the books with the two wills to the counter, we left the courthouse and went our separate ways, me to the nearby public library to hunt up the obituaries, him to make the rounds at several newspapers to arrange for next month's advertisements.

Like all big cities, Chicago had dozens of newspapers – dailies, weeklies, monthlies, foreign language papers for immigrants, even one for Negroes – but we stuck with the biggest ones for Carlotta's ads: the evening *Daily News*, the *Tribune*, the *Sun*, and the *Herald-Examiner*. We'd spent some effort designing an eye-catching ad two columns wide: Freddy had drawn a picture of a gypsy woman with a turban and dangling hoop earrings – the boy had a bit of the artist in his fingers.

Let Madame Carlotta, Chicago's Leading Medium
Connect You with the Spirit of Your Loved One,
Satisfaction Guaranteed
CAL-6949

Every so often we changed the wording and the typeface so readers wouldn't get so familiar with the message that their eyes skimmed past.

With Tommy bundled warm in my arms, I scurried across Randolph toward the public library where I could duck into a certain dark corner and nurse him before he took up wailing like a banshee. It was near noon but the tall granite buildings blocked the sunlight from reaching the streets, so it seemed like dusk. The wind blew my scarf back and stung my eyes. Inside the library, the high-ceiling rooms were deliciously warm. I fed Tommy and settled him on his stomach to nap in a quiet corner by a window while I tracked down the obituaries I needed.

Obituaries are another terrific tool for the mystic. In fact, there is more information in them than in most wills. But unless you know the date the person died and what newspaper the family preferred, it could take forever to find the paper that printed his or her tribute. I usually took the date the will was filed and started perusing newspapers backwards from that day, figuring most people would be quick to publish the obituary so everyone would know the when and whereabouts of the funeral. Probating the will would come shortly thereafter. I started with the city's largest paper, the *Chicago Tribune*.

Luck was with me that day! I found the Quillen obituary in the seventh newspaper I checked, upper right-hand corner, last page, November thirty-first date. As Tommy snoozed, I took notes: Herman Charles Quillen. Age forty-eight. Kinda young to die, but it didn't say what got him. Often it doesn't. Presbyterian. Assistant cashier with Midwest Savings & Loan. A home address – praise the lord. I'd check that out. Hobbies included ham radio, the Chicago Cubs, and coin collecting. Coins . . . maybe we could do the penny trick if I could find one dated 1876, the year of his birth. A lifelong bachelor with two sisters and a passel of nieces and nephews. Hmmm. No mention of the brother here either. This was becoming highly suspicious. Could our client be a stepbrother? Or a half-brother from another branch of the family? An illegitimate brother no one liked to acknowledge? Or more likely, was he no relation at all, merely someone posing as a brother? Was this something I should report to Officer O'Rourke? I needed to keep digging.

The only hair in my soup, as the French say, was Mrs Frederick Horde. Dead women were harder to investigate than dead men. With no will and no idea when she had died, I'd be looking for a needle in a haystack if I tried to find an obituary for her. I gave the matter some thought. Really, my only avenue was to look for the husband's name and make assumptions about the wife based on his information. Her son and daughter-in-law wanted to contact her spirit, but not her husband. Was that odd? Maybe he was an unbeliever . . . maybe he was dead too. I found a current copy of the *Chicago City Directory* and looked up Frederick Horde. Nothing. I went back year by year until I found him listed in the 1919 issue with an address and an abbreviation that said he worked as a railroad engineer. He probably died in 1919 since 1920 was the first issue that didn't include him. I would go by their house and have a look at the exterior – noticing something Carlotta could mention, something 'no one but a real mystic could know', like a picket fence or yellow shutters. That let clients conclude that this gypsy medium was the real McCoy, not someone who scammed gullible people out of their money. With any luck, I might encounter a servant coming or going, or a gossipy neighbor eager to chat with a young mother looking for a house to rent. It might not be as good as a will and an obituary, but it was the best I could do under the circumstances.

Mrs Frederick Horde couldn't wait. Her son was scheduled for Thursday's séance, tomorrow night. At that time we would also see Mr Quillen's invisible brother, the Ivan Chepurovs, who were hoping to hear news of their missing daughter Veronica, and the Peabodys. I'd already finished the Chepurov and Peabody investigations, but information on the others, Carlotta needed, and fast.

THREE

The next day dawned with clear skies and a bright sun, cheerful and warm enough to melt the icicles that dangled like daggers from the eaves. As I stood on the porch with Tommy snuggled up against my chest, one fell, nearly slicing off my ear, and shattered on the pavement beside my foot. The fright sent me scurrying out of range. A man across the street was cursing as he tried to start up his frozen truck. The engine wheezed like a TB victim. Above us, a woman flung open her window for a quick shake of a dirty rag rug. Three children shouted as they slid on a smooth patch of ice in the gutter, and the greengrocer on the corner lugged crates of carrots and turnips out to the cleared space on the sidewalk in front of his store. A train whistle blew in the near distance – long, long, short, long. I set out for the Horde's address on a street near Humboldt Park.

'If only we had a nice spring day,' I told Tommy who was having a fussy morning, 'I'd take you to the Lincoln Park Zoo. You're too little now, but come this spring or surely this summer, you'll be old enough to go to the zoo and see the wild animals. They have lions and bears and monkeys there – all free!' The appropriate animal noises jollied him into a smile. 'We'll have a grand time, you and me.' By then, I would surely have managed to beg, borrow, or steal a second-hand baby buggy. Carrying him like this couldn't go on much longer, not at the rate he was growing.

The late Mrs Frederick Horde had lived in the Humboldt Park area, so I hopped an electric streetcar that ran west along Randolph, then transferred to a northbound line, asking the conductor to let me know when I should get off to be closest to Le Moyne and Spaulding. Humboldt Park neighborhoods boasted blocks of neat houses and sidewalks lined with trees – bare today but leafy green in the summer. Lots of Polaks lived out here, and one of them kindly directed me to the Horde's address on Spaulding. A red For Sale sign was stuck in the front yard and a porch swing hung from the rafters. I knocked front and back, just in case a daily was inside cleaning. No answer. I peered in a few windows. Unfortunately, the heirs had removed the furnishings so all I could learn was the floorplan.

A voice from behind startled me. 'Hey there.' Caught snooping, I spun around to face a young man brandishing a snow shovel.

'Hello. I'm Mrs Maloney, looking to buy a house in this area,' I lied, shifting Tommy to the other shoulder. Nobody's suspicious about a woman carrying a baby.

'Frank Bart,' he said, leaning on his shovel. Tall and gangly in a coat that looked like it was made for his father, he sported the beginnings of a wispy mustache. Carlotta would have called him a boy in a hurry to grow up. 'Me and my parents have lived here for ten years.' He sniffled and wiped a runny nose on his sleeve. 'It's a good place to live, with the park so close. Used to be the Hordes lived there, but they both died. Him a few years ago, her last month.'

'Are there many children in the neighborhood?' I asked, pulling Tommy away from my chest and settling him on one hip.

His eyes squinted as he gave the matter some thought. 'Not so many . . . it's mostly older folks nowadays, on this block at least. But the park is full of kids.'

'I guess the Hordes' children are selling out?'

'Yeah. They got their own families and their own houses, and no one wanted to move back here.'

'Sons?'

'Yeah, two sons. Older than me. I didn't really know them.'

'You been inside?'

'A few times.'

'What's it like?'

The boy raised his eyebrows and shrugged, as if to say, *a*

house is a house. 'I dunno. Normal, I guess. Kitchen, living room, dining room. Far as I can recall, three bedrooms and the bathroom upstairs, like most on this street. Furniture's gone now. The sons sold what they didn't want. All I remember was brown. Brown walls, brown leather furniture. Brown rugs.'

'What about the Hordes?'

'That Mrs Horde, she was real nice. Used to bake cinnamon kuchen and bring us some. Man, that was the best stuff I ever put in my mouth.'

Perfect. With kuchen and the porch swing, I had enough detail for Carlotta or Freddy, if he should do the voice. 'Well, thank you for the information, Frank. I'll get in touch with the brothers and try to arrange a look-around soon.'

With a nickel ready in my pocket, I made my way to the nearest streetcar stop where I hopped an eastbound toward the lake. It took almost an hour to work my way south to the address where Herman Quillen had lived. It shouldn't have taken so long, but the snow banked along the sides of the streets had narrowed the lanes, squeezing motorcars, trucks, and streetcars into tight spaces. Horns honked at the timid drivers who held back and at the bullies who barged into the stream without waiting their turn.

When I found a five-story apartment building at Quillen's address, I groaned, fearing I'd wasted the trip – no details could be learned about the inside of an apartment from the outside – but I trudged up three flights just to make sure. I knocked on three hundred and five and a door opened, but not the one my knuckles had just rapped.

'You lookin' for Mr Quillen, he dead,' said a gruff voice behind me. An old hunchback with a gap where his front teeth used to be stood in his doorway across the hall from Quillen's apartment, looking like he'd been waiting all afternoon for someone to interrupt his solitude.

'I . . . yes, sir, I was. I'm a friend of his from the coin collecting society. I didn't know he had died . . . dear me. What happened?'

'Drank some smoke cocktail. Kills you pretty quick, smoke does. Nothing but wood alcohol. People ought not to drink spirits at all – it's against the law now, you know.'

'So I've heard. Does he have family nearby? Has there been a funeral?'

'You prob'ly missed it. He prob'ly been six feet under since yesterday. A molderin' in the grave, like John Brown in the song.' Helpfully, he sang a few bars before continuing. 'His sister has been coming to clean out his place so it can rent again.'

'She doesn't seem to be here now.'

He scratched his head. 'She here yesterday. She prob'ly be back tomorrow. She gonna sell most of his things. Needs the money. Poor lady, don't have no husband and Quillen helped her and her kids get by. She don't know what to do now that he's gone.'

'How sad! Isn't there a brother who can help out?'

'A sister what lives in Nebraska, but no brother. That Nebraska woman came last week to take away some stuff and went right home again afterward, leaving all the work to her sister here. I shoulda give her blue hell for that, but I kept my mouth shut. Need a man in that family to put things right.'

'Well, thank you, Mr . . .'

'Jepson.'

'Thank you, Mr Jepson.' I eased away before the garrulous soul could start singing again. I didn't need any more information to know that tomorrow night's client was a liar. Herman Quillen had no brother. What was going on? Nothing legal, that's for sure.

As I made my way back down the stairs, I nearly bumped into a stout, middle-aged woman, her hair tied back in a polka-dot scarf, taking each step as if she were carrying a load of wood on her back. Her vacant eyes stared past me as I approached. On a hunch, I spoke up. 'Hello. You wouldn't be Mr Quillen's sister by any chance, would you?'

She sent me a tired smile and straightened up. 'Why yes, hello. I'm Flora Masters, Flora *Quillen* Masters,' she said, rubbing her back. 'I've been working the past few days clearing out my brother's things.'

I held out a friendly hand to shake. 'How do you do, Mrs Masters. I'm Maddie Pastore from the coin collection society.' Rats! I should have given a fake name! 'I was sorry to read of his death in the newspaper.'

'You knew Herman?'

'Not very well,' I bluffed, 'but he was always courteous and seemed to be a hard-working gent. I heard there was a sister and stopped by to pay my respects, since I missed the funeral.'

'How very dear of you! But there's been no funeral, not yet. The police haven't released Herman's . . . Herman's . . .' She wiped her eyes with the back of her hand and sniffed back the tears. 'Care to come in for a quick cup of tea? I'd be glad to hear some kind words about Herman. His death was a shock to us, I can tell you.'

'Thanks. I could stand to set this one down for a few minutes too. My arms are aching, and he needs to be fed.'

She peered at Tommy who was sucking hard on his fist, the clue that told anyone who'd ever had a baby that he'd soon be wailing. Quillen's sister took her keys out of her coat pocket and unlocked the two locks on the door to three hundred and five. 'You can't be too careful in this place. I always thought this was a nice building, but I had to add this extra lock when I found someone had been in Herman's place after his death.'

'Gosh! Someone broke in?'

'Well, they didn't *break* in, at least there was no broken lock. Maybe they had a passkey or maybe they picked the lock. But it was obvious to me that someone had been in here.'

'How could you tell?'

'Herman was a real stickler for neatness. Typical bachelor, you know how they are. A place for everything and everything in its place, he used to say. So when I saw books laying on the shelves sideways and his closet door left wide open and his undershirt drawer in disarray – he always folded them in thirds, just the way Mother did – well, I knew someone had come in and messed up his things, like they was looking for something. First I thought of the coin collection and panicked, but it was safe under his bed, and I couldn't find anything in particular missing. Just messed up. So maybe I'm wrong. Anyway, I added the extra lock to be sure.'

'Good thinking.'

'He's a lamb, your little one. A boy?'

'Yes. Tommy.'

'I got eight myself. Six girls and twin boys. The boys come each day after school and help me take some of the boxes home.'

'I hope you don't have far to go,' I said, looking at the cardboard boxes stacked on the far wall of the living room, far too many to carry on the streetcar or the L. 'Or do you have a motorcar?'

She gave a sharp bark that told me better than words that motorcars were a pipe dream for such as her. 'With my boys, we can get everything we want home in a couple of days. I got a man from the secondhand store coming day after tomorrow to take all the furniture we don't want. Sit here, dear, and feed the little tyke while I make us some tea. So you're a coin collector too?'

'Well, really it was my husband. He died some months ago. I used to go along with him to the coin club meetings now and then, but I was never all that knowledgeable.'

'Oh, dear, so you're a widow too?'

I nodded. It was like being comrades-in-arms at the front.

'And with a little one. Tsk, tsk. I know all too well how hard a row that is to hoe. So Herman and your husband were friends?'

'Yes.' I was on safe ground here, since there was no one alive to gainsay me. 'My husband died last spring. Just before Tommy was born.'

'How sad! I hope you have family to help you out. It's so hard for a woman to raise children on her own. I work at the telephone switchboard, and twenty dollars a week barely covers our rent. Me and the kids, we relied on Herman to make up the difference.' To my dismay, her eyes welled up with tears that spilled down her cheeks. 'I don't know how we're going to manage without him. Financially or emotionally. I just don't earn enough jack to keep us all going . . .'

That was something I understood all too well. 'Surely he left you provided for?'

She wiped her eyes on her apron. 'He had some money saved at the bank where he worked. And his coin collection will bring something. I'll find a coin dealer to give me a price – maybe you know someone?' I shook my head. 'Well, we got a little breathing room, but the long run don't look good. But I don't mean to sound like that. It's not just the money I'm missing, honest. He was a good brother. He cared about us, and my kids adored him.'

Quillen's bachelor apartment was a modest affair with a spartan bedroom and a sitting room. No need for a kitchen. Bachelors ate their meals out. However, this one had an oilcloth-covered table in the corner where he kept a hotplate, some tea fixings, and a box of crackers. As I looked about the room, I could imagine him relaxing in the overstuffed chair after work, his feet up on the ottoman, reading the newspaper or one of the books from the shelves behind him and sipping his evening tea. From the looks of the place, there was little of value here that his sister could sell for more than a couple of fins. Maybe the two Chinese vases on the fireplace mantel? No doubt he could have lived better on his banker's salary if he hadn't had to support his sister's family.

'You have any relatives? A brother, perhaps?'

'Just a sister. Herman was our only brother. My sister lives in Nebraska. She came east when he died but since there's no date for a funeral yet, she went back home.'

Flora Masters was a nice lady. She worked hard, but no woman I knew earned a salary that could support a family of nine. We drank her brother's tea and talked while I nursed the baby. I managed to make some comments about Herman that pleased her, and she told me a bit about his job as assistant cashier at the bank. She had been surprised his death had come from poisoned liquor.

'Herman didn't drink.'

'Never?'

'Well, hardly ever. He never went to speakeasies. I found a bottle of whiskey above the sink. Good Canadian brand, not bootlegger's rotgut. I'm sure he had it since before Prohibition started. He wouldn't have bought anything illegally. That wasn't Herman. Straight as an arrow, he was. Crossed streets at the corners and such like. He used to warn me against drinking.'

'So how do you think he died? The doctor said—'

'I know what those doctors say, but I say they didn't know Herman. I don't know how he died. I been over it and over it in my head. All I can think of is that he didn't know what he was swallowing. Wood alcohol – they say you can't taste it so you don't know you're drinking poison.'

'He wasn't . . . um . . . he wasn't dispirited or discouraged or anything like that, was he?'

'Oh, no! Herman was a good Christian. He'd never consider killing himself, if that's what you mean. Never ever! And his life was going well. His job was good – he loved the bank and he loved my kids.' She began crying again.

I jotted down her address and telephone number and left her mine. I took my leave a short time later.

FOUR

'Welcome! Come in, Mrs Peabody,' Madame Carlotta gushed when she opened the door and found her client and me on the front steps. 'And Mrs Pastore, so nice to see you again. Do come into the hall and take off those heavy coats. What beastly weather we're having!'

But certainly not unexpected for Chicago in December, I thought, giving Carlotta's get-up a quick check. She was dressed even more flamboyantly than usual, wearing crinolines to pouf out her multicolored striped skirt with its fringed hem and a flowered blouse that left her fleshy forearms bare. A plaid headscarf covered all her gray hair except the one hank she dyed black with shoe polish for these occasions. Large brass hoops dangled from her ears, and on each arm she wore a dozen bangles, several with tiny bells she delighted in shaking. Mrs Peabody and I stomped the slushy cinders off our boots and joined the gathering. Tonight I was playing the role of a young widow trying to reach her late husband for advice on an upcoming move. I was the shill.

I had dressed for the part. No point in taking the risk that someone might recognize me later, so I dressed up older than I was with my long black hair in a bun covered by a hairnet and heavy spectacles. A severe gray half-mourning dress with no jewelry completed the effect. Even Baby Tommy had given me a puzzled frown!

'May I leave my pocketbook here on the divan?' I asked Carlotta, as a way of suggesting the other women do the same.

'Yes, of course, my dear. Hats too, and your coats on the hall tree. No distractions in the séance room! Your belongings are quite safe here.'

She introduced everyone. There was Mrs Alfred Peabody, the new widow who had entered with me; Mr Samuel Quillen, the mysterious 'brother' of the deceased banker; Mr and Mrs Ivan Chepurov, who were hoping to hear news of their missing daughter Veronica; and Mr Gerald Horde, son of the deceased, and his wife, Mrs Horde. I'd never met any of them, but I knew them all rather well from my investigations.

I stole a long look at Samuel Quillen – or whatever his real name was – sitting in one of Carlotta's velvet chairs. Clean-shaven, mid-forties, with his dark greased hair divided by a severe part, he sported a round gut and a ruddy, puffy complexion that suggested an excessive affection for beer during the mornings and hooch during the afternoons. When he talked, one gold tooth called attention to itself. Obviously uncomfortable among Carlotta's guests and her odd gimcracks, he lit up a Lucky Strike and took a deep drag, drumming his fingers on the arm of his chair. 'Are we all here now?' he muttered impatiently. 'Is this everyone?'

'We have a full table tonight,' simpered Carlotta in a low, whispery accent she considered her gypsy voice. 'Seven spiritual travelers into the Far Beyond. And one guide – myself!' She clapped her hands with excitement. That much was genuine. She couldn't wait to begin. Helping people was her all-consuming passion, and she was convinced that her spiritual efforts steered her clients toward happier emotional lives. 'Come into the Spirit Chamber, ladies and gentlemen. There's an ashtray beside you, Mr Quillen. Please extinguish your cigarette. Come take a seat, everyone, but first, feel free to look around the room. You must reassure yourselves that there are no secret drawers in the table or hidden compartments under the chairs. Take your time. And each of you must have a look inside the Spirit Cabinet over there in the corner to prove to yourself that it is empty. Sadly, there are so many false mediums out there that I feel obliged to prove my own impeccable honesty.'

Sometimes seating arrangements are important but tonight it didn't really matter as long as Carlotta saved me the chair on her left. As everyone began taking turns rapping on the table for hollow compartments and peering into the empty Spirit Cabinet, I said in a clear voice, 'Pardon me, Madame Carlotta, may I be excused for a moment to powder my nose?'

'Certainly, my dear. Up the stairs and straight ahead.'

She closed the séance room door so no one could see that I did not go upstairs. Instead I slipped through the hall back into the parlor to rifle the women's handbags. It didn't happen every time, but sometimes I found a clue that would give Carlotta or Freddy, in the room above, a trivial detail that could be worked into their patter during the séance. A photograph, a locket, a theater ticket, a letter – such tidbits had let us salt the gold mine in the past. If I found a nugget, I would sneak upstairs and tell Freddy or use a ruse to draw Carlotta from the séance room for a moment and whisper what I'd learned. But tonight the cupboard was bare. I returned to the séance room where Carlotta was ushering the guests to their seats and conveyed my lack of results with a brief shake of my head.

'Mrs Pastore, you haven't had the chance to examine the Spirit Cabinet,' she reminded me, waving her beringed fingers toward the ornate, inlaid cupboard in the corner.

'Oh, you all have already done it so I don't think . . . well, maybe I should. Thank you.' And positioning my body so no one could see my hand, I laid an 1866 Indian-head penny inside the box for Mrs Peabody to find later. It was the year of her husband's birth, something I'd learned from his tombstone, and would mean a lot to her. 'Yes, it's empty,' I said, and I took my seat beside Carlotta as she lit the bayberry scented candle in the middle of the table. With a magician's flourish, she closed the doors, shrouded the window with a heavy velvet curtain, and switched off the electric chandelier.

'Now let us all join hands to connect the circle of life . . . and bow our heads in prayer. Dear Lord, who commands the day and night, the heavens and earth, the past and future, look with favor, we beseech you, on our work tonight as we pierce the dark veil of death and commune with those who have crossed over to your everlasting glory. Amen. Now, as our savior Jesus Christ has taught us to say, "Our Father, who art in heaven . . ."' She liked to start with a prayer to reassure her clients that they weren't encountering devil worship or anything sinister.

As the soft chant filled the room, I took stock of the clients in the flickering candlelight. Unable to drum his fingers, Mr Samuel Quillen chewed on the inside of his cheek while his eyes darted about as if he expected a ghost to materialize in one of the corners. The Chepurovs had their eyes closed tight, while Mrs Peabody and the Hordes stared intently into the candle's flickering flame. Carlotta seemed to have fallen into a trance. After a very long silence, she spoke in a low, raspy voice, '*Ave verum corpus natum . . . vere passum immolatum in cruce pro homine* . . . O Michael, prince of the angels, greatest of the angels, deign to visit us tonight, I beseech thee . . . We are all believers tonight, believers who wish to commune with the spirits of our dear departed loved ones . . . You who escorts the souls to Heaven, you who commands the spirits . . . favor us tonight with the blessing of your presence. Are we not all believers?'

'We are,' I said, prompting others to chime in.

At that moment, a gust of air from nowhere extinguished the candle, prompting faint cries of alarm from two of the ladies. Freddy had opened the small trap door in the ceiling medallion above the chandelier and used bellows to direct a stream of air toward the flame. We were left in total darkness. The muffled sound of a bell floated above us. One of the men murmured nervously. Carlotta didn't miss a beat.

'Welcome, Michael, beloved of all angels. We beseech thee, blessed archangel, bring us the spirits of those who we wish to commune with tonight . . . *cuius latus perforatum . . . fluxit aqua et sanguine* . . . favor us with a visit from the spirit of Tommaso Pastore, beloved of his wife who is with us tonight . . . can Tommaso Pastore be found, O great archangel of God?'

Sometimes Carlotta liked to position me first so the evening would start with success. I'd played this part many times. The first time, I confess, I'd almost believed it was Tommy back from the dead, so realistic was Freddy's hoarse whisper. Tonight, she began with me and for about three minutes, I was the forlorn widow grateful to be speaking with her husband's spirit.

Then Carlotta took over from Freddy, using her gravelly voice. After a spate of Latin chants, she called on the archangel Michael again, asking if he would bring the spirit of the Chepurovs' daughter. 'O powerful archangel, can you bring us the spirit of Veronica Chepurov? Her mother and father miss her very much.'

This was a tricky case. The parents of sixteen-year-old Veronica were hoping Carlotta could tell them if their daughter was still alive and if so, where she was. The girl had run away with an older man over a year ago. They had heard nothing from her since, and they naturally feared the worst. The police seldom searched for runaways and certainly not those who were older than sixteen and had left on their own accord. My task had been to find an answer to their unanswerable question. Freddy had tried to help: he'd put out feelers to people he had known when he lived a beggar's life in the alleys of Chicago. He contacted prostitutes, hobos, and scavengers to see if anyone knew of the girl – was she working the streets? – but he'd come up empty. We couldn't hope to find her. We couldn't tell the parents whether she was alive or dead. The kindest thing we could do was give them hope.

'She isss not here,' said Carlotta, changing to her version of a middle-Eastern accent she believed came from Archangel Michael. 'She isss not here.'

'W-what does that mean?' asked Mrs Chepurov.

'If Veronica's not there,' her husband answered, 'she must still be alive on Earth. It's something, my dear. We must have faith that she will come home to us one day.'

It was not a very satisfactory conclusion, but it was the best we could do. Hopefully Veronica was alive and would contact her parents someday soon.

'I sense . . . I sense another spirit come down to us.' A long wait drew the tension tight as a drum. Carlotta mumbled some Latin in a soft growl. Above us, Freddy ran a bow across some violin strings, making an eerie, forlorn cry that seemed almost human. I chose that moment to raise my hand high above my head so that my palm faced the clients and waited for someone to notice.

'Wh-what's that?' said a voice.

'What?'

'There.'

A soft cry.

I waved my hand slowly back and forth. Of course, no one could see my arm, all they could see was the Undark painted on my palm. The radium paint glowed in the dark, displaying the distinctive cross-and-eagle symbol of an organization that Mr Peabody had belonged to for many years.

'It's the Sons of the American Revolution cross!' gasped Mrs Peabody. 'It's Alfred. My Alfred. Oh Alfred, where are you? How are you? I miss you so!'

Recently widowed, Mrs Alfred Peabody had written to Carlotta last week for a séance with her late husband. My research had turned up a will that contained several helpful details and an obituary that gave me the names of their six children and the cemetery where Mr Peabody was buried. At the cemetery, his tombstone bore a carving of the eight-pointed cross with an eagle on top, indicating he'd been a member of the Sons of the American Revolution. There was also a small gravestone nearby – their child who had died decades ago at the age of four months. 'The angels came too soon,' Carlotta would say. Walking past their house (the address was in the *City Directory*), I glimpsed a whimsical white gazebo in the side yard. Dropping these bits of information into her pronouncements would, I knew, make Carlotta appear omniscient. Whether Carlotta used them or not was yet to be seen.

There was no immediate reply to Mrs Peabody's outburst. Her husband's spirit had come into the room via the Undark paint, but I waited with nervous anticipation to see if Carlotta would speak. If she didn't – if enough silent time passed – Freddy would use the speaking tube to say a few words.

'Alfred? Alfred? Are you there, my dear?' implored Mrs Peabody.

A low hum came from Carlotta's throat, a good sign, for it meant she was getting ready to speak for a spirit. I squeezed her hand for encouragement. 'I . . . am . . . with . . . you,' she breathed at last, her voice little more than a whisper.

'Oh, Alfred! Are you in heaven? Are you happy there? What is it like?'

'Heaven . . . more colors than there are on earth, unimaginable colors, more vivid . . . angelic forces . . . There is no old . . . no young . . . no sick . . . the Lord is on his throne and angels like stars gather round . . . God wipes away every tear . . . no death, no sorrow, no crying . . . No more pain, for all former things have passed away.'

'Oh, Alfred, my dear!'

'I am home. Our dear baby Anna is with me . . .'

At the mention of the child who had died long ago – her name had been etched on the tiny headstone in the cemetery – Mrs Peabody gave a happy cry.

'We will not be parted for long . . . You will come home to the glory of God . . . where sin and violence do not exist. I wait to welcome you . . . into the house of the Lord.'

The lengthy lapses of silence and the repetition of Latin gibberish indicated that Carlotta was becoming tired. Only two more to go – Quillen and Horde. I tensed, remembering what happened when previous fakers had been confronted with the truth. An angry Mr Quillen might erupt in a violent outburst.

'O blessed Michael, prince of angels, there is one among us who wishes to contact his brother Herman Charles Quillen . . . *tantum ergo sacramentum* . . . can Herman Quillen be found?' Carlotta hummed her one-note tune and muttered more Latin, until at last, she broke off. 'I sense the spirit of whom we seek . . . he is among us . . . he is here . . . something disturbs him . . . something angers him . . . he will not speak . . . who speaks to him?'

Samuel Quillen cleared his throat and spoke up in a shaky voice. 'I want to speak to Herman. Is that you, Herman?' There was no response, so he continued, 'I . . . I . . . wish to know . . . that is, I have a question about money, the money he left. The money *you* left, Herman. You know what I mean. We can't find it anywhere and our sister needs it to feed her children—'

It was as we expected, the man was an imposter pretending to be Herman Quillen's brother in order to find out something about some missing money. It was not the first time greedy people had sought Carlotta's help in getting hold of money or learning which ponies would come in first at Hawthorne racetrack next week. Carlotta broke into Samuel's petition. 'Herman Quillen has gone. Herman Quillen has no brother. The archangel Michael does not communicate with frauds. He has gone as well.'

Releasing my hand, she left the table and flung open the parlor door in a dramatic fashion, letting in a soft light from the adjacent room. 'I am sorry, Mr Quillen,' she said haughtily, 'or whatever your name is, you are not welcome here.' The disgraced 'brother' pushed back from the table and spouted a mouthful of filth on his way out. I breathed a sigh of relief that he had not smashed something for good measure.

Carlotta continued. 'I regret to say, Mr Horde, that *that man* has ruined our connection to the spirit world. We cannot reach your mother tonight. I am very sorry. Please come again at a later date convenient to you, and I will try again. I beg your understanding.'

Everyone understood. The fake brother had spoiled the evening for some, but others were overjoyed at the connections they had made with their dearly departed souls. With due ostentation, I placed a ten-dollar bill in the basket in the parlor, a suggestion the others followed, more or less, as they left. To rid the room of that stale cigarette smell, I emptied the ashtray out the front door and left the book of matches Quillen left behind on the table where they would be useful lighting the candles.

We three met upstairs after Carlotta had removed her gypsy attire. As usual after these sessions, she was exhausted from the strain of reaching into the Far Beyond.

'Did I do it? I really felt I did it tonight. Do you think I did?'

Freddy and I exchanged uneasy glances. It was an odd game we two played, convincing the clients that Carlotta was a genuine mystic while at the same time convincing Carlotta that she was really reaching the spirits she so desperately sought. And there we were in the middle, unsure ourselves how much of Carlotta's revelations came from her imagination and how much came from the spirits. She believed – and we encouraged her – that Freddy's 'enhancements' and my research helped her break through to the Far Beyond, so she didn't view our efforts as complete fakery. We knew better but supported her delusions for obvious reasons: without Madame Carlotta, we'd both be on the street. But what made us most uncomfortable was the undeniable fact that at least once we thought that she really *had* communicated with the spirits, revealing important information none of us had any way of knowing.

'You seemed to leave us for a while,' I began, hedging my bets. 'Do you remember telling Mrs Peabody about heaven?'

'I . . . no, I . . . no, I don't. What did I say?'

'You described it as a perfect place without pain or sin or violence. She was so grateful to learn that her husband was with their baby.'

Carlotta nodded with satisfaction. 'Then I was successful. Praise God and thanks to Archangel Michael. Oh, and you were right, Maddie. You and Freddy were right. That phony Samuel Quillen was no brother to our Herman.' She often got very possessive about her spirits, as if they were her own family who needed protecting. 'Something's amiss there.'

'A man dies from drinking wood alcohol,' I said. 'There are three possibilities. One, he accidently got some bad hooch. Two, he knew what he was doing and wanted to kill himself. And three, murder. His sister said he'd never have killed himself, so I think we can toss that idea. I'd chalk it up to accident – I've certainly read enough of them in the papers recently – except for this so-called brother who is looking for his money.'

'And you said someone ransacked his apartment,' added Freddy.

'I'll bet it was our phony brother. He didn't find any money there, so he thought he'd try the spirit world.'

Carlotta shook her head sadly. 'The spirits never cooperate with criminals. At least, not my spirits.'

'So you think Quillen was poisoned on purpose?' Freddy asked me.

'It wouldn't have been hard to give someone a cocktail that was mostly smoke. They'd never know until it was too late.'

'But why would they do that?'

'To get him out of the way and take all the money.'

'But how did they expect to find out where the money was hidden? Dead men can't talk.'

'Maybe he lied to them. Then after he was dead, they discovered the money wasn't where they thought it was. I'll bet they're sorry he's dead now.'

'I think we should let that nice Officer O'Rourke know about this,' said Carlotta. 'He wanted our help, and now we can give him some.'

I was not so sure. 'We don't have much to go on.'

She waved her hand airily. 'That's his job, my dear, not ours. If there's foul play, it's the police who will make it right.'

Freddy shot me a look that conveyed his own, less rosy view of Chicago's finest.

FIVE

A visit to a Chicago precinct station assaults the senses. The constant din of raised voices, tears, protestations, and pleadings would rattle the hardiest factory worker, and a lady's scented handkerchief offers no protection against the stench of unwashed bodies beneath layers of damp woolen garments. This wasn't my first visit to the Maxwell Street station, so the shock had worn off even if my disgust hadn't. I picked my way over scuffed floors littered with clumps of filth and sand tracked in from the streets, past once-white walls pitted with nail holes from years of notices and advertisements tacked up by police officers, lawyers, bail bondsmen, and taxi drivers. Typewriters clacked, telephone bells jangled, doors slammed, voices rose and fell like waves on Lake Michigan's shore. From the second I arrived, I couldn't wait to leave.

'I need to speak to Officer Kevin O'Rourke,' I told the man behind the counter.

'His shift finished at three.' He glanced over his shoulder at the wall clock, looked to his right and his left, and lowered his voice so I had to read his lips to understand him. 'But you can probably find him at Yancey's. Blue door one block west.' He winked, and I realized he assumed I was some romantic interest. Geez Louise, really? With a baby on my hip? I thought about correcting him, telling him this was business, but what did it matter what he thought?

'Thank you,' I mouthed and jostled my way through the crowd and out the door where I could gulp the cold, fresh air.

I'd been to Yancey's before. Its signature blue door, nearly buried below street level, looked like it hadn't been painted since the Spanish-American War. Time and the elements had scraped off most of its once royal-blue paint. No sign announced its presence. A speakeasy, of course. Down the stairs I went.

Babies weren't exactly common in speakeasies, but since these joints had no operating laws they were obliged to obey, anyone with money was tolerated. You could find children in speakeasies drinking alongside grannies in babushkas who should have been home by the fireplace. Old men with palsied hands drowned their aches and pains in bathtub gin as they sat beside straight-as-a-stick flappers still in their teens. Many speaks developed a distinct personality to appeal to a specific customer, like musicians or longshoremen or teachers, or, in this case, working types who lived and labored in the immediate neighborhood. Its location near the precinct station made it a natural watering hole for off-duty cops. The floor was sticky, the light dim. No tablecloths or napkins bothered the coarse wooden tables. Drinks were served in a jumble of glassware of various sizes and shapes. The piano in the corner had no player – wrong time of day for entertainment.

O'Rourke spotted me through the haze of cigar and cigarette smoke and waved me over. He and the other man at his table stood when I approached. Nice manners. Their mothers would be proud.

'A pleasure to see you again, Mrs Pastore. I'd like you to meet my brother, Liam O'Rourke. Liam, Mrs Tommaso Pastore.'

My name sparked a flash of recognition in his eyes. It wasn't the first time that had happened. Tommy's murder had been front-page news in every Chicago paper two days running and on the inside pages after that, and it was only seven months ago. My own eyes darted back and forth between the two brothers, searching for the resemblance. They shared the same sturdy build and cleft chin, but not a lot more. Liam O'Rourke noticed my appraisal and grinned.

'Pleased to meet you, Mrs Pastore. And which of us do you take for the elder brother?'

Officer O'Rourke rolled his eyes but remained silent. He knew the drill. I studied their faces again, the square jaws, blue irises, sandy hair. Then it came to me – it was a trick question. They were twins, just not identical. 'I think you are the same age, but you can't expect me to guess who was born first.'

'Ring the bell, Mrs Pastore, clever lass! But I am the elder by half an hour, and sad to say this copper shows no respect for my greater degree of sophistication and worldly experience.' Officer O'Rourke rolled his eyes toward heaven again. 'I see you are out for a stroll on this fine day with your baby brother.'

The sound of my own laughter startled me. Laughing wasn't something I did very often. I tried to straighten my face at the outrageous compliment. 'No, Mr O'Rourke, this is my son, Tommy, named for his father.'

'A fine-looking boy, as all the world must agree. What is he now, about nine months?'

'Close to six. Does your greater experience include raising children of your own?'

'Sadly, I have not been able to persuade any eligible young lady to share my name. They all want me to take up steady employment like my younger brother here, and I am not so inclined.'

'He's a painter,' said Officer O'Rourke by way of explanation.

'But a painter is a fine profession. Surely there is enough indoor work during the winter months to keep you busy.'

'Alas, I am not that sort of painter. I am the canvas sort. And the public has not yet discovered my genius, so I must toil in a garret and beg for my beer.' So saying, he reached for his mug and took a swig.

'Well, I hope that in the years to come, I will be able to impress people when I tell them I once met the famous artist, Liam O'Rourke.'

He glanced at the watch on his wrist, a once-feminine accessory made masculine by the Great War. 'Gracious, look at the time. I can see that this lovely lady has some business to discuss with you, little brother, so I will leave you to it. Delighted to have met you and young Master Pastore. Good day to you.' And he downed what remained in his glass with a gulp, gave me an exaggerated bow, and left the speakeasy, his wet lips whistling a jaunty tune.

'Won't you sit?' said Officer O'Rourke. 'Please excuse my brother. He's always been the flamboyant one in the family.'

I set Tommy on the table. He could sit up by himself, as long as I steadied him with my hand. His big dark eyes surveyed the room, blinking solemnly as if he understood where he was and that it was important for him to remain quiet while his mother transacted her business.

'I stopped at the precinct station, but they sent me here.'

'What can I help you with?'

'You asked if Madame Carlotta would work with the police. Well, she wanted me to come today to tell you we think there is something fishy going on.'

'Is that so? Would you care for a drink?'

I should have ordered tea to warm me up, but beer was calling my name. He signaled to the bartender, and a mug of foaming brew appeared at my elbow. Sure sums up Chicago, doesn't it – a cop buying beer for a girl in an illegal speak?

'At one of our recent séances, there was a man who claimed he wanted to contact his dead brother to ask about a bequest. Carlotta suspected he was a phony and when he asked his brother's spirit about some missing money, she threw him out. She can't abide fakes.' That I could make that statement without blushing shows how far I'd come in the fakery business myself. 'I checked the deceased's obituary, and sure enough, Carlotta was right: he had only sisters. No brother. The dead man's name was Herman Quillen. He died from drinking wood alcohol, and we don't think it was an accident. I think – I mean, Madame Carlotta thinks – that someone, maybe this fake brother, made him drink it. Someone killed him to get his hands on this money, only – whoops! – found out afterwards it wasn't where it was supposed to be. Quillen being dead, the only option was to try to contact his spirit.'

O'Rourke watched me closely as he sipped his brew. When I stopped, he frowned and asked, 'That's it?'

'Well, not quite. I happened to meet Quillen's sister who was cleaning out his apartment, and she said it looked as if someone had searched the place before she got there. Maybe it was this fake brother, searching for the money.'

'Or maybe Mr Quillen was a messy housekeeper.'

'His sister said he was pretty neat for a man. And she said he would never have killed himself. That leaves murder.'

'What is this fake brother's real name?'

I squirmed. Some investigator I was! I should have tried to find that out. 'We don't know.'

'Do you know anything that would help us find him?'

I shook my head.

O'Rourke took another swig of his beer and stared at the hanging light above the bar for a full minute before turning his attention back to me. 'Thank Madame Carlotta for me, Mrs Pastore. I'll keep all this in mind.'

I felt like a schoolgirl being dismissed from the headmaster's office.

'But you aren't going to do anything about it,' I stated in a flat tone of voice.

'Exactly what would you have me do, Mrs Pastore?'

'Find the speakeasy where Herman Quillen was drinking, see if anyone else got sick or died from smoke that night, ask around if anyone knows about any missing money, find the fake brother . . .'

He tented his fingers against his chin and listened thoughtfully. I knew it was a pose. 'You don't know his name or address or anything about him.'

'He has a gold tooth.'

'Lots of men have gold teeth.'

I took a last gulp of beer and gathered up Tommy. 'Never mind, Officer O'Rourke. I can see you're too busy to investigate a murder.'

'Now, now, calm down, Mrs Pastore. Surely you can see you

have brought me no evidence, only speculation. A man has died of methyl alcohol poisoning – I remember the report from a week or so ago. There were no signs of violence. Chicago has seen an epidemic of poisonings from methyl alcohol in the past month. Someone wants the man's spirit to reveal where he might have stashed some cash. Interesting maybe, but it doesn't add up to murder.'

'You said that last time about the Weidemann murder, remember?'

'I remember. And I'll ask around at the station to see if anyone has heard anything about missing money or a man with a gold tooth.'

Too annoyed for politeness, I turned without thanking him and walked out the cellar, through the blue door, and into the cold.

SIX

The next day I went to the morgue. Not the dead-body morgue, the newspaper morgue. A while back, a librarian had told me that the big publishers kept back issues of all their newspapers, which wouldn't be much use in itself except that they had a filing system that worked like the library's card catalogue. You could look up a name or subject and find out the dates of any newspapers with relevant stories. And not only the date of the newspaper, but the page and column so you could find it fast. A real help for a spiritualist's investigator like me.

I put Baby Tommy down in the kiddie coop for his long afternoon nap, closed the top, and latched it shut. The kiddie coop was a godsend – my husband's friend Hank and his sister Rita had brought it over a week ago. 'I used it for all mine,' Rita had said. 'When the lid is fastened, they can't get out and nothing like bugs or pets can get at them through the screen.' I was grateful to have it in place of the dresser drawer he'd been sleeping in.

'I should be back before he wakes up,' I told Carlotta, buttoning up my coat, 'but if not, just give him a bottle of milk. There's some in the icebox.'

'Don't bother a bit about that, my dear. We'll be fine.' I no longer worried that Tommy would disturb the peace and quiet of Carlotta's home. I'd lived in her house for all of two weeks, but already she doted on Baby Tommy like he was her own grandson. Sure, she had grandchildren of her own, four or five of 'em, but they lived two thousand miles away in California, and she'd never seen anything but a picture. Tommy, she said, filled a hole in her heart. Even Freddy had fallen under his spell. He'd never seen a baby before, not up close anyway, and he couldn't get enough of my little boy.

'And can I bring two of your cookies for a thank you?'

'For that nice lady at the *Tribune*? Certainly.' She took a piece of waxed paper, wrapped the treat, and I was off.

Without the baby, I traveled fast, arriving at the *Tribune* building at Dearborn and Madison in less than half an hour. The elevator boy rode me to the basement, where I found myself alone with the morgue lady. I had met her last summer when I started this investigation gig. Stern-faced and reluctant to help anyone other than newspaper employees, she sent most civilians packing. For some reason, she took a liking to me. I was respectful and appreciative. Or maybe it was Baby Tommy.

'Good day to you, Mrs Waterman,' I began. 'If I'm not interrupting anything important, I would appreciate your help in locating any articles mentioning Herman Quillen that preceded his obituary on November the thirty-first.'

'Where's the little one today?' she asked.

'Napping. I travel so much faster without him.' Her expression soured. 'I'll be sure to bring him on my next trip.'

Grudgingly, she flicked through the card catalog and retrieved a newspaper from the stacks in no time. 'November twenty-ninth,' she said as she dropped the day's edition on the counter. 'Page fourteen.'

I moved to the large worktable and eagerly opened to page fourteen. At the bottom right, a grainy photograph showed two policemen standing over a man propped up against a brick wall in a garbage-strewn alley. Glass bottles littered the ground beside him. Under the byline of a reporter named Lloyd Prescott, the accompanying article read:

> Police responded to a concerned citizen's call in the early hours of yesterday morning to find the unconscious form of a well-dressed, middle-aged man slumped against a wall in the Near North Side in the vicinity of several illegal watering holes. Finding the man still breathing with no visible wounds, they summoned an ambulance which carried him to Cook County Hospital where doctors diagnosed alcohol poisoning. The gentleman was identified from his wallet as Mr Herman C. Quillen. Despite the best medical attention, he died three hours later.
>
> Nurse Fran Jacobs reported that this was the seventh such case the hospital had seen that week, with the result of two deaths and one paralysis. Quantities of poisonous wood alcohol, also known as methyl alcohol or smoke, have flooded Chicago's less savory drinking establishments through routes unknown, causing many accidental poisonings and deaths.
>
> Sources at the U.S. Treasury Department confirm that the law now requires a doubling or tripling of the amount of wood alcohol in all denatured alcohol formulae to discourage illegal drinking. The sudden increase in emergency room traffic substantiates this. Health Department officials have repeatedly warned the public that all forms of spirits are dangerous and should be avoided, as the law requires.

I thanked the morgue lady and gave her the cookies, implying that I'd made them myself. 'This reporter who wrote the story – Lloyd Prescott. Does he work in this building? I'd like to talk to him.'

'His desk is in the newsroom,' she said. 'But he's probably out on a call.'

'No matter. I'll just check as long as I'm here.'

'Up to five, turn left out of the elevator. Ask the receptionist inside the newsroom door which desk is his.'

Sometimes I'm lucky. Lloyd Prescott was in. His was one

of two dozen oak desks lined up in a cavernous room lit by large grimy windows and dangling light bulbs, where all the men seemed to be arguing, shouting on the telephone, typing, or rushing to-and-fro for no reasons I could discern. All except Lloyd Prescott. He sat tilted back in his chair with his feet propped up on the desk and a faraway expression on his face, so deep in thought he seemed oblivious to the chaos boiling around him. He was a young man of perhaps my own age, sporting a Douglas Fairbanks mustache and an old-school center part in his brown hair. He wore a rumpled double-breasted sack suit the color of strong coffee, a red-and-white striped bowtie, and battered, two-tone Oxfords with patched soles. I had to tap him on the shoulder before he noticed me.

Startled, he scrambled to bring his feet to the floor. 'Excuse me, miss. I didn't hear you come up.'

'Excuse *me*, Mr Prescott, for interrupting you. I hope I haven't disturbed you. You looked very deep in thought.'

'Sit, please. How can I help you? Or how can you help me?' He ran his fingers through his hair, making it stand up straight like a mad scientist.

'My name is Maddie Pastore. Mrs Pastore. I am curious about the death of an acquaintance, Herman Quillen, who was the subject of one of your recent articles.'

'I remember. Last week, was it?'

'Your article ran November twenty-ninth.'

'Another death-by-smoke cocktail. It's getting to be quite an epidemic. What of it?'

'What would you say if I told you that his death wasn't an accident.'

'I'd say I'm all ears.' He stretched one leg out, hooked the empty chair at the adjacent desk, and dragged it closer. 'Sit.'

'I believe his death may have been caused by someone else,' I said, pulling off my coat and scarf and laying my hat on his desk. 'In a word, murder.'

He whistled. 'Spill the beans, lady.'

'His sister says there is no way her brother would have purposefully killed himself, so that's out. She says he seldom took a drink of any sort, and she says his apartment was disturbed after his death, as if someone was looking to steal something.

Yet she noticed nothing missing, not even his valuable coin collection.' He was staring at me very intently, like he was trying to see through me and out the other side. I couldn't tell whether he was interested or not, but since he made no comment, I kept going. 'As it happens, I attended a recent séance where a man claiming to be Quillen's brother tried to reach his spirit to ask about the location of some money. Trouble is, Quillen didn't have a brother.'

Prescott whistled again. 'So what do you think is going on?'

'Did you know he worked at a bank?'

He shook his head. 'No. You thinking he robbed his own bank?'

'Maybe. But wouldn't the bank have accused him?'

'Not if they're afraid of looking foolish because an employee embezzled money. Which bank?'

'Midwest Savings & Loan.'

'Maybe I should talk to the bank president,' he said, picking up the telephone receiver. He paused, then laid it back in its cradle. 'On second thought, maybe I should visit the bank president.' Turning his head toward the edge of the room, he called, 'Norman!' It wasn't loud enough to penetrate the newsroom noise. He gave a sharp shout. Finally a skinny young man six desks down turned in our direction. 'Norm, what's the name of the president of Midwest Savings & Loan?'

Norman flipped through a file box for a few seconds before shouting back at us, 'Charles Randolph Hughes.'

'Write your name and telephone number here, Miss Pastore—'

'It's Mrs.'

'Yeah, yeah, write your number here and I'll get back to you if I have any other questions.'

'I'm coming with you.'

The mere thought horrified Mr Prescott. 'Don't be silly. This is business.'

'I am well aware of that. It's *my* business, and I want to know what you learn.'

'I promise to fill you in later. It could be dangerous.'

'Dangerous? We're going to a bank, not Verdun battlefield. I'll not cause any trouble. You can refer to me as your stenographer.' There was a pause as he considered my request, and before he could refuse again, I added, 'I have other information I can share if we're working together.'

'OK, sister,' he said, grabbing his coat and tossing me mine. 'You got a job as my stenog. Take this notepad and let's go.'

Hot on the reporter's heels, I scurried after him down the hall and into the elevator.

'Tell me more about this poisoned alcohol story. Your article mentioned the Treasury Department's new guidelines for denaturing spirits?'

'Um-hum. Happy story, huh? Your democratically elected government is poisoning spirits in ways that can't be filtered out for the express purpose of causing sickness, blindness, paralysis, and death in order to discourage drinking.'

'I didn't know alcohol was ever poisoned on purpose.'

'Industrial alcohol has been laced with wood alcohol at about a two-percent level for many years, even before Prohibition, to make it unfit for consumption. It's called denaturing. If it isn't denatured, then it will be taxed like liquor, which of course industrial users don't want. That's nothing new. When Prohibition started, chemists found they could filter the wood alcohol out and then flavor what's left to make it taste like gin or whatever they wanted. Some call it "white mule". Teetotalers don't like that, so they pressured the feds to start doubling or tripling the required percentage of wood alcohol.'

'When did this start?'

'Last summer. At first, the bootleggers said their chemists could overcome the new percentages – it's called re-naturing – by filtering it out just like they did the old. But they can't do it – hence the flood of patients into the hospitals and dead bodies into the morgue. You know, a year ago Chicago saw a few dozen people sick from alcohol poisoning each week with a death or two in there. Now, since summer, there are hundreds hospitalized each week with several hundreds of deaths so far. I'm keeping count for a big article in the new year. So far, I've counted three hundred and twenty-six fatalities and that's just at Chicago hospitals. Who knows how many unreported deaths there have been?'

'Who makes this stuff?'

He shrugged. 'Who doesn't? I've seen it come from tenement

stills, grocery store backrooms, bootleggers' warehouses, any place you can fit a still. Lots of people make bathtub gin at home. It's easy. All you need is some denatured alcohol, juniper flavoring, and embalming fluid and presto!'

'Why doesn't someone do something?'

'Someone tried. When doctors and coroners wrote letters complaining of the deliberate poisoning, a law was proposed to stop it, but the drys in Congress voted it down. They didn't dare vote against the Anti-Saloon League or they'd lose the next election. They justified it by saying it wasn't their fault if people chose to drink poison. They said no one would die if they just obeyed the law.'

'Well . . . that's true . . . but . . .'

'Of course it's true. But people want to drink, and they don't know when they've drunk white mule or a smoke cocktail. It doesn't taste any different from regular alcohol and it doesn't hit you for hours. By that time, it's too late. Besides, who really cares? It's a poor person's problem. The rich have enough money to buy the real McCoy smuggled in from Canada or Scotland or France. They don't have to drink bathtub hooch.'

'But . . . but that's awful.' I shuddered when I thought of Tommy's job, the one that got him killed seven months ago. He delivered booze to speakeasies for the Outfit, the gang bossed by Johnny Torrio and Al Capone. The job paid four times what he was getting when he drove a delivery truck for the Marshall Field's department stores, and he used to say it wasn't any different. But it was. People don't die from deliveries of sweaters or toasters. Had he been delivering white mule? I felt sick just thinking about it.

Lloyd Prescott slid one hand inside his coat pocket and pulled out a silver flask. 'I don't know why anyone would be such a simp as to drink liquor when they don't know where it comes from. I've got my own reliable source for this.' He tapped the flask and slipped it back into his pocket without offering me a swig. I thought of my former neighbors who made their own hooch in their backyard and bottled it in used Johnnie Walker bottles, but I said nothing. 'Come on, I'll pay your fare,' he said as we approached the line waiting for the L. 'Or I should say, the paper will.'

A thick pewter blanket of smog smothered the city that afternoon, making my throat sting with each breath. Except for the day after a severe storm, this was normal, but winters were the worst. During the long six months of freezing temperatures, fumes that belched daily from hundreds – no, thousands – of factories were magnified by tendrils of gray smoke pouring from hundreds of thousands of chimneys as homes and shops and offices burned coal or even wood to chase away the icy damp. What didn't blow away coated every surface with soot that no amount of rain would wash clean.

Watching Lloyd Prescott in action was a lesson in the power of audacity. Brash and charming in turn, he flashed his press pass and cajoled his way past a receptionist and a secretary right into the office of Midwest Savings & Loan's President Charles R. Hughes, a dapper gent in his sixties with gray hair, bushy gray eyebrows, and a gray double-breasted suit. No one looked more like a bank president than Mr Hughes, whose serene demeanor would calm any panicked investor or bankrupt businessman. It certainly put me at ease. Seemingly unperturbed at Prescott's pushy manner, he professed his eagerness to help with any questions the reporter might have. 'I am entirely at your disposal, sir,' he said, avoiding any eye contact with me, the lowly stenog.

'Right you are, sir,' began Prescott. 'I won't be taking much of your time. There are just a few questions I have about the death of one of your employees.'

'Poor Mr Quillen, yes, of course. What can I tell you?'

I whipped out my pad and pencil and made ready to take notes.

'What was his position, exactly?' asked Lloyd Prescott.

'Assistant cashier. He had been working here fifteen years.'

'And your opinion of him?'

'A good employee. A hard worker. Conscientious. Punctual. I can't recall a mistake he ever made.'

'Did he seem worried or discouraged about anything in his work or his personal life?'

'In his personal life? I wouldn't know about that. In his work, I think not. He was respected here. I believe he would have received a promotion in the coming year. At least, I mentioned his name to the board and suggested the new president consider him for a raise.'

'New president?'

'I have been president of this fine institution for twenty years. This is my last week.'

'You're retiring?'

'Yes. I gave notice four months ago to give the board of trustees time to hire a new man.'

'Would your impending retirement have meant for a change in Mr Quillen's job?'

'I see what you're driving at, young fella. You're thinking that he was despondent over losing some promotion and killed himself? Not possible. The most likely change would have meant a bump to a higher level.'

'Did he know about this?'

'Yes. He welcomed the opportunity.'

'Since his death, have you found any irregularities in the bank's ledgers? Any funds missing?'

'What are you insinuating? That Mr Quillen was embezzling money? Are you mad?'

Nonplussed, Prescott continued. 'It's been known to happen, sir.'

'Not at Midwest it hasn't. I've run this bank for twenty years and pride myself on the integrity of all its officers and employees.'

'You'll be leaving the bank in good hands then?'

'I certainly will. I wouldn't be leaving at all were it not for my wife who, I'm sorry to say, is in precarious health. Her doctor thinks getting away from Chicago's cold, damp weather would benefit her delicate constitution. We are leaving for southern California shortly – warm, dry air, you know – intending to investigate the climate of that region to see if we might move there permanently.'

We didn't need to hear the details of poor Mrs Hughes's ailments. Thankfully, Lloyd Prescott steered the interview back on track. 'Were you acquainted with Mr Quillen personally?'

'Outside of the office, you mean? No, I never associate with employees. Bad for morale. Favoritism and all that, you know.'

'You knew nothing about his personal life?'

'Afraid not. You might direct any questions of that nature to my secretary, Miss Stanley. She's been here longer than anyone. And now, if you have no further questions for me, I'm a busy man with only three days left to put my professional affairs in order before we leave for the Sunshine State!'

It took very little conversation with Miss Ruby Stanley before we understood who really ran Midwest Savings & Loan. A thin, fiftyish spinster, she wore her white hair in a bun on the top of her head, a bun pulled so tight it looked like it hurt. A silver chain with her spectacles fell like a necklace on her meager bosom. Her life revolved around the bank – *her* bank, she called it, and it did seem to belong to her. Miss Stanley knew every employee and every client. At some point in her life, she seemed to have worked every job in the bank, albeit without the title or salary, and she knew every procedure, every system, and how and why it had developed and altered over the years. It was Miss Stanley who trained the young men for their managerial positions and counseled them as they moved up the corporate ladder. Yet Miss Stanley remained a secretary. I caught on to this at once, for there had been a Miss Ruby Stanley at Marshall Field's, where I worked before my marriage to Tommy – a woman who ran the huge department store from her desk outside the manager's office, without the title or salary she deserved. A business was fortunate indeed to have a Miss Stanley to hold it together.

Once again, Lloyd Prescott waved his press credentials and hinted of his importance at the *Tribune*, and people – even sharp people like Miss Ruby Stanley – obligingly answered all his questions.

Miss Stanley confirmed that Herman Quillen had not seemed disheartened prior to his death.

'Has there been any money missing from the bank?'

Miss Stanley's eyebrows arched and her lips pursed. 'You are thinking Mr Quillen committed fraud and was discovered and then took his own life? You would be mistaken, young man. Herman Quillen did not embezzle funds from Midwest. I would know.'

Nonplussed, Lloyd Prescott continued. 'So his behavior showed no change on his last day or two at work?'

'Nothing out of the ordinary. He worked all morning at his desk,' she said, pointing with her spectacles to an empty oak desk across the room, 'lunched as usual at the diner across the street, and met with a client in the afternoon. I noted his desk was vacant at five and assumed he went to dinner.'

'There wasn't anything he was trying to avoid the following day, November twenty-eighth?'

I could see something flicker in her eyes as she considered her answer to his question. 'Well, we lost a major client on November twenty-eighth, but I don't think he knew about it yet. I myself only learned about it on the twenty-eighth.'

'He didn't know?'

'I am sure he didn't. When he didn't show up by afternoon, I assumed he had taken ill. I called his home to see how he was and to tell him about the client. However, even if he had known about it, we've lost large clients before. It's unfortunate but hardly the end of the world. It would not have sent him into some suicidal decline.'

'Who was the client?'

'A corporation by the name of Trask. Mr Quillen was their chief contact. They closed their account.'

'Did they say why?'

'They don't need to justify their actions to me, but if you mean, did they have some complaint about Mr Quillen, the answer is no.'

'Well, thank you kindly, ma'am—' began the reporter, but I cut him off before he could end the interview.

'Would you mind, Miss Stanley, describing Mr Quillen? What was he like?'

'What was he like? My, my . . . well, he was a kind gentleman, not terribly talkative. Steady. Devoted to his sister and her family . . .' She trailed off, obviously at a loss.

'How would you describe him? His features, I mean. Was he tall or short? That sort of thing.'

'Oh, I see what you mean. He was average. Average in height. Maybe less than average in weight. He wore spectacles. He covered his bald top by combing over the longer hairs from the side. Looked ridiculous but that's what some men do. And he grew a mustache last year.'

'Handlebar? Toothbrush? Pencil?'

She gave me an odd look. 'I suppose you'd call it a toothbrush style.'

In my role as a top-notch stenog, I wrote all this down, even though some of it seemed far removed from Quillen's death. Eventually we took our leave of Miss Ruby Stanley and made our way out through the bank's massive front doors. A light snow had dusted the ground while we were inside, making our footsteps visible on the sidewalk.

'What do you think?' I asked Lloyd Prescott as we were about to part ways. 'A waste of time?'

'Maybe. Maybe not. Obviously the missing money didn't come from his bank. Wonder how much money we're talking about? Hundreds? Thousands?' He shook his head. 'I'll keep thinking about this, but for today, I'm out of ideas.'

'Then you don't think I'm imagining things?'

'Maybe. Maybe not.'

'Do you want these notes I took?'

'Nah. I got it all up here.' He tapped his forehead. 'Keep the notebook.'

'Thanks. Here's the telephone number where I can be reached.' I scribbled Carlotta's number and tore off that sheet. 'Before you go, can I ask a newspaper question?'

'Shoot.'

'Does the *Tribune* have lady reporters? You know, like Nellie Bly?'

'Sure, ever since Nellie Bly, every paper wants a stunt-girl reporter. Back in the day, we had Nora Marks – she did that big exposé about ten-year-old boys being held in Cook County jail.'

'I remember. That was ages ago. What about today?'

'Today? Well, we got a lady reporter who takes care of the society page. And another who does a column on home economics for the women's section.'

'But news reporting?'

'It's too rough for women.'

'It wasn't too rough today.'

He gave me a condescending smile. 'Sister, you ain't seen nothin' today. I deal with fistfights, drunks, murderers, and dead bodies spilling blood all over the gravel. I been slugged, thrown in the gutter, and pushed down the stairs of City Hall by a politician I won't name. Trust me, news reporting is no place for a girl.'

I nodded as if I believed him. Truth be told, I *did* believe him, but it didn't matter. I couldn't help thinking how I was going to use my newfound knowledge to improve my investigations.

On the way home, I stopped at the police station to see if Officer O'Rourke was there. He wasn't. I wanted to tell him what we had learned at the bank, even though it wasn't much, so I left a message with Carlotta's telephone number on it asking him to call me. It sure was handy having a telephone.

SEVEN

Lloyd Prescott called the following day. My heart leaped – I thought he had some news about our case. Fat chance.

'You left your scarf on my desk yesterday. Well, on the floor actually. It fell off the desk.'

I hadn't even noticed it was missing. 'Oh, no, I'm sorry. I'll come by later to get it. Thanks for letting me know.'

'Hey, did you know there's another Mrs Tommaso Pastore in Chicago? I guess that isn't so surprising. There must be half a million wops in this town.'

My body turned to wood. My mouth opened but nothing came out.

'Hey, you still there?'

Finally: 'Yeah.'

'I couldn't find the telephone number you gave me, so I checked the *City Directory* and called that one. It's not you. Got some maid who said wrong number. Is that your mother-in-law or something?'

'No.'

'Well, never mind. Lucky I found your number in my other pocket, since you're not in the directory, are you? I'll leave your scarf in my upper right desk drawer, in case I'm not here when you come by.'

Another Mrs Tommaso Pastore. *The* other Mrs Tommaso Pastore. Not the real Mrs Tommaso Pastore – I was the real Mrs Tommaso Pastore. She was the legal Mrs Tommaso Pastore. Or so the lawyers said, but what did those jerks know about anything? I was the only one who mattered. I was the only one that Tommaso Pastore loved. I was the only one who had his son.

Not a day passed that I didn't think about *that woman*.

I tried not to. Ever since that day last spring, when the lawyers told me there was nothing I could do about getting back our house and all the money she stole from us – the thousands of dollars Tommy and I had saved in three separate banks – I'd tried to shove her out of my head and out of my life, to look forward, not backward, to take care of Baby Tommy and build a new life for the two of us. Legally, all the lawyers agreed, everything belonged to her, the other Mrs Pastore. Our marriage wasn't legal, they said. Bigamy, they said. That was nonsense. Tommy and I had been married by a justice of the peace and I had the papers to prove it. Maybe Tommy had committed bigamy, but I hadn't. My marriage was legal, and anyone who tried to tell me Baby Tommy was a bastard would feel my fist in their face.

But it was impossible to forget the cozy house where Tommy and I had been so happy, the little bedroom we'd painted yellow for the baby, the checked curtains I'd sewn for the kitchen, and the davenport, rug, and easy chair we'd bought from Sears for the living room, a matching set. Now all of it belonged to the woman he'd married before me, the woman he'd never mentioned, the woman he'd neglected to divorce before we were married at City Hall. I hadn't believed the lawyers, not for the longest time. I still couldn't really digest what had happened. How had he never mentioned her to me? How had he not remembered to divorce her first? He said he would protect us, me and the baby to come. He didn't. I hated him for that, but I still loved him. And I missed him every single day. More at night, in the dark, alone.

We had never met, me and this phony Mrs Tommaso Pastore. When she took my house and my bank accounts, it was all done through lawyers and policemen and bankers. She could pretend I didn't exist. I couldn't return the favor.

There was one thing of ours that thieving tramp didn't get. I got precious Baby Tommy. I got what mattered most. And every time I looked at his sweet face and saw my husband's eyes blinking back at me in wide wonder, I knew I'd won the war, even if I'd lost all the battles.

But now she'd come back, pushing into my life from outside. No more pretending she didn't exist. The new *City Directory* listed her under Tommy's name, not me. With nothing but a room at Carlotta's, I hadn't been listed in the new directory at all. Tommy was listed in last year's, at our old house address and our former telephone number, but I wasn't there either. Wives don't get listed, only widows or spinsters with their own home or telephone. So now this miserable slut had a line in the directory. A line that should have belonged to me. The injustice of it all roiled my stomach.

Mid-morning on Monday, with Baby Tommy riding in a shawl around my neck, I set out for the library to start my investigation of Carlotta's new clients. But personal business first: I picked up the latest edition of the *Chicago Area City Directory* and flipped to the Ps to see what that reporter had found. There she was, bold as brass, like she deserved the name. Mrs Tommaso Pastore on South 53rd, Cicero. CI2-4457.

Just looking at the words made my heart hammer something fierce. For several minutes, I wrestled with my better half. What should I do? Did I dare? What would happen? What did I want to happen? My better half lost. An overwhelming power took possession of my mind and body, drove me out of the library and down the steps, and compelled me onto the southbound bus toward Cicero.

Cicero is the first suburb west of Chicago. It was a peaceful factory town until Johnny Torrio and Al Capone moved their gang there to get out from under the Chicago police. Being smaller, the Cicero police were easier to buy off, and within the span of one election, the Outfit controlled the mayor and all the elected officials who mattered. To get to Cicero required a change of buses, but within no time, we were driving through the leafy streets of Cicero's quiet residential area, passing signs that read 'Whites only within city limits after dark'. A quick question to the bus driver was all I needed to find out which stop was nearest my destination.

'It's only a coupla blocks from here, lady,' he said, pointing with his thumb. 'That way, and past the school. You'll run right into 53rd.'

And I did. I turned left first, but hadn't walked more than half a block along haphazardly shoveled sidewalks before I realized the numbers went the other way. Shifting Tommy to the opposite shoulder, I turned and retraced my steps.

Tidy houses with small front yards lined each side of 53rd Street, mostly brown brick, mostly two stories, mostly pretty new. Most had a fenced plot of land out front where the woman of the house grew flowers or tomatoes in the warmer months. A few had a car parked at the curb. Not much different from the darling little house Tommy had bought for us after we were married. Had he bought this one for *her*? I couldn't bear to think about it.

My feet slowed as I approached her number on the left. I crossed to the opposite sidewalk to get a longer view. Smoke drifted lazily from some of the neighbor chimneys but not from hers. A young couple came out of the house on my right arguing loudly about someone's sister. An old man across the street walked his large, black poodle who barked at the mailman with his leather pouch. Were they looking at me? Could they tell that I didn't belong here?

I bit my lower lip nervously as my thoughts ping-ponged back and forth. I wanted to see the house; I wanted to see her; I couldn't bear to see either one. I wanted to get closer; I wanted to run home. Tommy started to fuss, so I used that as an excuse to stop and sing a soft nursery song. He wanted the breast. I bounced him a little until he settled back down. I'd have to find a warm, private spot very soon.

Her house looked much like its neighbors. It had a narrow porch with an old wooden chair in the corner. Someone had shoveled the walk to the front steps. The curtains in the front room – probably the living room – were open. If I'd gone closer, I could have looked inside. Did I dare?

It dawned on me that the absence of smoke coming from the

chimney probably meant there was no one home. Maybe she worked. Maybe she had a job. But she wouldn't need a job, not with the bank money she had snatched from Tommy and me. And the money she got from the sale of our house and all its furnishings. And what did that reporter say: a maid had answered her telephone? Licking my chapped lips, I looked up and down the street. The houses were nice, sure, but not the sort where families could afford a regular maid. Maybe a colored cleaning woman once a week? I hated her.

Was she home? Did I dare ring the bell and pretend to be lost? Pretend to sell magazines? I couldn't just stand here in the cold and wait to see if she came in or out. It could be hours. What on earth had I been thinking, coming all this way in the middle of the morning on a whim like this with no plan?

A nearby church rang its noon bells. I continued to the end of the block, shaking from the cold or nerves or both, then turned and walked slowly back, like a mother out for some fresh air with her baby. Still no sign of life from her house.

How stupid to have come all this way!

Suddenly from around the corner came a stream of uniformed children, walking, skipping, running in twos or threes, kicking the snow, jabbering and pushing as they surged along the sidewalk like an incoming tide. Of course, lunch hour. The youngsters had come from the Catholic school I passed earlier. I stepped aside just in time to avoid being run over by the first wave of boisterous boys and watched as they split up, one to this house, another to that.

One of the lads, a dark-haired child of six or so, pushed past me and crossed the street without looking both ways. As I watched in mounting horror, he dashed up the front steps to *her* porch, opened *her* door, and disappeared inside.

A son? Tommy had a son with that woman? My knees turned to jelly and I sank to the hard-packed snow. It couldn't be true. Surely he would have known about a son. Surely he would have told me.

Of course it wasn't true. I told myself sternly that there were lots of reasonable explanations for a boy living at that address. The woman who lived there had a younger brother. Or her older brother and *his* son lived with her. Or her sister and her son.

She took in boarders. The boy was adopted. He was just visiting. I had the wrong house. She had moved away last month and this was another family all together.

Snuggled at my chest, Tommy whimpered unhappily. It was cold out, but not freezing and for once, no wind was blowing. I moved to the steps of the house across from hers and settled in to nurse Tommy and wait until the children returned to school.

It was less than an hour before the boy reappeared. As if a bell had rung to signal the end of lunchtime, children burst from their homes and began the short walk back to their classrooms, this time moving slowly on reluctant feet. Down the steps came the boy, across the street, pausing to wait for a friend three or four houses away. I struggled to rise, stamping away the cold, and said in what I hoped was a cheerful, unthreatening voice, 'Hello there! I'm a bit lost. Which way is the bus stop?'

'Around the corner just a ways,' he replied, peering at the bundle at my chest. 'Is that a baby?'

'It sure is.' I took a deep breath. 'His name is Tommy. What's yours?'

'Vincent.'

'Vincent what?'

'Pastore.'

I bet my fake smile looked like death's grin. 'Tommy isn't even one yet. How old are you, Vincent?'

'Six. I'm in first grade.'

At that moment, the friend came running up to him; he and Vincent scampered off without another word.

EIGHT

Everyone knows staying busy keeps your mind off your troubles. I knew it too, but I can tell you, it's hard advice to follow. There was nothing I could do right now about the boy – who, after all, might just as well have been a Pastore cousin or something else rather than my husband's son – so I plunged doggedly back into the problem of Herman Quillen's suspicious death by smoke. It had been over a week since the man died, but still, maybe someone at the speakeasy where he drank it would remember him. That way, I might learn how he got the rotgut or, more to the point, who he was with when he got it. If I only knew which speak to visit!

William Dever (Square Deal Dever some called him) was mayor of Chicago then, but before him, it was Big Bill Thompson, one of the crookedest politicians ever to run a city. He and Al Capone were buddies. Big Bill never even tried to enforce the liquor laws, heck, he had his own speakeasy, a floating bar at Belmont Harbor called the Fish Fans Club. Chicago's speakeasies operated right out in the open, none of that secret knock or 'Joe sent me' password stuff to get in. A newspaper once wrote that there were seven thousand illegal bars in Chicago. Personally, I didn't see how they could come up with a number like that and call it even close to accurate, but the point is, there were lots and lots of them, and it was no trouble finding one because they had no need to hide.

So I took Tommy home and put him down for the long afternoon nap and went out again, this time alone, to the street where the newspaper said Herman Quillen's body had been found. I looked up and down the alley for the nearest speak. Nothing. I scouted around the corner, figuring he might have staggered a few feet before he fell over and died, and saw that there were two close by: Bedouin to the right and Lamb Chop to the left.

Three sailors lurched out of the Bedouin, laughing like they'd just heard the biggest joke in the world. They staggered toward me. One put two fingers in his mouth and gave a wolf whistle, so I turned toward the Lamb Chop and slipped inside. They didn't follow.

At the top of a rickety staircase, a naked light bulb burned just strong enough to light up the sign of a fat white lamb and an arrow pointing to a second flight of stairs. My feet followed the music – an oboe from the sound of it – and I pushed open the greasy door, only to blink in surprise at the unexpectedly sumptuous sight. A couple of crystal chandeliers dangled above marble-topped coffee tables surrounded by clusters of crimson velvet chairs and divans. A piano and oboe playing the mood from the corner muffled the low buzz of conversation and the clink of glasses from the bar – exactly the sort of class dive a banker might frequent. I had not taken two steps onto the plush carpet before a man dressed up like a butler in the movies swooped down on me and eased me out of my coat.

'A solo table for you, madam, or are you meeting someone?'

Startled by the unexpected attention, I flubbed my lines. 'I, uh, I was just, that is, I was wanting to speak to the bartender, or . . .' Too late, it occurred to me that this butler fella might be the better person to quiz. I needed to get more astute at this questioning business.

'Certainly, madam, if you'd like to order your drink yourself.' He motioned with his arm toward the bar. I followed the gesture.

The mid-afternoon crowd was light. No doubt the pace would pick up after work. Most customers were men, and most turned to look at me as I passed. Conversation was low. A good-looking young man with weightlifter arms and a cigarette between his lips nodded to me from behind the bar. 'What'll it be, lady?'

I regained my poise. 'Some information, please. Were you working here last week? On November twenty-seventh, to be precise?'

'Mighta been. Whatcha lookin' for?'

'Information about a man who was in that night. I know it's a long time ago to expect anyone to remember, but this was a middle-aged fella with spectacles and a mustache, dressed in a suit like . . . like these men . . .' I paused, realizing that there was little to distinguish Herman Quillen from anyone else likely to patronize this place. I took another tack. 'Did you hear about the man the police found in the alley near here twelve days ago?'

'Yeah, sure. Died from smoke.'

'I was wondering if he might have been in here that night—'

'And drunk smoke here? Forget it, lady. He was never here.' And he turned his back on me and resumed wiping glasses.

'I'm not suggesting he drank the poison here. I'm sure that didn't happen. I'm just trying to learn where he was that night, if he was with anybody.' This was getting me nowhere. The bartender wouldn't even turn around. I tried my questions on the butler. His friendly face turned ugly and he steered me firmly out the door.

What had I expected, asking lame questions like that? No one wanted to be accused of serving Mickey Finns. I would have to improve my story at the next stop or face more of the same.

A block away, the Bedouin beckoned. No staircase here; this tiny joint was located in the parlor of what had originally been a house. In fact, the owner probably lived on the second floor. A widow, maybe, making ends meet by opening her own little blind pig and decorating it like something out of *The Sheik*, with fabric draped above like a tent and big oriental rug cushions to sit on. Maybe she was making her own gin in the bathtub or on the back porch. Back when he was alive, Tommy told me that building a still was pretty easy and that he might do it one day.

The Bedouin held half a dozen low tables with cushions instead of chairs. Two women sat in the corner, their legs curled comfortably under them. They dismissed me with a glance and returned to their conversation and cocktails. A woman wearing an exotic robe came out of the back room when she heard the bell on the door. 'What'll you have, darlin'?'

'I'm looking for information, please. You may have read about a man whose body was found in the alley over there?'

'Yeah, I heard about him. Died after drinking some poisoned hooch.' Her eyes narrowed.

'Yes, that's the one. He was my uncle. The police said some Good Samaritan had tried to help him, but sadly, wasn't able to save him. My mother is his sister, and she sent me to ask around to see if I could find out who that good person might be. She would like to thank him and offer a token of her appreciation for his efforts. Or *her* efforts. So I'm wondering if you remember a balding, middle-aged man with a toothbrush mustache and spectacles coming in here the night of Wednesday, November twenty-seventh.'

The two women paused their conversation to listen in to my story. The server shook her head. 'Sorry, darlin'. No one like that came in here that day or any day. I get mostly ladies here.' She glanced at the two in the corner to see if their drinks needed refreshing, then disappeared into the back room. Strike two.

In the distance, a church bell rang twice. I had another hour before I needed to get home. These days Little Tommy napped reliably from one to three o'clock, sometimes longer. I hadn't left him alone – Freddy was at the house if he should wake up earlier – but I figured I had time to hit at least two more joints. My theory was to target the speakeasies nearest the alley where Quillen's body was found, and then work my way back toward Midwest Savings & Loan, which was located only about five blocks south. I had passed at least ten speakeasies in those five blocks. The nearest were Kasbah, a large, raucous joint a block down the street, and Watson's, a basement dive that smelled of spilt beer and urine. I couldn't imagine a banker at either one. No one working there could either.

By early December, every corner of Chicago had surrendered to the Christmas frenzy. Sidewalk crowds on State Street bunched in front of the famous windows of Marshall Field's, where I had once worked as a sales clerk, ooohing and aaahing over the fantastical scenes depicting snowy German hamlets, Alpine villages, Holy Land crèche scenes, and other Christmases around the world, all populated with frolicking farm animals and miniature children in native garb. Huge wreaths hung from the gaslights lining the main commercial thoroughfares. Even the more modest establishments welcomed holiday customers with garlands of greenery, strands of colored lights, and red bunting on the front door, and every window display included signs urging customers to come inside and see the wonderful array of Gifts for Mother or Best Children's Toys at Lowest Prices. Strangers who would never normally speak greeted one another with a smile, a nod, a tip of the hat, or a cheerful 'Merry Christmas!'.

Beyond the commercial blocks, homeowners who could afford to spend a week's wages on a string of Edison electric lights outlined their doors or windows with those colored globes. Those with thinner pocketbooks cut snowflakes from white paper and poinsettias from red and taped them to the window-panes. Others hung holly wreaths, tissue paper Christmas bells, and chenille roping about their doors in expressions of holiday merriment. The markets were full of seasonal vendors, mostly Negroes or recent immigrants, hawking boughs of greenery and cut trees, tall and short, snatched from the nearest forest and carried into the city on open trucks or horse-drawn wagons.

I wanted none of it.

I resolutely looked past every bit of festive decoration until the sheer volume of it all made ignoring it impossible. Every strand of tinsel, every pine wreath, every bit of gaiety made me sick to my stomach. All of the peace-on-earth-goodwill-toward-men crap mocked me, resurrecting memories of last Christmas, that happy time when Tommy was alive before a bullet stole our future, when we looked forward to our new baby boy or girl to be born in the spring, when we lived in our cozy house with its smell of yellow paint drying in the nursery and the fresh-cut pine tree in the living room decorated with paper cornucopias and painted birds I'd made and a box of twelve, paper-thin, glass ornaments from Germany that Tommy bought me. Where was all that now? Did *she* have them? My fancy German ornaments I'd put away up in the attic, did *she* have those now? The mere thought of it made me want to throw up.

My grief only grew sharper when I got back to Carlotta's house, thinking myself safe from reminders of the season. There she was in the parlor with Freddy hammering together a wooden stand to hold the small fir that leaned against the door. Before they could see my tears, I fled to my room where I hugged Baby Tommy until he fussed in protest.

'I'm sorry, little man,' I said, gathering my composure while I consoled him with my breast.

Carlotta followed me upstairs. 'Is everything all right, Maddie dear?'

'Fine. Just fine. I'm feeding the baby. I'll be down later.'

'We can wait for you to help us decorate the—'

'That won't be necessary. I'm not . . . I'm just not very interested in Christmas this year, Carlotta. Thank you, though.'

'I understand, dear. I understand.'

And I think she did. That was Carlotta's gift – or maybe it was better labeled a curse – to understand the heartache of those who grieved. That was what had propelled her into this late-in-life vocation as a mystic, her desire to lighten the burden of those who grieved for departed loved ones. Which was most of us, come to think of it, in one way or another.

I had to be strong for Baby Tommy's sake, if nothing else. He was all that mattered in my world. I'd tough it out through this holiday season. I'd get past the next one too. And maybe, just maybe, one of these years when Tommy was four or five or six, I'd summon the strength to take him to see the Marshall Field's windows and sit on Santa's knee and maybe we'd decorate a tree with little paper ornaments that we would make together, and I'd find some joy seeing Christmas through his eyes. For the time being, I reminded myself sternly, I was a working girl with plenty of work to do.

That thought led to another. I'd forgotten about the most obvious lead in this peculiar business of Herman Quillen's death – the fake brother. I should have been tracking him, not running around after my late husband's long-ago strumpet. But how to find a man whose real name I didn't know, whose place of residence I couldn't find, and who I'd seen only once? All I had to go on was his appearance: a middle-aged man with dark hair, a ruddy complexion, and a gold tooth. How many men out of Chicago's two and a half million people matched that description? Hundreds certainly, maybe even thousands.

'Mommy's going to buck up now and be tough,' I told Tommy as I changed his diaper and buttoned him into a clean white gown, a hand-me-down that I'd washed and ironed just last night. Still in the box of donated clothing was a christening gown, beautiful in spite of a few torn seams that would easily mend and some yellow stains that hardly showed. 'Why haven't you repaired me?' the garment seemed to reproach me. 'Why haven't you washed and ironed me and dressed Tommy in my finery and taken me to the baptismal font? Soon he will be too big to wear me.' Shaking those thoughts out of my head, I buried the gown deeper in the box where I couldn't hear its accusations. Not now, later. I couldn't deal with that now.

Chin up, I joined Carlotta and Freddy in the living room, determined not to spoil their joy.

'No, thanks, Carlotta, I'll just sit here and watch,' I said, settling into the red velvet armchair and surveyed the gangly, lopsided fir. 'You and Freddy have chosen a lovely tree. And so fragrant!'

'Well, it was a bargain, and we can face that bare part toward the corner and none the wiser. Look what Freddy has made!'

The boy proudly held up the daisy chain he'd concocted with strips of colored paper and flour paste. I had the distinct impression he had never done anything like this before in his life, and it made me even more determined to show him a merry Christmas, no matter that I couldn't share the joy.

Tommy struggled to get down from my lap, so I set him on the rug and played peek-a-boo with his favorite toy, a stuffed felt bunny with very big eyes and floppy ears that had been in the box of hand-me-downs from Hank Russo's sister. Tommy would celebrate his six-month birthday soon, right before Christmas. These days he was turning over and scooting a few inches on his tummy, but I could still set him down and expect him to stay put. It wouldn't be long before he was doing a proper crawl and that easy expectation would end. For now, he just rolled on his back and waved his hands and kicked his feet. As I glanced about the room for some small object he could hold, my eyes fell on the matchbook on the end table beside me.

Eureka! The matchbook. The one that the fake Quillen brother had left. It was one of those advertisement matchbooks that they give away to smokers. This one had a red cover with shiny gold words that read 'Twin Anchors' and two golden anchors that crossed at the top. Inside were the matches, of course, plus an address on Rush Street in the Near North Side and a telephone number.

NINE

An hour later Tommy and I stepped off the Michigan Avenue streetcar that ran parallel to Rush Street. A short walk took us to the down-in-the-mouth front of Twin Anchors with its crossed anchor sign swinging boldly from a wrought-iron arm. I knocked. No peephole. No password. No answer. There was no need – the door was unlocked. All were welcome. Twin Anchors did not fear the police.

The smell of fresh beer made my mouth water. A glance about the large room was enough to classify the joint as a better-than-average watering hole. Little daylight filtered through its narrow windows, but candles spaced along the bar helped give the place a warm glow. An upright piano stood in one corner, mute for now. As the evening wore on, a colored jazz musician would no doubt drop in to entertain.

Joints like this filled up at night but were almost empty at mid-afternoon. A few customers lounged carelessly at round tables along one side of the room, but I noticed every one of them had their backs to the wall. Two men sat on barstools arguing about a race at the Hawthorne. A burly bartender stood behind the bar wiping glasses. He saw me and stiffened, probably surprised to see a woman with a baby.

He was roughly my own age with the broad shoulders of a longshoreman, a wide smile that revealed even teeth, white as porcelain, and obsidian eyes that gleamed in the dim light. 'Well, well, what have we here? Madonna and child, straight from Raphael's brush. Right here, madonna.' He gestured to the empty table closest to the bar. 'Plenty of room for you and the babe.'

I wasn't sure of the reference but figured it was a compliment, so I smiled back and sat Baby Tommy in one of the chairs. The man came out from behind the bar and helped me out of my coat and gloves. 'What can I bring you today, madonna?'

'I've come for some information, but I'll have a beer too, please.'

'Coming right up.'

He brought the mug to my table. 'May I?' he asked, and without waiting for my response, sat down beside me and stuck a toothpick in his mouth. 'Who's your friend here? Boy or girl?'

It was a fair question and I took no offense. All babies wear white dresses and few have any hair. 'A boy. My son, Tommy.'

'Well, he's a healthy tike, ain't he? Can he have this?' He held out a miniature spoon. Tommy snatched it eagerly and gave an open-mouth smile so big you'd have thought he'd been handed a golden rattle.

Nothing melts a mother's heart faster than a kindness to her child. 'How thoughtful! Thank you so much.'

'I know little ones. My brother has two. Roy's the name.' He stuck out his right hand and we shook.

'Maddie.'

I didn't give my last name on purpose. It wasn't awkward because he didn't give his, but my hesitation came from the fact that I was sitting in a joint in the middle of North Side Gang territory where my husband – a driver for Torrio's south-side Outfit – had been murdered not that long ago. Since all the papers had covered his death, it didn't seem wise to toss his name around in case it was remembered in these parts.

'Aha! Short for Madonna?'

I chuckled. 'I'm afraid not. Short for Madeleine.'

'Madonna suits you better. A Madonna and boy child, just right for this time of year, no? So, what can I do for you, Maddie Madonna?'

'Information?' I laid a silver dollar on the table and pushed it toward him. Scowling, he pushed it back. I'd insulted him. Best to come straight to the point. 'I'm looking for a man who comes in here occasionally. I don't know his name, but he's middle aged with slick dark hair and a gold tooth. Does that ring any bells?'

Roy frowned and looked around. There was no one near enough to overhear our conversation, and maybe that mattered to him. 'I guess so,' he replied with a shrug. 'Could be . . . Why do you want to know?'

'I'd like to ask him some questions.'

'How come? That his?' He pointed to Tommy with his thumb.

'Heavens, no! I'm a respectable widow!'

'What, then?'

'I'd rather ask him directly, if you please.'

'I'm sure you would, but that's not how things work here. You need to give me some more information before I give you any.'

Now *I* looked around the room. No one was paying us any mind. Roy's dark eyes met mine in a stare that never blinked. If I wanted answers, I had no choice but to trust him.

'He came to a séance. I was there too. He wanted the medium to ask the spirits about some missing money, money he was looking for that wasn't his. She doesn't take those kinds of questions – no questions like who's going to win the World Series. It offends the spirits.'

'She for real, this medium?'

'I think so.'

'You ever talk to any spirits?'

'My husband. Sometimes. Anyway, she made the gold-tooth man leave.'

The customer on the barstool turned toward us and knocked his empty glass on the bar. 'Hey, Romeo,' he called. 'Another whisky, if you can drag yourself away from the dame.'

Roy untangled his long legs and ambled behind the bar. A few minutes later, he was back, toying with another toothpick. 'So now you're trying to find the missing money?'

'No! I don't care about the money.'

'You're one-of-a-kind.'

'The money might be connected to the death of a friend of mine. This friend, he died a few nights ago from drinking smoke, maybe by accident, maybe suicide, maybe . . .'

'Murder?'

'Yeah, and I think this gold-tooth man knows something about how my friend died.'

Roy gave the toothpick a real workout while he thought over what I'd told him. 'Sorry, Madonna. Can't help you.'

'Can't or won't?'

'Both. You need to steer clear of the gold-tooth man and this place too, if you get my meaning.'

'Why don't you spell it out for me?'

'He comes in here now and then with Hymie Weiss, and you know who that is if you read the papers. You need to forget about this before you or your little one gets hurt.'

Only a few weeks back, henchmen from Johnny Torrio and Al Capone's Outfit had gunned down Dean O'Banion, boss of the North Side Gang, in his flower shop. A struggle was going on over the succession. Maybe 'war' was the better word. Meanwhile the Outfit was taking advantage of the chaos to grab some of North Side territory. Gang violence, normally held in check by a desire for mutual preservation, had spiked dramatically as the battle for the streets escalated from handgun potshots to shotgun sprays from moving vehicles. Hardly a day went by that the papers didn't feature a dead body or two on the front page. Who would take O'Banion's place? Most of the money was on Hymie Weiss – Hymie the Pole, some called him. Not to his face. A friend of my late husband once told me that Weiss was the only man alive that Capone feared.

Confusion reigned at the Maxwell Street police station when I entered later that afternoon. The cops had dragged in a group of spiffy young men who were shouting and stumbling and demanding lawyers. I couldn't push my way through that bunch without harming Tommy so I waited, my arms aching from the baby's weight, until three officers had herded the group through the door to the cellblock. Working my way to the counter window, I asked for Officer Kevin O'Rourke. At last I had some solid information for him.

'It's not a name exactly,' I began when O'Rourke led me to a quiet corner, 'but it's enough that you could run him down and ask some questions. He's a regular at Twin Anchors and almost certainly involved with the North Side Gang. Roy – that's the bartender – said he comes in sometimes with Hymie Weiss.'

O'Rourke looked thoughtful. 'I guess I shouldn't be surprised. Where there's missing money and a suspicious death, there's bound to be gangsters.'

'Is it enough? Can you investigate the gold-tooth man now?'

'I can talk with some of our contacts in that part of town. I know the owner of Twin Anchors – he's the harbormaster at Monroe Harbor whose job gives him access to oceans of liquor pouring in from Canada. I'll start with him. Thank you, Mrs Pastore, but please, no more "help". You did right to leave the Twin Anchors the minute you heard Weiss's name. He's a nasty piece of work.'

'I'll take your advice, sir.'

'I'm glad you stopped by. I was planning to telephone Madame Carlotta to see if I could attend one of her upcoming séances.'

My heart stopped. To cover my shock, I made a big deal about settling Tommy on a nearby desk and straightening his little hat while my thoughts raced. This could not happen. Officer O'Rourke at a séance spelled disaster. Probably put us out of business. I had to think of something, fast. Or no, I didn't. I had time to figure out a plan. Carlotta could find out what he wanted. She could stall him. As long as I got home first, before he could reach her.

'You know she'll be pleased to assist the police in any way she can. But she's not home right now. She'll be home later this evening, if you'd like to talk with her about her calendar. I'm afraid I don't know when her next séance will be, or if she even has one planned. They aren't regularly scheduled.'

'I understand. Thank you, I'll talk with her tonight.'

TEN

'Geez Louise, what are we going to do?' Freddy slapped his hand to his forehead, grasping the threat at once. 'He's a cop, for Pete's sake. A smart cop, too, not your average flatfoot. We can't risk any of our enhancements on him. And when we say to look around the room and no one ever notices our tricks, he's sure to find some of them. The cut floorboards, the hole in the kitchen wall . . . oh my god, I won't be able to use the speaking tube!'

'Don't panic, Freddy. He's skeptical, all right, but not necessarily a skeptic. Remember what he told us, that some cops in his precinct were believers and some were deniers and some were undecided. I took that to mean that he himself was undecided, which is better than being certain like Houdini. But criminy, what if he's read the book?'

A Magician Among the Spirits was Harry Houdini's attempt to prove that all mystics, mediums, spiritualists, fortune tellers, and telepaths were charlatans. As the world's greatest magician, he possessed skills that let him attend a séance and figure out how the medium and her cohorts were pulling off their various scams, and his book, published earlier this year, exposed many of their tricks. Some of which were *our* tricks too. I'd mined the book for ideas to use in our own séances, banking on the likelihood that no Spiritualist would buy a copy of Houdini's work in the first place. In fact, Houdini himself admitted that many believers were so convinced that they were in contact with genuine spirits, they explained away his revelations as exceptions to the rule. Yes, they would say, that particular medium is a trickster, but the one I go to is genuine.

'We have to come up with a way to keep Officer O'Rourke from coming,' Freddy said.

'Impossible. We can stall him for a few days, sure, but it would be far too suspicious if we refused to include him in a séance. We just need to have a plan. And we have time to work something up.'

'You're right. Still, if there was some way to—'

'Wait! I know! Tomorrow night is Miss Bridenbaugh, isn't it? The one with the twin sister. Just her. No one else. She's an easy client. We won't need much in the way of enhancements to get her to speak with her twin. What if we invited O'Rourke to that one and played it straight?'

We tossed around some ideas, added me to the séance, and came up with a reasonable plan.

'It's good, Maddie. It's good.'

'I'll tell Carlotta that O'Rourke's going to call her tonight and she can invite him to Miss Bridenbaugh's next session. And we'll be very, very careful.'

The next morning I bundled Tommy into a thick sweater and wrapped him in a blanket. 'Where are you going so early?' asked Carlotta.

'Out for a walk. There's something I need to do, something I've been putting off for too long. I won't be long.'

The strain of planning O'Rourke's séance got to me and for some reason, I had to settle this baptism business once and for all.

Whenever anyone asked about Tommy's baptism, I'd say I'd been too busy to schedule it, but that inevitably led to warnings about his immortal soul if he should die unexpectedly. Nothing like that kind of remark for cheering up a new mother! If I lied and said it was coming up soon, I got questions about dates and which church and who were the godparents? If I said I didn't go to church anymore, people wanted to know why not and would then admonish me about putting my own selfish desires ahead of my boy's spiritual welfare. The real reason wasn't anything I could admit to anyone, ever.

Picking up Tommy, I marched down the front steps and made my way to the Catholic church nearest Carlotta's house, which was St Patrick's on West Adams. I knew where it was, although I had never been inside. Now, on the first floor of the rectory where the parish secretary's office was squeezed in between a tiny library and a conference room, I learned the name of the priest.

'And is Father Matthew here today?' I asked the secretary, a pale, thin woman with a bossy manner that evaporated when Baby Tommy babbled nonsense at her.

'Isn't this a darling!' she exclaimed, tickling him under the chin. 'A boy?'

I nodded. 'Six months old. I've come to ask about a baptism.'

'Well, Father is in the sanctuary finishing with confessions. You could sit here or you could go on into the church and wait until the last parishioner left.'

Speaking to the priest in the office where Miss Bossy Secretary and who-knows-who-else could hear me was not part of my plan. 'Thank you. I'll wait for him in the church. Say bye-bye, Tommy.' And I waved his little arm for him.

Heating a big church like St Pat's would have cost more than a collection plate full of gold coins, so it was hardly a surprise that the temperature inside the church was only marginally warmer than the streets of Chicago. But Tommy and I were bundled up in our coats, hats, and scarves, so we planted ourselves in the pew nearest the confessional booth where he could lie on his back and kick while I examined the jewel-like colors in the stained-glass windows and the stone walls that rose like cliffs into a vaulted sky. It wasn't twenty minutes before the last parishioner finished her confession. I don't know how long he'd been on confession duty, but Father Matthew emerged from the booth looking like a shell-shocked soldier staggering out of the trenches. Perhaps the confessions had been unusually grim that day. Well good, maybe that would make my sin seem mild by comparison.

'Good morning, Father Matthew.' I stood respectfully. 'I wonder if I could talk to you a moment about a baptism.'

His priestly vestments made this small man seem larger and more authoritative. He was only in his thirties, but his hair had nearly disappeared and his back was bent as if he had spent his whole life hunched forward in prayer. 'The secretary can help you with the schedule.'

'I have some questions first, if you please.'

'Well then, sit down and let's talk.' At that moment, another priest, much older and bald as an egg, entered the sanctuary and approached the altar, his soft soles making little sound on the cold slate. Father Matthew called to him, and they spoke briefly about the Communion wine – at least the church didn't have to worry about how to keep a supply of wine on hand. Churches and synagogues were exempt from the Prohibition laws, a necessary loophole exploited by countless unscrupulous fake priests and fake rabbis. After a few moments, the bald priest busied himself about the altar and Father Matthew returned his attention back to me.

'I gather this is the baby who needs the holy sacrament of baptism?'

'Yes. My name is Mrs Tommaso Pastore. I am a widow. This is my son.'

He held out his hand. 'Pleased to meet you. I'm afraid I don't recognize you. Are you new to the parish?'

'Not new to Chicago, but yes, I'm new to this part of the city.' I thought it unwise to mention where I boarded, in case the good father took a dim view of Madame Carlotta's spiritual competition. I stopped, unsure of how to begin, thinking perhaps I should have gone into the confessional with him first.

He sensed my hesitation. 'What is it, Mrs Pastore? What is the problem?'

There was no good way to approach the subject. 'I-I was married . . . my husband is dead. Dead of a bullet. Last May.' I couldn't help it; I teared up and choked. Father Matthew patted my arm and waited patiently while I regained my composure. Swallowing hard, I continued. 'After he was buried, the lawyers told me . . . they told me . . . they said he had been married before. I didn't know. They said he had another wife. She took everything that was ours. They called it bigamy. My mother said . . . she said my son is a bastard. She said the Church wouldn't baptize a bastard . . .' I couldn't help it. I just broke down and sobbed.

Father Matthew put a compassionate hand on my shoulder until I could speak again before he asked, 'Who married you, my dear?'

'A justice of the peace. At the courthouse. It was legal. I have the papers.'

'I'm sure you do. And you're sure he never had the first marriage annulled?'

'The lawyers investigated everything.'

'First, as to your question about the baptism,' he continued, 'it matters not at all whether the baby is legitimate or illegitimate. In Matthew chapter nineteen, verse fourteen, Jesus says, "Suffer little children, and forbid them not, to come unto me: for of such is the kingdom of heaven." He didn't say bring only those whose parents were legally married.' The priest lifted Tommy into his lap. 'He's a fine, healthy boy, Mrs Pastore. What is his name?'

I hadn't realized I was holding my breath, but now a wave of relief washed through my body, and I let out a long sigh. He didn't judge Tommy. He didn't judge me. He didn't say what my mother had said: that I was a whore and Tommy was a bastard. Carlotta was right when she told me never to mention the marriage issue again. The priest wasn't going to talk – he continued to call me Mrs Pastore even after I told him about the bigamy. As long as I said nothing, no one would ever know. Nothing would hurt my little Tommy.

'I gave him my husband's name: Tommaso Pastore. And for a middle name, mine: Duval.'

'Well, Mrs Pastore, if you have godparents chosen, we can baptize him any day you wish.'

He walked back to the office with me and we settled on a date and time for the baptism. A huge weight lifted off my heart, but I was still strung tight as a bowstring with Officer O'Rourke's séance coming up tonight.

My job was getting information about dead people, information that would help Carlotta convince her clients that she was communing with their spirits. Getting information about *living* people was something completely different. Especially when that living person was a policeman and nobody's fool. O'Rourke had asked to visit a séance; it was possible that he intended only to observe the goings on in Carlotta's spirit chamber. But if he had a spirit he wanted to contact and decided on the spur of the moment to test Carlotta's powers, we were up the creek. Freddy didn't dare use his usual enhancements, and I had only a few hours to come up with something – anything – that Madame Carlotta could use that would convince this very observant cop that she was a genuine clairvoyant.

Chicago's *City Directory* had two and a half columns of O'Rourkes, but fortunately only one named Kevin. No Liams, but I figured that was a nickname for William and there were twenty-one Williams. I cross-referenced the addresses to see if any other O'Rourkes lived at Kevin's address. No matches. The address was a weak lead but it was also my only one. I had to hurry.

If anyone were to mention to O'Rourke that a young, dark-haired woman with a baby had been hanging around outside his house asking questions, he'd be on me like a flea on a dog. So I left Tommy napping in the kiddie coop with Freddy in the next room, borrowed Carlotta's red-hair wig that she hadn't worn since she discovered turbans, put on a pair of plain-glass spectacles, and hopped a westbound bus toward the cop's address.

Officer O'Rourke lived in a row house on a street of row houses in a neighborhood of row houses, all built of identical brick, two stories with a basement and a front porch just wide enough for a chair. Of course no one was on their porch on a cold December day like today, but many had decorated them with wreaths on the door and paper Santas in the picture window. No such frivolity for O'Rourke. His house was bare of Christmas frippery.

I looked up and down the street for a For Sale sign – something that always provided a good springboard for questions – but no one on this street was planning to move any time soon. So I tucked myself into a corner across from O'Rourke's address to wait for someone to come in or out of an adjacent house. If anyone grew suspicious, I'd say I was waiting for a ride. Pedestrians passed me by with heads down against the wind, walking dogs, pushing baby carriages, carrying sacks of groceries. No one gave me more than a glance.

After an hour or so, two girls who looked about fifteen came down the sidewalk. One started up the steps of the house two down from O'Rourke's, the other continued toward the corner. Quickly, before the first girl could reach her porch, I slipped out of my corner and called out to her.

'Excuse me, miss,' I said, pulling a piece of paper from my pocket and adopting my confused face. 'I'm looking for a widow, Mrs Nancy Murray, who lives at number four hundred and fifteen here. I've knocked, but there's no answer. Have I got the right address?'

The girl came back to the sidewalk. 'What name did you say?'

'Murray. Nancy Murray. She told me to come to her house at this address' – I pointed to the paper – 'but there's no one home.'

'That's four one five all right, but I don't know that name. There's a man who lives there, a cop.'

'Hmm, well, does he live alone? Maybe my friend rents a room here?'

She shook her head. 'I don't think so. No one comes in or out but him.'

'Maybe my friend is a relative. Does he have any family that visits?'

The girl considered this for a couple of seconds. 'There's a mother who comes by every so often. She's old but nice. In the summer she sits on the porch some evenings. Could that be your friend?'

'Is the policeman's name Murray?'

'No, it's O'Rourke. So I guess that isn't your friend. Sorry I can't help you.'

'Well, never mind. Must be my mistake. Thanks anyway.'

I waited another hour. While plenty of people walked along the sidewalk, none went in or came out of any of the houses near O'Rourke's. Time to attack from another direction.

The nearest church was two blocks away. It was Catholic,

and to my certain conviction, the Irish O'Rourkes were Catholic. I climbed the stone steps beside the church to the quiet patch of frozen ground dotted with gravestones and ambled through the rows, casting my eyes right and left, looking for a marker that read O'Rourke. A memorial with dates would tell me something about the family history of our policeman. Chances were slim, of course, but if the O'Rourke family had lived in this neighborhood for any length of time, there would be monuments to their dead.

There were none. A precious half hour wasted.

'All I've been able to learn,' I reported to Freddy and Carlotta, 'is that he isn't married, he lives alone in a brick row house, he has a twin brother, and his mother visits.'

ELEVEN

I nearly didn't recognize the man who knocked on the door at eight that evening. Minus his jaunty cap and dark blue coat with its shiny brass star, Officer O'Rourke had turned into ordinary Mister O'Rourke, a transformation that startled me because, I realized ruefully, I hadn't looked much past his uniform until that very moment. Curiously, he seemed younger without it, perhaps smaller, and more vulnerable. A regular person instead of an authority figure. I wondered how old he was. Older than me, maybe not by much.

'Do come in, officer.' I motioned him into the parlor that served as Carlotta's waiting room. 'I'll take your coat and hat.' Handing me his fedora, he pocketed his gloves and ran nervous fingers through his sandy hair before slipping out of his overcoat. Either the cold air had colored his cheeks bright red or he was embarrassed to be here. Probably both.

'You can wait here until Madame Carlotta's other guest arrives,' I told him.

'Will you . . . uh . . . will you be attending the séance tonight too, Mrs Pastore?' he asked, fingering his too-tight collar.

'I don't normally,' I said, which wasn't true, but I didn't want him to think I was as heavily involved in Carlotta's business as I was. For all he knew, I was nothing more than Carlotta's boarder who occasionally attended one of her séances, and I wanted to keep it that way. It was important that Carlotta seem to work alone. 'But Madame Carlotta asked me to join her tonight, since you've come as an observer. If you object, I'll be happy to retire to my room upstairs.'

'No, no,' he assured me hastily. 'I'm glad to see you, to have the opportunity to bring you up to date on something. Something about your gold-tooth man. I dug into that information you gave me and tracked him down, or rather, I dropped in at that bar and asked around. I found out who he is.'

'Who?' I asked eagerly. Why was everyone so eager to keep the man's name a secret from me?

'All you need to know is that he's one of Hymie Weiss's boys, a very dangerous man, an enforcer they called him. A ruthless killer. The way we figure it, Quillen crossed someone in the North Side Gang somehow, someone who took offense and arranged for his death.'

'You think he stole some of their money?'

'Possibly. Or maybe he was honest and refused to do business with them. We'll never know. The police don't get involved in gang murders.'

'But why not?'

'They don't get solved. There's always a cover up, and no one talks.'

Like a punch to the gut, I heard what he didn't say. Who really cares if gang members kill each other? Good riddance to bad rubbish. No one was ever going to find out who shot my husband, my Tommy. They weren't even trying. He didn't matter.

'But it must have been about money,' I protested. 'Or else that man wouldn't have pretended to be Quillen's brother trying to find out where the money was.'

'Most everything's about money when you come right down to it. But Quillen's bank isn't missing any, so it's likely gang money.'

'Are the cops trying to find it?'

Officer O'Rourke shook his head. 'It's not our problem. Look here, thanks to Madame Carlotta, we now know who killed Quillen: your gold-tooth fella who came to the séance. He was probably sorry he'd done it after he realized Quillen had hidden some money and he couldn't beat the information out of him.'

'So arrest him!'

'No point. Don't you see? There's no hard evidence, and he'll have an alibi. A dozen guys'll raise their right hands and testify that he was in church or visiting his sick mother in Gary. And if a bystander was stupid enough to say they'd witnessed something, they'd be dead before the trial could convene. What makes no sense to me is how he could be dumb enough to come here, trying to get the spirits to talk, but . . .' He held up his hands as if to ward off my protestations. 'But I'm not into all this Spiritualism stuff so maybe I shouldn't judge. In any case, I wanted you to know that you were right. Quillen's death was murder, and thanks to you, it's solved.'

'Except where is the missing money?'

He shrugged. 'It's a gang problem, Mrs Pastore, and you don't want to get within spitting distance of that. Digging any further will get you dead as Quillen. Hymie Weiss will find his money, sooner or later, hopefully without any more murders, but don't count on it. In any event, the police are finished. Case closed.'

I drooped like a deflated balloon. Case closed, huh? Where was justice for Mr Quillen? Even if he was in cahoots with the North Side Gang, that didn't mean his killer should get off scot-free, did it?

Evidently it did. Just like it meant Tommy's death would go unsolved and unpunished. His killer was probably walking the streets right now, free as a lark. It wasn't right. It wasn't fair. And there was something else bothering me – but a knock at the door drove that thought out of my head and brought our conversation to an end.

Miss Bridenbaugh had arrived. The séance began moments later when Madame Carlotta glided into the room, jangling her bangles and swirling her skirts, and invited us into her Spirit Chamber.

Miss Bridenbaugh was a regular. Every week or two, she made an appointment and every visit brought her success in reaching the spirit of her twin sister. She was a known quantity, as good as a shill, easy to slot into virtually any mix of people, and a sure thing whose presence brought as much credibility to Carlotta's performances as my own. The perfect client for O'Rourke to observe.

Freddy and I had spent hours readying the room and discussing the format of this unusual séance. 'We can't afford to mess this up,' I told him time and again.

'I'm scared,' he admitted. 'The cops . . .'

'I know how you feel about cops. Don't worry. We're not going to make any mistakes,' I said firmly, determined to sound more confident than I felt.

The safest strategy was the simplest: do almost nothing. O'Rourke was an observant skeptic who could be counted on to give the séance room a thorough search before Carlotta launched her monologue, and as an experienced cop, he was far more likely than our regulars to uncover our little tricks. We disguised the peepholes in the wallpapered walls with carefully cut out bits of the patterned paper. We put a room-size rug over the trap door that Freddy had cut in the center of the floor so that even if O'Rourke lifted the edges, he would see nothing. There was no need to alter the spirit box because we would not be using it, nor would we use the speaking tube from the ceiling or blow the candle out with bellows. Our table had never been rigged, so that piece of furniture could remain as it was for inspection, but we replaced the hidden-compartment chair with another chair from the kitchen. Freddy would not be playing his eerie violin music or delicate chimes from the floor above. I would not be doing my water trick or tapping. This séance would rely wholly on Carlotta, with the exception of one necessary bit of subterfuge I hoped was foolproof.

As always, Carlotta invited her guests to search the room before taking a seat at the table. I promptly sat in the chair next to hers and held my breath as O'Rourke cased the joint, as they say in the pictures.

Taking his time, he inspected each piece of furniture and the spirit box, ran his fingers lightly over the walls, examined every exposed floorboard, peered behind the velvet curtains that covered the windows, and rapped on the table and chairs. He made the mistake most people do of ignoring the ceiling, but if he had thought to look up, he would have seen nothing but a gaudy chandelier hanging from a chain fastened in the center of a fussy ceiling medallion. Finally – finally! – he sat down. I exhaled.

Carlotta began as she always did, with the Lord's Prayer 'to put people at ease', followed by several minutes of monotonous Latin mumbo jumbo. I wondered briefly what we would do if ever a client understood Latin, for her words were merely random snatches of chants and prayers and songs that she had absorbed during decades of Catholic services, but that worry could wait for another day. At last she blew out the candle and called on her spiritual guide, the archangel Michael, to bring forward Miss Bridenbaugh's twin, then slumped into a trance-like silence. Seconds passed. Nothing. Normally that was Freddy's cue to provide some whispered words or music from the ceiling, but not this evening.

Eventually Carlotta roused herself enough to inquire, 'Are you there, Miss Bridenbaugh?'

At that, I let go of Carlotta's hand and raised my own to show the Daughters of the American Revolution symbol – a wagon wheel surrounded by stars – that I'd painted on my palm with Undark radium paint. That Undark is terrific stuff, invented during the Great War to make watches for our soldiers with dials that glowed in the dark. Waving the glowing DAR image slowly above my head as high as I could reach, I waited for Carlotta to answer herself in Archangel Michael's raspy voice. 'I come to bring the transmutable blue flame, to deliver a simple message, to assist you to continue forth in your soul's journey. The one you seek is here.'

That was enough for Miss Bridenbaugh, who from there on did most of the talking, keeping her sister's spirit up to date on family matters. Their second cousin had lost his bid for alderman in November's election; their grand-nephew was to play the part of one of the three kings in the Christmas pageant; their brother had at long last announced his son's engagement to the young lady he'd been courting for six years. When she'd exhausted her news, I lowered my arm to imply that the late Miss Bridenbaugh had floated back to the Far Beyond.

That should have signaled the end of the séance, but as I feared, Officer O'Rourke had other ideas. Without warning, he spoke.

'Madam Carlotta, if you please, could you contact the spirit of my mother?'

It was a test, of course. If what the girl on his block had told me was true, his mother was alive and visited his house on occasion. If she was mistaken and the visitor was an aunt or an old friend, we were about to be exposed as frauds. I held my breath as I waited to see how Carlotta would handle the question. I'd given her everything I knew about O'Rourke. It was up to her to sense the best way forward. I gave her hand an encouraging squeeze.

'Her name?' she rasped.

'Nora Ryan O'Rourke.'

I held my breath again. Moments later, Archangel Michael responded. 'She isssss not here. She isssss not here.' At which, Carlotta snapped herself back from semi-consciousness and pronounced the séance over. 'Michael has left us,' she said simply.

When I brought the light up, I watched O'Rourke's face. Confusion creased his brow, but he asked no questions, made no comments. Did we make a believer out of him? I thought not, although he couldn't deny the truth of Carlotta's pronouncement. His mother's spirit was not in the Far Beyond, because she was still among the living.

TWELVE

Chicago is a big city, the second biggest in America with two and a half million people, so you'd think running into someone accidentally would be long odds. Truth is, most people stick to their own neighborhoods for shopping, working, and recreation, so it wasn't such an amazing coincidence that I nearly collided with Liam O'Rourke on the Roosevelt Road sidewalk a few blocks from my home that Wednesday. Or so I thought at the time.

Nattily dressed for motoring in a tan polo overcoat atop a striped gray suit, he tipped his felt fedora in a gentlemanly fashion and bid me good day. 'And where are you heading this brisk morning, Mrs Pastore?' he asked, guiding me by the elbow to a sheltered spot under the awning of a nearby dry goods store where we were out of the stream of pedestrians.

'Tommy and I are going to the library to fetch some new reading material.' That wasn't my real aim, of course, but the artist would be scandalized if he knew how I used the library to snoop into the private lives of Carlotta's clients. Oh for the days of yore when my Marshall Field's job allowed me to be honest about what I did for a living! 'What brings you out on such a frigid day?'

'A different sort of cultural excursion, if you will. I'm on my way to the Art Institute. Have you been there?'

'Twice – once when I was a schoolgirl and another time with my late husband. It's a lovely place for strolling and seeing the beautiful paintings. Is that what you do, look for inspiration?'

'You might say that.'

'What do you paint?'

'Do you mean what medium do I use?' I could only nod – the only mediums I knew were Spiritualists. I had no idea what he meant but was loath to confess my ignorance. 'Oils usually, although I've played about with watercolors recently. Not very successfully.'

'And do you paint nice pictures or the new modern art?'

He grinned. 'Doesn't the new modern art deserve the adjective "nice"?' Now I was flustered. I hadn't meant to insult him. He smoothed over my confusion with a reassuring answer: 'Never fear, Mrs Pastore. You would recognize my subject matter: portraits, still lifes, an occasional landscape. At the moment, I'm working on a landscape of the Chicago skyline in winter.'

'It sounds lovely,' I said, hoping he wouldn't ask me anything like who my favorite artists were. I couldn't have named a single one. The art world was for rich people or starving artists. I was neither.

'Would you like to see it? My motorcar is just around the corner. I could take you there for a quick look and then drop you at the library. Save you the walk.'

'Oh, but I couldn't trouble you—'

'I pass by the library on the way to the Art Institute, so it's not out of my way at all.'

'I . . . well . . .' Why ever not? An automobile ride would be a luxury, and I didn't mind saving the dime for the streetcar. There was that tiny voice in my head asking whether an unchaperoned woman should accompany a single man anywhere indoors, let alone his studio, and didn't artists have a reputation for seducing their models? But Liam O'Rourke was brother to a police officer, for heaven's sake, and he seemed very much the gentleman. And I was no model. Besides, Tommy was there to chaperone us. Shifting him to my other hip, I answered, 'Sure!'

He reached out both arms. 'Why don't you let me carry the young gentleman? We'll go along more easily that way.' Tommy's eyes opened wide at being handed off to a stranger, but he made no protest. Neither did I.

Liam O'Rourke's Lincoln sedan was waiting for us a short block away and before I knew it, we were motoring north past the public library and into a neighborhood of large older houses that had been divided into apartments. O'Rourke parked the sedan along the curb and helped us out, just like a chauffeur would.

'My studio is at the top of this building, I'm afraid. Let me carry the baby. It's rather a lot of stairs.'

We climbed a fine marble staircase to the second floor, a modest oak stair to the third, and narrow, bare pine steps to the fourth-floor attic, a space originally reserved for servants or storage or the family's mad uncle. The pungent scent of varnish met us before he had even unlocked the door, and we moved from the dark hallway into the light-filled studio.

Liam O'Rourke's rented room fit the description of the starving artist's garret to a T: the floorboards were speckled with every color of paint imaginable. Canvases of varying sizes lay about, some blank, some partially used, some leaning against the wall, some stacked on the floor or perched on easels. On a big messy table lay dozens of squeezed paint tubes, three artist palettes, tin cans of mysterious liquids, and pots of brushes. Rags stained with oils and pigments littered the floor. A low cot in the corner suggested that the artist might live here too, or at least nap here on occasion.

'I see why you rented this place,' I remarked, looking through the glass at the bare trees outside the window. 'All these windows really brighten the room. It gives the space the feel of a treetop playhouse.'

He laughed. 'My exact thought when I first saw this place. I had to do a bit of renovation – the skylights and windows are my own additions. An artist needs good light above all else.' He lay Tommy on the corner cot and motioned me over to an easel that held a painting of the city skyline on a winter's day, gray and misty. Tacked beside it was a black-and-white photograph of the view that looked as if it had been taken from a boat on Lake Michigan. 'It's a work in progress, but I hope you can see where I'm heading.'

'It's very nice,' I said, feeling completely inadequate. It *was* nice, but I lacked the vocabulary to say anything more intelligent. 'I don't know what to say. I could never dream of making anything this lovely.'

'You could if you had lessons.'

'Did you? Have lessons, I mean.'

'Not growing up. But I've always liked to draw. Then, when I was in the army in France, I had the chance to visit Paris on leave. Even during the war years, it was the art capital of the world, stuffed with painters, sculptors, and photographers of all abilities and nationalities. When the war ended in '18, I stayed and soaked up as much as I could from the men and women I considered real artists. Then one day, I realized I was a real artist too. Not as talented as some perhaps, but more talented than others. Come, let me show you some of my finished pieces. This one' – he pulled out a picture of a table set with a blue-and-white plate that held several lemons and a lime – 'and this' – he indicated another still life with fruit piled beside a pitcher – 'are complete.'

'Will you sell them then?'

'Aye, there's the rub! Finding buyers isn't easy. I have an arrangement with the owner of an art gallery on Adams Street, near the Art Institute, who exhibits a few of my paintings and even sells one on occasion. My portraits sell best because they are commissioned.'

I looked around the room. 'I don't see any portraits.'

'Alas, I have no commissions at present. Unless . . .' He glanced over at Tommy who was cooing softly in the corner. 'What about . . .?'

'Oh, no, thank you very much but I could never afford such a thing.'

'I wasn't thinking of a painting, rather a sketch. Of you and the baby. Madonna and child. Right now. It won't take long.' I shook my head, but he wasn't finished. 'Have you had Tommy's photo taken?'

The cost of a photograph was well beyond what my thin purse could afford. 'No,' I told him, 'but I will have one, one day soon.'

'Until that day comes, you must have a sketch, a reminder of how he looked at six months. Come, sit on this chair and hold him in your lap, facing me. The light is right. It won't take long, I promise.'

Ignoring my feeble protests – honestly, a picture of Tommy as a baby would be something to treasure all my life – he handed Tommy to me and positioned the rush-bottom chair just so, by one of the windows. In seconds he had whipped out a sketch pad and the sound of his artists' pencils scratching the paper filled the silent room. I held Tommy as tight as I could, hoping O'Rourke understood that babies didn't sit still for anyone. He worked fast, his blue eyes shifting rapidly from Tommy's face to his sketch pad, back and forth, back and forth like a tennis ball over the net. As the minutes passed, Tommy grew increasingly squirmy.

'There!' he said at last and, with a flourish, handed me the stiff paper. I gasped when I saw what he'd done. It was the spitting image of my precious little boy, my baby, with his wisps of hair, his two bottom teeth, and his dimpled cheeks, yes, but it was the eyes that stunned me. They were my husband's eyes, beautiful, dark, and as recognizable as if he'd been the one to sit for the portrait instead of our son. The flood of emotion made my eyes water.

'What is it? Aren't you pleased? Did I get something wrong?'

I blinked hard. When I could find my voice, I managed to croak, 'No. No, it's perfect. A wonderful likeness. It's just that . . . his eyes. I always thought Baby Tommy had his father's eyes, but here, you've drawn my husband's eyes exactly.'

THIRTEEN

Father Matthew was waiting for us in St Patrick's narthex on Thursday afternoon. I'd stuffed Baby Tommy into the hand-me-down christening gown that was too small for him, and I'd fed him right before we left so he wouldn't fuss when the priest performed the rites. Beside me, Carlotta had on her best hat and gloves and Freddy wore his one suit with the trousers that bared his ankles.

'Are these your godparents?' the priest asked, looking doubtfully at Freddy who was clearly too young for the responsibility.

'Father Matthew, let me introduce Carlotta Romany here, who will serve as godmother. Freddy is a cousin. The godfather will get here any minute now. It's Hank Russo, who was a good friend of my late husband.' Best not to mention that Hank had worked with Tommy making deliveries for the Outfit. And still did.

Before Father Matthew could say another word, a second priest entered the narthex and hobbled toward us on unsteady feet. I'd seen him the last time we were there; the old man must've been eighty if he was a day. We hadn't spoken then, but he made a beeline for me now.

'Excuse me for interrupting, but are you Mrs Pastore?' He squinted and blinked his old, weak eyes.

'I am, Father—?'

'Francis. I saw your name in the records book and wanted to take the opportunity to introduce myself. You are the widow of Tommaso Pastore, the young man who was killed last spring, are you not?' A lump stung my throat and I could only nod. 'I thought as much. I remember your husband. It was six or seven years ago when I was in a different parish, but I remember counseling him about his marriage. I never saw him again, so I am glad to see that you and he reconciled. And you have a new baby! What a blessing!' He looked around with a puzzled expression. 'Is your older child here today too?'

Six or seven years ago, Tommy and I hadn't even met. He would have been seeking advice from a priest on his marriage to *her*. It took not a second for me to realize that Father Francis thought I was *her*, Tommy's former wife. I swallowed my disgust and managed to stay calm. Here was a chance for some information!

'I'm afraid you're mistaken, Father Francis. My name is Madeleine Pastore, and I married Tommy just three years ago. This is our only child,' I said as I handed Baby Tommy to Carlotta and took the old priest's arm, guiding him to a dim corner where we could talk in private. 'But if you please, may I ask you something?'

'A second wife? Oh, excuse me, my dear. I see, I see. So he was able to get an annulment after all? I didn't know.'

I confessed right out of the starting gate that some people thought my marriage to Tommy had been invalid. There was no reason to be coy with this priest – Father Matthew knew the truth already. I told Father Francis how I had learned about the other woman, the one lawyers said was the legal Mrs Pastore, and how she had taken all our belongings and money. He listened with a grave expression and when I had finished, I begged him to tell me whatever he knew about this murky part of Tommy's life.

Father Francis might be old as Methuselah, but his memory – at least for events long gone by – was still sharp.

'He came to me in the spring, asking for advice on an annulment. I don't remember the year, but it was spring, because we sat outside in the churchyard on a bench under a willow tree that was just beginning to sprout its tender leaves. He said, "Father, back in New Jersey, I married this girl when she told me she was carrying my child. After a few months, I came to Chicago for a job and was going to send for her as soon as I had a place for us to live." Well, then, he told me that a cousin sent him congratulations for the new baby, a baby that wasn't due for another two months. When his wife failed to write about the new baby coming early, he grew suspicious and rode the train home without telling her he was coming. What did he find? A baby born earlier than could possibly be his – a big baby, not premature at all. He asked me if he could get this marriage annulled, seeing as how it took place under false pretenses.'

'And? What did you tell him?'

'There are several valid reasons for annulment, one of which says that if one party was intentionally deceived about the presence or absence of a quality in the other party in order to obtain consent to marriage, an annulment is possible. I advised him to pursue this at the archbishop's office.'

My heart pounded wildly. 'And did he?'

'I have no idea, my dear. I was transferred out of that parish to this one, and I never saw him again. But you said the lawyers for this first wife ruled that she was the legitimate wife, so perhaps he took my advice no further. Or perhaps he did and the lawyers weren't Catholic – by which I mean they didn't know to check the church records for annulments.' He raised his eyebrows in a suggestive way as if urging me to do just that.

'Thank you! Thank you, I will do that! Right away!'

'The archbishop's office is open on Monday, my dear. Ah, look, Father Matthew is signaling to us. I believe your son's godfather has arrived. Shall we join them?'

I was so excited about this revelation that I could hardly focus on what Father Matthew was saying about the baptism service. Surely Father Francis was right and Tommy had applied for an annulment! Surely there was a record of this in the archbishop's office! Surely I would be confirmed as Tommy's legitimate wife and the stain of illegitimacy would never soil Baby Tommy's future! Surely I could find a lawyer who could get back my money and my house! Soon that evil woman would pay for her sins and her greed!

And the other revelation almost escaped my notice – that woman's child, Vincent his name was – he wasn't Tommy's son after all. Vincent may have Tommy's name, but he wasn't Tommy's son. I had Tommy's son, his only son, and I didn't have to share that with anyone. I nearly danced with happiness.

Our little group moved to the opposite end of the narthex where the marble baptismal font stood. The priest instructed Hank Russo and Carlotta where to stand and then began the formal questions.

'What name do you give this child?'

'Tommaso Duval Pastore,' I said, relishing the sound of the French and Italian together. Tommy was a genuine American, a mix of different nationalities.

'You have asked to have your child baptized. In doing so you are accepting the responsibility of training him in the practice of the faith. It will be your duty to bring him up to keep God's commandments as Christ taught us, by loving God and our neighbor. Do you clearly understand what you are undertaking?'

The massive church doors swung open on creaky hinges and two big, dark-suited men barged in. Their eyes swept the narthex and the nave. Finding it empty except for our small party, they positioned themselves at either side of the door like suspicious sentries guarding the palace gates. Two more big men entered next, their hands clutching something bulky in their overcoat pockets, escorting a fifth man, squat and stubby with a fedora pulled low over his eyes. Eyes that gleamed when they caught sight of me.

Alphonse Capone.

Anyone with an ounce of sense was afraid of Al Capone, Johnny Torrio's second-in-command at the Outfit, and I had pounds of sense. My husband had known him only slightly, but he once told me that Torrio had originally brought Big Al to Chicago to be his chief enforcer, a job Al enjoyed so much that when he was promoted to Number Two and ordered to delegate murders to underlings from then on, he complained about missing all the fun. I'd had a narrow escape recently when he tried to offer me, the poor widow, his 'protection'. Turning down a volatile killer who could see insult in the twitch of an eyelid was no mean feat, believe you me. And the fiasco at the following week's séance when he failed to reach his dead brother's spirit nearly cost Carlotta and me our lives. Scarface Al Capone was the very last person I wanted to see entering the church. I nearly lost my lunch.

'I hope I'm not too late,' he said, as if anyone would dare to scold him. Handing his hat to one of the bodyguards, he lumbered up to the font, keeping the two thugs elbow-close. 'Good day to you, Mrs Pastore. I heard Tommy's son was being baptized today and made up my mind that I was going to honor your late husband by standing godfather to his boy. It's the least I can do for Tommy Pastore – a good man – and we take care of our own.'

His words echoed through the narthex until they died against the thick stone walls. My mouth fell open. The very idea of this murderer, this piece of criminal filth, promising God to give my boy a Catholic upbringing in my absence was more appalling than anything I could comprehend. No way in hell would this gangster be my son's godfather! After several awkward seconds, I swallowed hard and managed to speak.

'Th-th-thank you, Mr Capone. Th-that's very kind of you. But we already have a godmother and a godfather, Tommy's good friend Hank Russo. You're – you're welcome to stand with us while the priest, uh, while the priest finishes . . .' I looked toward Father Matthew for help but he remained stubbornly mute. He knew who he was dealing with, the coward.

'Nonsense,' replied Capone, dismissing my protests with a wave of one hand as he shrugged off his overcoat, revealing a dead black suit with a narrow pink strip and a pale blue shirt. A ruby pin tacked down his orange striped tie. 'Russo will step aside,' he said.

Hank didn't need to be told twice. He literally stepped aside, as if making room for the Outfit's second-in-command to move closer to the font.

'It's important for Tommy's boy to have the best,' continued Capone, licking his thick lips. He was chewing gum. I could smell the Dentyne. 'The best is me, who can give the kid a future, who can protect him when things go wrong.'

'I'm sure we won't have any problems like that, Mr Capone. Baby Tommy will be—'

'Not today, sure, but what about his future? Nobody's gonna beat up this kid on the street or give him any lip when he has big Al Capone for his godfather, ya know?'

'But Hank's family has given us the—'

'And should anything happen to you, God forbid, Mrs Pastore, I will be there to take him under my wing like he was my own son and make a man of him. A man his father would be proud of. On my word, he'll have a job – a paying job – when he's twelve.'

'But we've promised Hank—'

'Sure, sure, I understand. But a boy can have two godfathers, can't he, Father? God doesn't mind that, does He?'

'Ah . . . no, of course not,' replied the gutless priest. If he had disagreed, if he'd said we were already too far into the ceremony to change, if he'd given any sort of religious reason, we might have broken free of this farce. But he didn't.

Carlotta, too, had been silent throughout this exchange, her expression one of frozen horror. Now she reached over to my hand and squeezed it. If she meant to send a message, I didn't understand it.

'Well then, we're all good, right? And here,' he said, handing the priest an envelope. 'Here's a donation to the church, Father. A big one. For the poor. Now let's get this show on the road. Give us the short version. God knows I don't have all day here.'

FOURTEEN

I was determined to be at Holy Name Cathedral's office the minute they unlocked the door. Too keyed up to sleep, I was running on nerve alone, desperate to discover if Tommy had applied for and maybe received an annulment from the Vatican. A piece of paper that would restore our marriage and our son to legitimacy. But right after breakfast, a telephone call from Lloyd Prescott put paid to those plans.

'We neglected to do something,' said the reporter. 'We need to go back to Midwest and talk to their tellers. Find out who was working the windows that day. Maybe they remember something about Quillen and money. Is my stenog coming with me?'

'Can't we go later? I have something to do this morning. Something that won't take long.'

'What?'

'Well, nothing much really. I just need to check into some paperwork at the cathedral office.'

'That can wait an hour, can't it? I've got an appointment at the bank with the tellers at nine. We gotta be finished by ten when the bank opens to the public. We'll be out by then and Holy Name Cathedral isn't far.'

I nearly said no, but he was right. My annulment search could wait an hour.

Miss Ruby Stanley met us at the bank's back entrance at the stroke of nine. 'Waiting in the lobby are the three tellers who were working on November twenty-seventh,' she said, her voice frosty with irritation and her heels clicking with sharp disapproval on the polished floor as we traveled along the hall toward the main lobby. 'We usually have four but one quit and his replacement wasn't hired until after that date. I don't know how you managed to get permission to waste more of our time, but the board wanted it, and we follow the board's instructions to the letter. However, I assure you that there is simply no way for money to vanish from this bank without our knowledge. Embezzlement is impossible. We have too many controls.'

'Could you explain those controls?' asked Prescott.

'Humph, I already did.' Click, click, click went her heels. 'All right, I'll make it really simple this time so even you can understand. A patron comes in to deposit or withdraw. A receiving teller accepts his cash, counts the currency and specie, checking it as the count is proved so there is little possibility that a package of currency will remain in the pocket of the person bringing the deposit to the bank, either through thoughtlessness or otherwise. He writes a deposit slip or, for withdrawals, hands the patron his cash and writes a withdrawal slip. The slips and cash are collected at day's end when they are checked by the head teller and then by the paying teller who is the custodian of the bank's cash. The amount is posted to the depositor's account on the ledgers. The paying teller then gives all the information to the head cashier or his assistant, which was Mr Quillen, for another review. The head cashier sends them to me for yet *another* review, after which I send the report to the president.'

'Sounds like you'd need the entire staff to be on the take to make embezzling work.'

Goaded beyond endurance, she stopped short and glared at him. 'Such may be the ethical standards in your profession, young man, but I assure you, they are not in ours. Now, did you want to speak with the tellers separately or together?'

'Separately, if you please,' replied Prescott, unchastened. Nothing phased that man.

'Mr Cassell will be first, then. The receiving teller.' She motioned to a heavy, middle-aged man with no neck and bulging eyes and pointed us to an empty desk in the far corner of the lobby. Lloyd Prescott introduced himself and me, explained that we were putting the finishing touches on an article about Quillen's death and needed to ask just a few questions. I whipped out my pad and pencil.

'Did you handle any deposits or withdrawals of any large amount on November twenty-seventh?' the reporter asked.

'I'm sure I did, sir, but without more details, I cannot be more specific. How do you define "large"?'

'Let's say in excess of a thousand dollars.'

'I'm sure there were. That isn't an unusual amount.'

'More than ten thousand, then?'

'I don't remember any in particular. Often the larger transactions are – or were – handled by Mr Quillen, the assistant cashier.'

'Did any of that day's clientele strike you as strange?'

'Strange?'

'Unusually nervous? Careless? Inept? Suspicious in any way?'

He shook his head. 'Not that I recall, sir. If I had noticed anything amiss, I assure you I would have notified the head cashier or Miss Stanley right away.'

I wasn't supposed to open my mouth, but the questions slipped out. 'The teller who quit recently, who was that?'

'That'd be Bill Tucker.'

'Did you know him well?'

'Not well. He worked here less than a year.'

'Did he quit before or after the twenty-seventh?'

'The week before.'

'Why did he leave? Was he fired?'

'No. He said he'd come into some money and didn't need to work anymore. His father died, he said.'

'Did you believe him?'

'Why wouldn't I?'

Lloyd and I exchanged a meaningful look. That would be something to check. The reporter cleared his throat and resumed the questioning. 'If you wanted to embezzle ten thousand dollars from Midwest, how would you go about it?'

His eyebrows shot up in surprise. 'It's not possible. Any discrepancy would be noticed by another teller or by the head cashier.'

'Suppose you pocketed the money and destroyed the deposit slip.'

'The patron would have a receipt and a pass book entry to prove his deposit.'

'And no patrons have come forth to claim their account is short?'

'You'll have to ask Miss Stanley that question.'

'Suppose you withdrew more than the requested amount and pocketed the difference?'

'The client would have a withdrawal slip and see that it didn't match the record.'

'I see. Well, thank you, Mr Cassell.'

After we questioned Mr Faverton and Mr Blum with similar results, the reporter looked at his watch. It was nearly ten.

'Well, that wasn't a very productive outing, was it?' he asked me.

'Are you going to check on that fourth teller's father? To see if there really was a bequest?'

'Sure, no problem. Bill Tucker. Obits. Easy as pie. I'll let you know if anything suspicious turns up.'

'Are we finished?'

'Sure are.'

'I have another question for Miss Stanley, if you please.'

Lloyd Prescott's irritated look made me think he would refuse this impertinent intrusion into his realm, but he relented. 'Go ahead.'

We stood over Miss Stanley's desk waiting for her to look

up and acknowledge our presence. I felt like a naughty pupil waiting for a rap across my knuckles with a ruler. I cleared my throat and said 'Excuse me' twice before she looked up.

'Is it true that Mr Quillen usually handled the larger transactions?' I asked.

'Occasionally Mr Quillen would leave his desk and assist special patrons, yes. It gives the important patron a sense of receiving extra service.'

'Did Mr Quillen handle any unusual transactions that day, his last day, whether deposits or withdrawals?'

Wordlessly she went to the shelves behind her desk and brought forth a ledger book as large as a world atlas. Flipping back a few pages, she came to the twenty-seventh and ran one finger down a middle column. 'Yes, two that day. A deposit for Apex Inc. for $630,622 and a withdrawal from Wilson Brothers Construction for $272,000.'

I looked at Lloyd Prescott. He looked at me. 'Apex Inc?' he said. 'That's a North Side Gang company. They own betting parlors. Brothels. Did you know that, Miss Stanley?'

She sniffed. 'The origin of the money isn't the bank's business, Mr Prescott.'

The grandfather clock in the lobby chimed ten. Out of the corner of my eye I saw a stern-faced employee stride to the front door, throw the bolt, and let half a dozen people shuffle out of the cold into the warm bank. I paid them no mind until I heard one of the men shout, 'Nobody move!'

Of course like everyone else, I spun around to see what was going on, then froze when I understood.

Jeez Louise, it was a bank job.

Three or four or five men spread out into the bank's lobby – initial confusion made it hard to tell robbers from patrons since all the men were swathed in dark overcoats, hats, and mufflers. One threw a sack over the grill to Mr Cassell, the nearest teller, and barked instructions. Something about him seemed familiar . . . yes, I squinted to be sure. It was the fake brother Quillen who had been to our séance last week! He wasn't facing my direction, so I couldn't see his gold tooth, but I was pretty sure it was the same man who had sat on our sofa and then across from me at the table that night, the man who asked the spirits where the money was. This was the North Side Gang. Maybe the very same men who had killed my Tommy.

'Fill it up,' he ordered, pulling a gun out from under his coat with his free hand. He acted like the leader. The others stood sentry, watching employees and patrons alike with cold eyes and twitchy trigger fingers eager for an excuse to shoot.

Beside me, Lloyd Prescott could hardly contain his excitement. 'What luck!' he whispered hoarsely. 'This is so jake – an exclusive on a genuine bank job!'

Not feeling quite as lucky, I could only watch in dismay as the teller pulled open drawers and stuffed bundles of cash into the sack. No one was looking directly at me, so I inched closer to the desk. I would be ready to drop behind it if shooting erupted.

'Maddie,' hissed Prescott, 'look at Miss Stanley over there, cool as a cucumber. Bet the old bag has seen more than one of these in her lifetime.'

Miss Stanley was, as Lloyd said, the picture of calm, standing behind her desk in a pose that reminded me of an irritated classroom teacher glaring at her naughty pupils. One of the robbers had planted himself across from her desk, but his eyes were on the tellers and not Miss Stanley, so he didn't notice her hand reaching into the kneehole, just under the center drawer. I noticed. So did Lloyd.

'Look! She's—'

I jabbed him with my elbow to shut him up. He got the message.

'Hurry up!' shouted a nervous robber as Mr Cassell passed the bag to the next teller, Mr Blum. Blum moved so quickly he dropped bundles of cash on the floor. Confused, he turned to their leader and asked, 'Shall I pick them up?'

The gold-tooth man fired a warning round into the ceiling. 'Faster!' His eyes swept the room, moving with slow deliberation from one person to the next. Fearing he would recognize me from the séance, I ducked my head and turned away as his gaze came closer, then covered my mouth and nose with my hand and coughed. When I dared look up again, his attention had shifted back to the hapless Blum who was scooping up fallen bills with shaky fingers, taking more time than if he'd moved carefully. I wondered about that.

No one stirred, no one spoke, no one seemed to breathe; the only sound was the steady ticking from the lobby clock near the stairs. Seconds stretched into one minute, then two, as Blum passed the bulging bag to the third man.

Noise from outside the bank turned heads. Car doors slammed. More than one. Rough voices blasted through a megaphone.

'We've got the place surrounded, boys. Come out with your hands up and no one gets hurt.'

The gold-tooth man raced behind the counter but instead of snatching the money bag, he grabbed Mr Faverton, the teller who was holding it, and pulled him close for a shield. With his gun in his other hand, he dragged the hapless fellow toward the door. The other robbers didn't need directions – they were not giving up. They were taking hostages to ensure a safe getaway. The one nearest Miss Stanley's desk seized her by the collar of her starched shirtwaist and nearly lifted her off her feet.

'Open the door!' ordered the gold-tooth man, waving his gun toward one quivering patron. Standing well behind the thick door lest the police mistake him for a robber and shoot, the man opened it slowly, wide enough for the gangster to stand on the threshold with his hostage in front of him like a Roman shield. 'Stand back! We're coming out and these guys gonna eat a bullet if anyone gets in our way.'

The robbers made it through the door with their hostages, one by one, until the bank lobby was nearly empty. Suddenly brave, Lloyd Prescott dashed to the window just as the first gunshots were fired. I was close behind him.

I don't think anyone ever figured out who fired first, but a volley of gunfire erupted as the robbers tried to climb into two automobiles parked at the curb. Panic ensued. Lloyd gasped as several men dropped to the ground, wounded, dead, or just seeking cover, I couldn't tell. The cops swooped in on the remaining robbers, clubbing one with nightsticks as they hauled him into a paddy wagon. In the melee, one gangster managed to throw off his human shield, fire a few rounds toward the cops, and duck into a getaway car. Rubber tires screeched as he tore off. Valuable seconds were lost as the police scrambled to send two patrol cars after him.

'Dear god,' breathed Lloyd. 'That's Miss Stanley on the ground.'

From a distance came the sound of an ambulance siren.

FIFTEEN

After routine questioning, the police released us along with the bank patrons. Lloyd Prescott hustled off to his typewriter to bang out his big scoop – his eyewitness account of a bank heist that failed. In the end, I managed to learn that the bank was out no money (the sack of banknotes had been dropped on the pavement and was promptly retrieved) and no one had been killed, although several men were hospitalized with bullet wounds. Miss Stanley emerged from the commotion bruised but unbowed – after downing a bracing shot of whiskey that someone pulled out of a drawer, she insisted on returning to her desk. 'This is not my first robbery,' she remarked tartly. Evidently not: it was she who knew to press the emergency call line to the nearest police station that alerted them to a robbery in progress. Two of the bank robbers were in police custody. Two had escaped by automobile, but they would soon be apprehended. Or so the cops assured us.

'Did one of the men in custody have a gold tooth?' I asked, wondering if he was one of those who got away. They didn't know.

Incredibly, the lobby clock chose that moment to strike eleven. It felt as if hours had passed since Lloyd Prescott and I had arrived, and it wasn't even noon.

By the time I got home to feed Baby Tommy, my hands had stopped shaking. Feeling bold, I telephoned the local precinct to fill Officer O'Rourke in on the robbery details. The bank wasn't in O'Rourke's precinct, but when it comes to cops, word travels on invisible telegraph wires.

'I was there,' I reported. 'One of the robbers was the same gold-tooth man who came to our séance.'

'Louis Roth was there?'

Ha! He slipped. Now I knew the gold-tooth man's name. 'Yes, I'm sure it was Roth – he seemed to be their leader. I don't know if he was one of the ones who got away.'

'Must've been. He isn't in jail.'

'Now you'll have to investigate, right?'

'There's a special unit that investigates bank robberies. I'm not in it, so no, I won't be working that personally. But I'll make sure they know someone in the bank recognized Roth. What were you doing at the bank that morning? Coincidence?'

'Um, sort of. I was with that reporter, Lloyd Prescott, who's digging into Quillen's death. Now he gets an eyewitness story about the bank job. We believe the heist is related to Quillen's death, since Roth figures in both.'

'Mrs Pastore, now that the authorities are involved, you step aside, hear me? When I asked you and Madame Carlotta to help the police, I didn't mean for you to put yourself in danger investigating murders. I meant communicating with the spirit world. These are ruthless men. They don't hesitate to kill when they're cornered. Word on the street says Roth is trying to find a hundred-thousand-dollar stash of gang money that's gone missing. And while no one thought it was bank related at first, now we do.'

'A hundred thousand dollars! Since Roth couldn't get the spirit of Herman Quillen to tell him where the money was, he must've figured the quickest way to get it was to rob a bank.'

'Which didn't work, so he's bound to be desperate. Promise me you'll leave this all to the cops?'

'I promise.' And I meant it. Baby Tommy was my first concern, and he needed a mother to raise him right, not a godfather. I was through with this investigation. I'd done my part and then some.

I hung up the receiver feeling a satisfying sense of closure. Carlotta and I had helped the police, just as we said we would. There was nothing more either of us could do. The police were hot on the gangsters' trail. We could read about their findings in the newspapers like normal Chicagoans.

It was only then that I remembered the archbishop's office.

Putting a clean diaper on Tommy, I wrapped him in a thick

blanket and set out for the Holy Name Cathedral humming a nursery song in his ear. I had just survived a bank robbery unscathed. Surely this was my lucky day.

Until it wasn't.

Never mind the details, the cathedral files contained no record of my husband ever applying to Rome for a divorce or an annulment. My last hope was crushed. Too depressed to return home, I stumbled into the cavernous cathedral and collapsed in a rear pew, alone and in complete silence, breathing in the years of candle wax and incense, letting the tears come where there was no one but Baby Tommy to know. It would have meant everything in the world, that piece of paper. Legitimacy. Respectability. A future for little Tommy. Everything.

A few parishioners entered the cathedral, sat a while to meditate or knelt to pray, then left. They didn't look at me and I returned the favor. I thought about lighting a votive candle in memory of the dead, but I wasn't feeling overly generous toward my late husband at that moment and besides, candles were too much a feature of Carlotta's spooky séances to mean much to me anymore.

The way I figured it, Tommy had been young and naïve, maybe nineteen or twenty, an easy mark for an older woman who found herself in a family way with no one to put a ring on her finger. So she seduced the young lad, convinced him it was his, and got him to the altar. When he went to Chicago for a job, she must've thought she had it made. Or maybe she sent him, to get him out of the picture at the crucial time. All she had to do now was have the baby quietly and when he returned, tell him it was two months younger than it was. Birth certificates can be altered – I knew that from one of my brothers who'd changed the date on his own. But Tommy had shown up back in New Jersey unexpectedly. The truth spilled out. Must've been quite a brawl – Italians don't fight quietly. He returned to Chicago without her. The conniving little tramp must have followed shortly thereafter or maybe a few years later, who knows? Tommy asked Father Francis about annulments and divorces and then neglected to follow through. Why, I'd never know. He couldn't have forgotten. Maybe it was too expensive. I've heard you have to make a hefty donation to the church for such relief. Maybe he figured no one would ever know, so why bother? Whatever the reason, he didn't get around to it, and here I was today.

Skies darken early in December, especially in the city where the tall buildings act like mountains blocking the sun. When I finally left the cathedral and headed back to Carlotta's house, the sun had dipped below the skyline and the bank clock on State Street read four thirty. By the time I'd stepped off the streetcar, twilight had turned to dusk and I still had a good many blocks to walk home, most of it with a bitter wind off the lake stinging my cheeks.

For the first few blocks, the sidewalks were busy with pedestrians, and gaslights brightened my path, but as I came closer to Carlotta's street where gaslights were scarce, the neighborhoods became eerily empty. I clutched Tommy tight when a mangy mutt followed me for a whole city block, menacing my ankles until he finally slunk away. Several times strange noises made me glance over my shoulder, but it was only rats scurrying along the gutters, looking for refuge in the warm sewers. I breathed a sigh of relief as we reached our block of sturdy brick row houses, each with its own sturdy brick staircase leading to a raised first story. There was no one in sight as I approached.

Until a figure materialized from behind the stairs of the house next to Carlotta's, like a specter created from the shadows.

'Well, well,' said the specter, 'if it ain't my old séance gal, Widow Pastore. Evenin', ma'am. And how's the little one tonight?'

I skidded to a halt. A glance around the deserted street told me I'd get no help from bystanders. He stood between me and Carlotta's staircase. There was no way I could outrun him with the baby in my arms. I prayed that Carlotta or Freddy or someone who lived in one of the adjacent houses would see me out the window and step outside, giving me the chance to slip past him to safety.

Nothing doing. Louis Roth leaned his face so close I could see his gold tooth gleam even in the dark. His pointy chin and beady black eyes made me think of a fox. Holding Tommy hard against my chest, I took a step back. I didn't have to glance around to know that there was no one within shouting distance. The street was dead as a morgue. There was nothing to do but bluff my way past him and get up the steps before he could do us any harm. I stepped right. He followed my movement, shifting left to block my path.

'What's your hurry, little lady? No time for a chat? Me and you got a problem we need to talk over.' One dirty finger reached out and pulled the blanket away from Tommy's face. Batting away his hand, I squeezed Tommy even closer against my breast.

'What is it you want?'

'That's better. Now, let's see . . . someone at the séance told the cops I was lookin' for money from a dead guy, and the cops come lookin' for me down at Twin Anchors, and word of all that gets around to Hymie Weiss, who now thinks maybe it was me behind the snatch of his hundred grand, or maybe I was trying to get the money on the sly and keep it for myself. I swore it wasn't me who took it in the first place. I said I was trying to find out where it was so I could give it back to him, and he nods like he believes me, and then he says he don't care who did what, he just wants the money back. So you see our problem.'

'I . . . I don't understand.'

'He thinks I have the money or at least that I learned where it is at your séance. If I don't get him the money and quick, I'll be pushing up daisies come spring. Now, here's the thing. I didn't know Herman Quillen, the sap who stole the money. I wish I'd killed him, but I didn't kill him, and I don't know who did, and I don't care who did. I just want the money.'

'I don't know where it is either. I'm no detective. The cops are investigating. They'll find it.'

'No, no, no, doll, you need to smarten up. We don't want them to find it, do we? That won't get it back to Hymie Weiss. We want *us* to find it, see? You and me. I tried at the séance. I tried at the bank this morning. You were there, doll. I saw you. You were trying to find it too, weren't you? Don't deny it. Now you try again. Ask again with your gypsy woman. Herman Quillen took that money and he knows where it is. Get me back that money and nothin' bad will happen to the kid here, got it?'

What had Al Capone promised me yesterday? Maybe that loathsome gangster would be good for something after all. I swallowed hard and fought back.

'How dare you threaten my baby! If you think I'm helpless and alone in the world, think again. My boy's godfather is Al Capone from the Outfit, and he won't take kindly to your threats.'

Roth barked a coarse laugh and spat on the pavement. 'Capone? You think I give a rat's ass about any of those faggot Capone boys Torrio keeps close? The minute that Scarface punk hears the name Hymie Weiss, he's pissin' his pants. Get me the money and be quick about it. A shame if something should happen to your kid.'

SIXTEEN

'Don't tell Carlotta about this,' I warned Freddy after relating what had just happened with the gangster and his threats. I'd been telling myself over and over that Louis Roth wouldn't really hurt Baby Tommy. Or me. He was all bluff and bluster. No one would harm a baby. Just to be sure, though, I would leave Tommy safe at home as much as I could rather than risk taking him with me. Still, finding that money would be my all-around best bet. 'I don't want to worry Carlotta unnecessarily. I don't know what else I can do for Roth other than visit some more speakeasies near where Quillen's body was found. Maybe tomorrow I can learn something about his final hours. Like, maybe he was seen with someone who later killed him. Maybe the person who killed him learned the location of the money and already has it. If I can find out where it is, I don't have to get it back myself. The gangsters can get it back.'

'I'll come with you.'

'No. I wanted you to know what was going on because I need to leave Tommy here tomorrow morning. He'll be napping. Just don't leave the house with him or anything like that.'

Freddy looked shocked that I would even think such a thing. 'I'd never take him anywhere without you.'

'I know, I know. I just want someone here to be aware of the danger he's in – we're all in for that matter – in case Roth decides to burn down the building or turn on the gas.'

Working with what I'd learned from Lloyd Prescott, I burnished my credentials as a girl reporter for the *Tribune* and set out to scour more speakeasies between the bank and the alley where Quillen had died. It was Saturday morning and every speak I came across was open. Some were quiet with only a couple of last night's drunks sleeping it off in the corner, others had your early morning boozehounds and even a few coffee drinkers huddled around dirty tables. A few had Victrolas playing lazy jazz. All reeked of alcohol, beer, and tobacco. I carried a pad and pencil like I figured a real reporter would and told bartenders and waiters that I was working with Lloyd Prescott on a story about Herman Quillen. The line got me more cooperation than any of the others I'd used.

Cooperation, yes. Information, no. No one remembered the man I described and honestly, who could blame them? It had been more than two weeks now since Quillen's death. Lots of river under the bridge since then. And describing him was hard. He was so damn average!

At last, as I was leaving the Tree Club, a classy joint three blocks from Midwest Bank, my luck changed. I'd been talking with the bartender, a pudgy older gent who remembered the story of Quillen's death but not anyone fitting Quillen's description. I had just thanked him and headed to the door when a waitress edged over, a bottle blond with crimson lipstick, her tray resting on one ample hip. 'I heard what you said to Kenny,' she began. 'I think I served the man you're talking about.'

'Really? Kinda skinny, middle-aged, comb-over? Toothbrush mustache?'

'Yeah, I think so. I really didn't pay much attention to him. It was the other fella.'

'He was with someone?'

'Yeah, maybe that's the man you're looking for, huh? A fat older fella with a nice suit. Laughed a lot. They were celebrating because he was retiring, and I remember them because they ordered one drink each, then the fat man finished and paid the bill and left me a fin, saying it was for any more drinks the other fella wanted and I could keep the rest, and well, the other fella didn't want any more drinks and he left soon after, so I got to keep the whole five bucks. Biggest tip I've ever had in my life.'

The bank president! It had to be. What was his name? Charles Hughes. He had a big belly and was counting the days 'til retirement. So Hughes had been drinking with Herman Quillen on the night he died. Why hadn't he mentioned that fact when Lloyd Prescott interviewed him? Surely that was suspicious.

'What were they drinking, do you remember?'

'Sure, I do. Top-shelf whiskey – Irish label – and if you're thinking there was poison in it' – her voice turned hard as stone – 'you're dead wrong because both their drinks came from the same bottle and others drank it that night too, and no one died but that Quillen fella so don't go thinking he got any of that rotgut here. This is a respectable joint.'

'No, no, I didn't think that. Not at all. He probably bought something off someone in the street later on that night. We'll probably never know. Thank you. Thank you very much.' I gave her a silver dollar and wished it was more.

I raced home to the telephone to call Lloyd Prescott.

'I have a scoop!' I said, proud of my reporter lingo. 'Quillen was seen with a man who sounds like the bank president, Charles Hughes. Remember him telling us he was retiring? Leaving town for California? It didn't sound suspicious at the time but now . . .'

'You're damn right it sounds suspicious. We need to collar him right away. Here, let me grab the – wait a sec. I'm looking up his address. Hope he hasn't left town yet. Damnit all to hell, the *City Directory* doesn't list an address for Hughes.'

'It doesn't?'

'Well, it gives the Midwest Savings & Loan address as if it was his home. That's a dodge right there.'

I gave this a half second's thought. 'What if we see if the bank has a home address for him? I'll bet Miss Stanley does.'

'Good girl. I'll call her – no, I'll go in person. The old bat hung up on me last time I called. You coming?'

Of course I was. I needed to find the money before the police did.

An hour later, Lloyd Prescott and I met at the bank. We didn't warn Miss Stanley that we were coming this time. We just walked up bold as brass.

'Miss Stanley!' he exclaimed as if he was astonished to find her sitting behind her desk. 'How delightful to see you! We happened to be in the neighborhood and thought we'd drop by for some quick information. Seems the *City Directory* incorrectly listed Mr Hughes' home address as the bank's and we were certain you would have it at your fingertips.'

She scowled. 'Mr Hughes has retired. He no longer works here.'

'Very true, but we need to talk to him before he leaves for California. If he hasn't already left.'

'I'm afraid I can't help you.'

'That's too bad.' He turned to me. 'Well, I guess we'll just have to get the police to track him down.'

Miss Stanley's eyes grew big as dinner plates. 'What do the police have to do with this?'

'They don't *have to* have anything to do with this, Miss Stanley. We could bypass the cops if we had his address.'

With lips pressed in a tight line of defeat, she scribbled on a pad of paper and tore off the sheet with a snort. Handing it to Prescott, she got up from her desk and stalked into the back room.

'What a charmer,' he muttered. We were making to leave when a thin man with a long face, a slack jaw, and jug-handle ears stood up from his nearby desk.

'Don't be too hard on her,' he said, taking a few hesitant steps toward us. 'The old gal's been through the wringer since the robbery. Hasn't gone home but to sleep. There's been an audit going on, and she finds it all highly insulting. She's been grumbling all day. "We don't need outsiders telling us what's going on in our own bank," she keeps saying.'

'So there's no money missing?' I asked. Lloyd glared at me. I know I wasn't supposed to talk but the words just slipped out.

'Not a dime. If you ask me, one of those gangsters told his boss he deposited the money and took off with it himself. I can tell you, it never came through our system.' He twirled his pencil with his fingers, then stuck it behind his big ear. 'There was one odd thing though.'

'What's that?'

'That week – the week Mr Quillen died – the vault had an unusual proportion of its currency in small denominations.'

'Small denominations?'

'Ones, fives, tens.'

'What's strange about that?'

He shrugged. 'Nothing, I guess. It's just odd. We've never been so short on large bills before. Doesn't mean anything.'

SEVENTEEN

The Near North Side is the oldest part of Chicago and the place where the richest people live. The fanciest shops are there and lots of skyscrapers too. Along the Gold Coast, millionaires like Potter Palmer build turreted castles surrounded by green grass lawns that slope toward Lake Michigan's gentle waves. The people who live in the Near North Side have gardeners and maids and cooks and butlers and nannies and chauffeurs to drive their Duesenbergs and Rolls Royces. They have their clothes made at fancy boutiques and dine at restaurants in luxury hotels like the Blackstone, the Palmer House, or the brand-new Drake. Driving through Near North Side neighborhoods felt like flying over dreamland in a magic carpet. When Lloyd Prescott and I rattled across the State Street bridge in his Ford Runabout, it was obvious to any onlooker that we didn't belong there.

'Here's Oak Street,' he said, turning left. 'Watch for the house number.'

'There!' I pointed, not at a number but at a house where a hatless man was huffing and puffing, trying to install a For Sale sign at the curb. Not an easy job, seeing that the ground was covered with a foot of snow and the soil was rock hard. 'What's going on?' I asked Prescott. 'They're moving? Didn't Hughes tell us they were taking a trip to California?'

'He said they were checking the California climate to see if they might move there. Because his wife's health was bad or something. Maybe they made up their minds already.' He pulled the motorcar over to the curb and rolled down his window. 'This the Hughes' residence?'

Leaning on his pickax, the man wiped his brow with his coat sleeve. 'Yes, sir. You in the market for a house? This one's not ready for showing yet, but I can give you an early peek.' I expect he was just being polite because the dented flivver must have shouted what sort of price range the likes of Lloyd Prescott could afford.

The stately Hughes mansion looked like something out of my old fairy-tale picture book with its exposed timbers criss-crossing a white stucco exterior. Set back from the street and overarched by four towering trees, bare now of leaves, it was bordered by gardens that I imagined burst into a rainbow of flowers each spring. It was a house full of romance. A house that smiled.

'No, we're looking for Mr and Mrs Hughes. They home?'

'Nope.'

'They're moving, huh?'

'Yep. Soon as they pack up their things. Taking a long time, with just them doing the work. Servants all skedaddled. I'd help 'em myself but I got four houses to show tomorrow.'

In a quiet voice, I said to Lloyd, 'Tell him you know someone who does that kind of work, cheap.'

Giving me a queer look, he called to the agent. 'I know someone who can do that kind of work cheap.'

'How cheap?'

'A dollar a day.'

'Mrs Hughes would be glad to have that help. You send your man here tomorrow morning, early. I'll tell Mrs Hughes when she gets home.'

'You can count on it, mister.' He rolled up his window and pulled away from the curb. 'What in heaven's name are you thinking, Maddie? Surely not you. Hughes met you at the bank. He'll recognize you right off.'

'No, he won't. He barely spared me a look that day. You did all the talking. For extra insurance, I'll wear a wig and cheaters.'

'They'll be expecting a man.'

'I'll blame the misunderstanding on the agent. Listen, Lloyd, I'm a good worker. I know how to pack merchandise. They'll have no reason to complain about me. And we'll just see what I can learn.'

So that's how I came to work at the Hughes' house the following morning, dressed like a man in overalls with Carlotta's wig on my head and her fake spectacles on my nose and sturdy shoes on my feet. Opening the back door at my knock, Mrs Hughes gave me the once-over and scowled at my cheery greeting.

'The estate agent said he was sending a man.'

'Did he, ma'am? I'm sorry he misunderstood. I'm sure you'll be happy with my work. I did a lot of packing when I worked for Marshall Field's, so I know how to take good care of your valuables. Give me a try for an hour or two and if you're not satisfied, I'll leave with no pay, no complaints.'

Mrs Hughes was a plump, big-bosomed matron in her fifties with her thick silver hair arranged in a twist at the nape of her neck. No make-up adorned her plain face – of course not, women of her era scorned cosmetics as tools of harlots and actresses. Evidently the proscription did not include perfume – she reeked of jasmine. Her pale cheeks could have used some rouge. Her squinty eyes would have benefitted from a bit of eye pencil. Her hale-and-hearty voice showed no trace of sickness.

'Well . . . all right. Come in.' Over her shoulder she called to her husband. 'Charles! Charles, the packing helper is here. It's a . . . it's a woman.' A faint answering call came from the bowels of the house. 'Leave your wraps here, dear. What did you say your name was?'

'Madeleine Duval.'

'Well, Madeleine, go directly into the library. Through that hallway and bear left. My husband will put you to work.' She looked at me rather doubtfully. 'I hope you're strong.'

'Very.'

The interior of the house kept faith with its English exterior. I had never been in such an elegant home, but they all looked like this in my head with dark paneling, floors of polished wood or tile, flocked wallpaper, and ceilings decorated with stuccoed swirls and floral designs. I wanted to pause long enough to admire every detail but dared not keep Mr Hughes waiting.

Standing in the midst of hundreds of leather-bound books, the master of the house looked more like a befuddled scholar than a former bank president, dressed in rumpled trousers and a white turtleneck sweater. As soon as he'd ascertained my name and Marshall Field's credentials, he waved his arm toward one wall of floor-to-ceiling bookshelves and barked, 'All those books need to be packed into those boxes. Each box goes to the front porch. A man is coming this afternoon to pick them up. Nothing on these shelves' – he pointed to another wall with only a couple of shelves – 'goes with them. Those books get packed into the boxes and stacked in that corner. Is that clear?'

'Yes, sir.'

'Make no mistakes. I'll be back to check on you shortly.' He strode from the library. Breathing a sigh of relief that he hadn't recognized me, I climbed the ladder to the top shelf and got to work.

It took most of the morning to pack up the Hughes library, but I managed to lug the last box out to the porch before the man with a truck came to haul them away. Where to, I didn't know or care. My arms ached. Maybe this hadn't been such a grand idea after all. I had learned nothing so far, working in that room all by myself. With Mr and Mrs Hughes busy in other rooms, there was no opportunity to engage in casual conversation. As soon as I'd finished with my assignment, I retraced my steps back to the kitchen, taking the liberty of peering into every room along the way. There was an enormous entrance hall, a formal parlor, a south-facing sun room, a dining room that could have seated an entire women's club for luncheon, and a curving staircase that led to numerous second-floor bedrooms and, as I would soon learn, a third-floor maids' quarters. Marks on the bare walls indicated where paintings and mirrors had recently hung. Divots in the Persian carpets revealed where the heavy furniture had stood.

In the kitchen, Mrs Hughes was putting a silver tea service into Pacific silver cloth bags.

'May I have a glass of water?' She nodded and I helped myself. 'The library is finished. Can I help you here?'

'Well, yes, I suppose you can. You said you know how to pack merchandise. Fetch some more newspaper from the garage and start wrapping this china.'

Soon we had developed a routine: Mrs Hughes would hand me a porcelain plate or a Meissen figurine or a glass candelabrum and I would wrap it in newsprint and lay it snug in a box as she noted the item on her master list. At first, she watched me carefully to make sure I hadn't exaggerated my abilities. Once reassured, she pursed her colorless lips with satisfaction. 'You'll do.'

I didn't let the companionable silence last long.

'It's awfully cold today. I hope you are going somewhere warmer than Chicago.'

'Hm. Yes. Mexico.'

'Mexico!' I nearly dropped the demitasse cup I was holding. Mr Hughes had told us California. Jeez, they were fleeing the country! It would be hard for the police to find them once they'd crossed the border. 'I mean, gosh, it's so, well, exotic. How exciting! And you're taking all your belongings with you?'

'Gracious me, no! Most of the furniture has been sold to antiques dealers. The paintings too. I never cared much for those dreary old things. Most of these things belonged to my husband's parents who owned the house before us. We're taking very little with us. I look forward to furnishing my new house with lovely new Mexican pieces.'

Mrs Hughes proved quite chatty once you got her going, and in short order I learned more than I ever wanted to know about what she intended to buy once she reached their destination. It sounded like there'd be no limits to her Mexican spending spree. The word California never came up. Why had her husband lied to us that day at the bank?

I had not finished when Mr Hughes interrupted to summon me upstairs to the bedrooms where he had boxed up bedding and linens. 'Carry these down to the garage,' he ordered. 'They'll be picked up tomorrow. Then you can roll up these rugs and stack them in the front hall.'

As soon as he left, I scouted out the upstairs rooms. Just as I'd figured, there were bedrooms and two modernized bathrooms – the kind with the white porcelain sink, toilet, and tub in the same room – but there was also a study and a dressing room with some furniture still in place. I searched all drawers and built-in cupboards, hoping for . . . what exactly? Incriminating papers? Bags of money? A half-empty bottle of methyl alcohol? Something that would indicate where the money was so I could give it back to Roth. Something that would count as proof so I could tell Officer O'Rourke who'd poisoned poor Mr Quillen.

Most rooms had already been cleaned out.

My stomach told me it was well into the afternoon. No one had offered me anything to eat so I downed another glass of water and started hauling boxes down the stairs. By the time darkness fell, my back ached and my arms throbbed, but I put a smile on my face and asked for my dollar. 'Shall I come back tomorrow?'

'Yes,' said Mr Hughes. 'You've been a great help. Tomorrow should finish us up.' I let myself out the back door and trudged through the night toward home. Two days of smelly diapers waited for me in the enamel diaper pail. My least favorite chore. They'd already been rinsed in the toilet and soaked in water with bleach to keep the stink down, but the hard part lay ahead. I'd spend this evening scrubbing them one by one at the washboard in the cellar sink, then boiling them in the huge stewpot on the kitchen stove, then running them twice through the wringer to squeeze out every last drop of water. Diapers dried fast in the summer on the outside line, but this time of year, there was no place to hang them except the cellar. Sometimes the next batch needed washing before the first batch had dried.

Freddy met me at the door before I could climb the steps. 'Carlotta's in the kitchen,' he said. 'Tommy's upstairs. We waited dinner for you. We were sure you'd be hungry.'

'Starved. I didn't have any lunch. How was Tommy? Did he eat all right?'

'Yeah, he chowed down the cream of wheat and the mashed yams like he'd never seen a meal. Slept two hours in the morning and three in the afternoon. What about you? Did you learn anything?'

'That the Hughes are not going on a trip, as Mr Hughes told Lloyd Prescott and me. They are moving. And not to California, but to Mexico! That liar told us it was all because Mrs Hughes was so sickly that her doctor recommended a dry warm climate, and guess what? Mrs Hughes looks fit as the butcher's dog.'

'So the day was a bust?'

I gave him a weak smile as I hung up my coat. 'I got my dollar. And I'm going back tomorrow. Probably for no reason, but things certainly sound suspicious. Maybe I can learn the name of the Mexican town that they're going to. That might give the police some way to track them if they get away before we can prove he's the embezzler. Give me a few minutes to nurse Tommy and I'll be down for dinner.'

I directed my weary legs to the stairs, wondering how many flights I'd climbed that day. Down the hall I walked and into the front bedroom Tommy and I shared. There he was, in his kiddie coop, cooing softly as he waved his hands and feet in the air, the cutest baby God ever made.

And above him, hanging with a noose around its neck, dangled Tommy's little felt bunny with a hatpin pierced through his eye.

EIGHTEEN

'Is this some kind of joke?' I demanded, my voice trembling with rage.

Freddy straightened up from his slouch on the sofa and peered at the vile object I was holding. His eyes widened, first in confusion, then in horror. No one could have faked such facial expressions. Carlotta squinted at the item in my hand, reached for the spectacles lying on her bosom, and struggled to focus. I brought it closer and dropped the thing in her lap.

'What's . . .? How . . .? Where did you find this?'

'Hanging over Tommy's kiddie coop.'

She and Freddy exchanged baffled glances. Obviously, they were as much in the dark as I was.

Carlotta fingered the horrid little toy. 'You don't think that we—?'

'No, of course not,' I said, feeling guilty because I had thought exactly that, at least for a few moments. 'But it was hanging over his head. Who was in the house today?'

They exchanged glances again.

'No one,' said Freddy.

'No salesman? No milkman?'

Carlotta shook her head. 'It's not the milkman's day. No, Maddie, no one's been inside today but us.'

'No iceman? No delivery boy?'

'No one.'

'Not even a neighbor come to borrow something?'

'No.'

'Well then, did you go out?'

'Not with the baby. We would never leave here with the baby.'

'Did either of you go out today? I'm thinking the house might have been empty, just for a moment.'

'I ran to the post office around noon,' offered Freddy, 'and I stopped to buy some string and candles at the hardware store. But Carlotta was here the whole time, weren't you?'

Carlotta nodded. 'I never set one foot outside.'

I looked about the parlor and considered the layout of the house. 'Someone must have come in while you were here. Someone must have crept up the stairs without being noticed. When was the last time you checked on him?'

Freddy answered. 'I looked in on him around four to see if he was awake. He wasn't.'

'Did you see this hanging there?'

'No, but to tell the truth, I wasn't looking for anything like that. I was just looking at the baby's face to see if his eyes were open. I can't say for sure if it was there then or not.'

'What's going on, Maddie?' asked Carlotta, reminding me that I had told her nothing about the threat from Louis Roth.

'I'm sorry I didn't tell you sooner, Carlotta, but I didn't want to worry you,' I began, taking a few minutes to bring her up to date on Roth's threats to me and Baby Tommy. Suddenly she looked older, shaken – exactly what I had wanted to avoid.

'You know I keep the doors locked all the time, even when we're home,' she said weakly. 'Here, give me the baby while you and Freddy check the doors. And every window. Right now.'

We began in the kitchen and worked our way through the main floor. It was as Carlotta had said, the back door was securely deadbolted. Windows are rarely opened in winter, but we checked the locks on each one in the kitchen, middle room, and parlor. All were secure, as was the front door deadbolt.

'It's impossible for anyone to get into the second story without a ladder,' said Freddy, 'but let's check those windows too.'

There were three rooms on the second floor and a bathroom at the end of the hall. The bathroom window was cocked open for ventilation, but it was too tiny for anyone larger than Tommy to climb through. Carlotta had the quiet room at the back of the house with one window that overlooked the alley. It was locked. The middle room that served as our enhancement room and Freddy's sleeping place was the same. The front room that Tommy and I slept in had a window overlooking the street. Its lock was securely fastened. Anyone trying to sneak in that way would have had to raise a ladder that blocked the sidewalk and climb up it in full view of nosy neighbors.

'What about the cellar?' Freddy asked.

Our cellar ran the length of the house, with the coal furnace in back and Carlotta's laundry sink and washboard in front. Its hardpacked dirt floor had been covered in part with a thick canvas painted and varnished like a floorcloth, but the space was still grimy and dark. It had four high windows so narrow that they barely lived up to their purpose of letting in a little daylight. These were covered with sturdy iron bars. I clicked on the electric bulb that dangled in the middle of the room, then rattled each bar to make sure none were loose. 'I doubt these have been open since the house was built. Help me try the cellar door,' I said crawling up the cement steps to the double doors that opened outward into the back yard.

The sole purpose of the barn-like double doors was to enable coal deliveries. The coal man would come by truck, pull up as close as he could, and ring for Carlotta to bring out the key to unlock the cellar door. Then he would dump a load of those black rocks down into the basement bin beside the furnace that heated water for the radiators. It was Freddy's job to keep the furnace fed throughout the winter and shovel the ashes onto our icy front steps and sidewalk.

We pushed up against the cellar door. It seemed solid. Its lock was on the outside. I looked around in the dim light. I hadn't been in the cellar since I last washed Tommy's diapers, which hung from the clothesline like limp dishrags. 'You were the last person down here, Freddy. When was that?'

'Um, I fed the beast this morning after you left the house.'

'Does anything seem different to you?'

He looked around and gave it some thought before replying in the negative.

'I'm going to check the key,' I told him.

The key to the cellar door padlock was safe and sound on its nail inside the broom closet. Slipping into my coat, I stepped outside to make sure the padlock itself was fastened tight. It lay there, all shiny and secure.

'This makes no sense,' I said, so frustrated my hands were trembling. 'Someone was in this house. I know it. Someone did that to Tommy's little bunny as a warning to me. They can't fit down the chimney. They didn't come through the windows or the locked doors. What other explanation is there? It must have been Louis Roth. Who else could it be? And how did he get in?' The helpless feeling robbed me of any feeling of safety I once had.

Carlotta and Freddy could only shake their heads. Tommy smiled and kicked his feet in the air. He knew. He saw the man – or woman? – who came in his room, who took the little bunny out of his kiddie coop and tied the noose around its neck. He watched that person ram a hatpin through the little bunny's eye and swing its body back and forth over his head. Tommy knew.

All I knew was this: Tommy wasn't safe in his own bed.

NINETEEN

I could no longer fool myself that Louis Roth was bluffing. His threats couldn't have been plainer if he'd nailed them to the front door. Somehow he was able to enter our house and creep around unnoticed while two people were home. For the life of me, I couldn't figure out how, but he'd done it, and my baby wasn't safe. I got his message, loud and clear.

Find the money. His own life depended on it, therefore, so did my baby's.

Freddy agreed with me that the money had to be with Charles Hughes. Charles Hughes had downed celebratory drinks with Herman Quillen the night he was murdered; Charles Hughes had the means to embezzle the money from his own bank in cahoots with Quillen; Charles Hughes was making a quick escape to a foreign country where he'd be forever beyond the vaunted long arm of the law. He'd lied about his destination and his wife's illness. As best I could figure, he'd conspired with Quillen to skim off some of the deposit made that day by Apex, Inc., a business run by the North Side Gang. Not all of it, just some, so it wouldn't be noticed in the chaos following Dean O'Banion's murder last month. How they'd accomplished it, I'd no idea. But the timing was perfect. O'Banion's death left the gang temporarily leaderless. The top-dog spot was up for grabs, available to anyone ruthless enough to snatch it. Smart money was on Hymie Weiss, O'Banion's best friend, but evidently he hadn't consolidated his authority yet because Bugs Moran was a contender. Chicago's other gangs, like the Outfit and the Gennas, scented blood. It was a good time to grab more territory, to settle old scores. Every day the newspapers carried stories of gang violence, violence that screamed in-house turmoil.

'I have to go back to the Hughes tomorrow,' I told Freddy and Carlotta.

'If the stolen money is anywhere, it's there,' the boy agreed. 'I could go with you.'

'No, I need you here to protect Tommy.'

'We weren't much good today.'

'But now you're alert to the danger. And the house is secure.'

'Freddy can carry down his kiddie coop,' suggested Carlotta, 'and we'll keep him here in the parlor with us. We'll be beside him every minute of the day, so you needn't fret.'

I blinked back the tears. Except for my husband, I had never felt love from anyone like this, not even from my blood relations. I'd lived here for all of three weeks and already it felt like family. 'I'm so grateful . . .' I managed to choke out as I gave Carlotta a big hug.

Freddy blushed at the emotional display. 'Aw, women!' he snorted in disgust.

I tossed and turned in bed that night, all the while trying not to make any noise that would wake Tommy, but sleep wouldn't come. Something was nagging at the corners of my brain. Something was missing. Something was wrong. I couldn't shake the feeling that I'd ignored something important. When I finally slept, I dreamed horrible dreams about locks and doors and being shut up in tiny dark places, unable to get out to save Baby Tommy.

Suddenly I bolted upright in my narrow bed. The shiny cellar door lock! That was it!

Wasting no time, I slipped out of my bed and into my shoes and shawl. I heard a nearby church bell chime three, but this couldn't wait 'til daylight. I had to know *right now* if Roth or any of his gangster cohorts could break into this house again.

Taking care to avoid the third step from the top that shrieked like a banshee, I crept downstairs, holding fast to the handrail. A little glow from the corner gaslight seeped through the parlor window, but the kitchen was pitch black. The broom closet door made a click and squeak when it opened, but nothing loud enough to disturb Carlotta or Freddy's sleep upstairs. I ran my fingers along the doorjamb until they felt the nail with the padlock key. A minute more and I found Carlotta's flashlight.

On tiptoes I made my way to the kitchen door, eased back the deadbolt, and wiggled the door ajar, bracing myself for the scraping sound it made whenever it was wrenched open. I paused, listening hard, but no noise came from upstairs. I breathed a sigh of relief and stepped into the frigid night air.

The Big Dipper shone bright in the clear sky like one of those dot-to-dot puzzles in children's play books. Moonbeams bounced off the packed snow. With the flashlight in one hand and keys in the other, I surveyed the back yard and made my way along the beaten snow path to the cellar door where I crouched and reached for the shiny padlock, my warm damp fingers sticking briefly to the frozen metal.

Suddenly, he was behind me, looming over me with a massive weapon of some sort. I spun around just in time for reflexes to kick in. My body threw itself to one side with no instructions from my brain. The club missed my head by a hair, striking a heavy blow against the wooden cellar door. A hollow thud broke the stillness of the night. Someone shrieked – me no doubt, but absurdly, it was a soft shriek, as part of my brain was still concentrating on being quiet. I threw up my arms to shield myself from the next blow, and prepared to let loose a shattering scream that would wake the entire block, when I heard a familiar voice.

'Jeez, Maddie, what the hell are you doing?' Freddy lowered his baseball bat and reached for my arm to help me up. 'Are you OK?'

'My god. Freddy,' was all I could manage.

'I'm sorry, I'm sorry! But I heard someone downstairs, and then I saw someone trying to get in the cellar door and I thought . . . I thought . . .'

Of course he did. Brave boy, he was trying to protect us. I couldn't be angry.

'It's OK. I'm OK. Don't worry . . . I was . . .' I took several deep breaths to stop shaking, then continued. 'Look, I think I know how someone got into the house this afternoon.' And without explaining more, I tried to insert the key into the padlock. I tried several times, both ways, but it wouldn't slide in. 'This isn't the right key, see? And look at the padlock. You can't see it very well but when daylight comes, you'll notice it's all shiny and new. Not like this old key. It's a different padlock.'

'What do you mean?'

'Someone came here with a tool to cut through the padlock—'

'Like a bolt cutter?'

'Yeah. He cut the old lock that went with this key and came in through the cellar door. When he left, he put this new padlock in place so we wouldn't notice it was gone. And he kept the key to this one so he could get in easy next time.'

'But how did he get all the way up to your room while we were in the parlor?'

'Think about it. Where does Carlotta usually sit?'

'In her red velvet chair by the window.'

'Right, facing the window for the light and because she likes to watch the people in the street. You were lying on the sofa, right? You can't see the staircase from there either, because it faces her chair. He could have sneaked up the cellar stairs and then peeked around the corner to see that neither of you were looking in his direction.'

'I'd've heard his footsteps on the stairs.'

'Carlotta wouldn't – she's hard of hearing. You might have if you were thinking about it but you didn't. Maybe you were out of the house then or out of the room or maybe you were napping or maybe he was just really quiet on stocking feet. However he did it, he got upstairs and back down to the cellar again without anyone noticing. Come on, let's get inside before we freeze to death.'

Freddy looked askance at the cellar door. 'He has the key. And if we replace the padlock, he'll just cut it again.'

'Right. But we can add a strong deadbolt on the inside of the cellar door. That'll stop him. First thing tomorrow, you go to Brewster's Hardware and buy a thick slide-bolt latch. No, buy two. Screw them into the cellar door. That way, if he tries his key or uses the bolt cutter, the doors will still hold.'

I returned to bed. Freddy insisted on sitting up the rest of the night, his baseball bat in hand, just in case.

The next morning, I retraced the streetcar route to the Near North Side, arriving at the Hughes house before eight. Mr and Mrs Hughes were in the kitchen finishing their coffee and breakfast. Their greeting was friendly enough but no one offered me as much as a cup of coffee. Never mind, I'd been smarter today. I'd brought a bread-and-cheese lunch in my pocket.

Moments after I arrived, a Ford pulled into the driveway and the real estate agent knocked on the back door.

'Don't get up,' the agent said as Mr Hughes made to rise from the table. 'I've just dropped by to have you sign these papers.' He rummaged through his briefcase as he looked around the kitchen at the stacks of boxes, empty and full. 'How goes the packing? Will you be finishing today? I've been putting off several potential buyers, you know.'

'You're welcome to bring them inside any time,' Mrs Hughes said, but the agent shook his head.

'You know I can't do that until you're out and the place is put in order. Anyone viewing the house as it looks today will come away with an unfavorable impression. Even if someone is interested, it will lower the offer. No, we'll wait 'til everything is empty and clean.' He turned to me. 'You'll come back after they've gone, won't you, Miss Duval, and clean? Top to bottom, the whole place needs to sparkle. Windows too.'

'I'm not sure I can—'

'There's double the pay for you.'

'Thank you, I'll let you know.'

'You do that.' He turned back to Mr Hughes and laid some documents in front of him. 'This is authorizing me to bargain on your behalf up to ten percent of the list price – although I have no doubt I can get the full amount for you, sir, your asking price is more than reasonable. Sign here. And this one authorizes me to transfer the money to that bank in Mexico . . . sign here.'

My word, they were leaving sooner than I thought, before Christmas, before the house was sold, even before the money was in hand. A strong urge to peer over Mr Hughes' shoulder moved me several steps closer until I was almost close enough to read the name of the Mexican bank, but Mrs Hughes sent me a withering look and snapped, 'Time to get to work, Maddie. This is men's work. You and I will start upstairs this morning.'

Half a dozen large trunks were waiting for me, ready to be packed with personal items destined for Mexico, so Mrs Hughes and I began by clearing the dresser drawers first, then the coat closet, dressing room closets, and linen closet, layering pieces of tissue paper between the folds of the clothes, coats, and shawls, and wrapping shoes, one pair per cotton bag. There was enough there to outfit ten women for the rest of their lives.

'Will you have reason to wear these furs and warm coats?' I asked with as innocent a tone of voice as I could muster. 'I thought the climate in Mexico was warm year round.'

'Some parts of the country have seasons.'

'And mountains too, I imagine. I've never been to Mexico.'

'Neither have I.'

'It's a big country, isn't it? Which part did you say you were moving to?'

She gave me a frosty glare. 'Look here, Maddie, this trunk has room for more. Go bring me what's on hangers in the closet across the hall.'

And that's how I found the money.

TWENTY

I'd given plenty of thought to that money over the last two days. One hundred thousand dollars was a whale of a lotta dough, enough to set up just about anybody for a fancy rest-of-their-life. I'd earned twenty dollars a week at Marshall Field's and Tommy had brought in thirty making deliveries, which is why he jumped at the chance to earn more than triple that delivering booze for the Outfit. I knew from the Want Ads that carpenters made about fifty and painters and plasterers about sixty, but those were skilled union jobs that paid better than most. I had no idea what a bank president earned, but I strongly suspected that one hundred thousand was enough to tempt even the saintly Charles Hughes to dip his sticky fingers into the honey pot. No matter what snooty Miss Stanley said about the bank's surefire accounting controls, I'm sure Mr Hughes – that clever liar – could find a way to embezzle funds without anyone knowing.

A hundred thousand dollars. I tried to picture just how much space that amount of cash would take up. Of course it would depend on the denomination of the bills. One hundred thousand dollars in one-dollar bills would fill several suitcases, I imagined. But how unlikely for Charles Hughes to be so stupid as to take all of the money in one-dollar bills? If he stole it in one-hundred-dollar bills, there would be only a thousand of them. With five-hundred-dollar bills, only two hundred, a quantity easily carried in a handbag. One of the tellers had said he noticed an unusually large number of small bills in the vault that week and a shortage of large ones. It didn't mean much to me then, but now I saw its significance. Hughes must have taken small bills from the North Side Gang deposit – their money was made in gambling, prostitution, and bootlegging, all transactions conducted individually in smaller bills – and exchanged them in the vault for larger denominations. Easier to transport, sure, but harder to spend and more quickly noticed. My bet was on a mixture of bills: some five-hundreds, some thousands, and some twenties, fifties, and hundreds. Bigger than a handbag, smaller than a suitcase.

Which was exactly what I found in that closet: a new, red leather valise, lying on the floor beneath Mrs Hughes's dresses. I picked it up for closer inspection, shook it once – it felt the right weight and consistency for paper money – clicked open the clasp, and cracked it open. Money! I caught only a glimpse of some bundles of green bills before a furious voice shot over my shoulder like the crack of a whip.

'What do you think you're doing, miss?' he barked.

I snapped shut the lid and spun around, my heart in my throat. 'I-I-I was just getting Mrs Hughes's frocks, as she directed.'

Gone was the jovial bank president. This Mr Hughes snatched the valise out of my hands and glanced hurriedly inside to see if the contents had been violated. Then he turned to me, his face contorted with fury. 'You're dismissed, you little thief. Leave at once.'

'I'm sorry, sir. I've taken nothing.' I held out empty hands.

'Only because I interrupted you.'

'I was just moving the valise and it fell open . . .'

He hauled me up off my knees and shoved me toward the stairs. 'Get out before I call the police, you lying tramp.'

I scurried down the stairs and out the back door without a word to the bank president's wife, who stared after me with a confused frown. She'd hear about the reason soon enough from her two-faced husband.

The minute I reached home, I grabbed the telephone and rang through to the Maxwell Street police station. There was no time to waste if we were to catch this thief – and murderer? – and return the money to the bank. There it would go back into Apex, the North Side Gang account, which should satisfy everyone, including Louis Roth. But Officer O'Rourke was on patrol, and there was no one else I trusted, so I left the message that Maddie Pastore had vital information for him and drummed my fingers while all the things I needed to tell him buzzed like bees in my head.

'I thought you'd never call!' I exclaimed when he finally did. 'I have important news. I've found the stolen money!'

'I'm listening.'

'You said there was a special unit to work on bank robberies. I need to speak with them at once!'

'Where is the money, Mrs Pastore?'

'It's at Charles Hughes's house. The bank president who retired.'

'And how did you come to find it at the Hughes house?'

'I was working there. Just for a day or two, helping them pack for their move. Just to see what I could learn. And boy, did I!'

'You promised me you had stopped your investigating.'

I took a deep breath. 'Yes, well, I *had* stopped, but then I had to start up again, but I didn't want to, honestly, but that awful thug Louis Roth came by my house and threatened my baby if I didn't find the money because Hymie Weiss was blaming him for stealing it, and unless he got it back fast, he was going to be killed, and I couldn't—'

'Hold on, hold on there, Mrs Pastore. One thing at a time. Roth threatened you?'

I nodded, forgetting that he couldn't see me through the telephone line. 'And then to make sure I believed him, he broke into our house past the cellar locks and hung a toy over my son's crib with a hatpin through its eye to show me he could get to my baby any time he wanted so I had to try or else.' And to my horror, I burst into tears.

Officer O'Rourke waited patiently while I gathered my wits and slowed down.

'And so I took a job helping the Hugheses pack. In one of their closets, I found a red valise with money in it. I didn't get a good look but there were definitely several bundles of banknotes. You need to tell the special bank-robbery police to hurry to their house and arrest them before they leave for Mexico. That's where they're going, not California, and by the way, Mrs Hughes isn't the sickly woman Mr Hughes made her out to be. And Hughes lied about something else. He said he never saw Herman Quillen the night he was murdered, but he did. They had drinks together at the Tree Club a few hours before Quillen's body was found.'

'Thank you, Mrs Pastore, I'll pass this along. Meanwhile, you should have told me right away when Roth threatened you. I'll talk to the precinct captain and see if he'll post a man to guard your house tonight.'

'Oh, thank you! That would help us all sleep better tonight.'

'If he can't spare a man, I'll be there myself as soon as I'm off duty.'

Freddy came into the parlor as I hung up the receiver. 'Is everything all right?'

I gave a long sigh. 'Yes, I think so. The cops will arrest Hughes now, before he scarpers off to Mexico, and the money will go back to the bank.'

'But Roth?'

'I know, he said it had to go to him, but I can't do that, try as I might. This was the only way. The money will go back to the bank and into Hymie Weiss's Apex account, so the result should be the same. I did the best I could.' I just hoped Louis Roth saw it that way and left us alone. A cop outside tonight would provide temporary comfort, but no one could expect that arrangement to last forever.

Freddy put a thin hand on my shoulder. 'No one could have done more. And now, I have a surprise for you.' He turned toward the hallway and called Carlotta, who came from the kitchen drying her hands on a tea towel. 'Go get Tommy, Maddie. I just heard him. He's awake. I have something for both of you. I'll be right back.'

I climbed up the stairs. Freddy headed to the cellar. When I returned with Tommy, I heard weird noises coming from the cellar stairs, rhythmic bumping and some knocks against the wall as Freddy struggled with something large. Mystified, I sat on the sofa beside Carlotta.

'Do you know anything about this?' I asked.

'Not a thing, dear. Although he's been acting very mysterious since yesterday.'

The boy stuck his head around the corner to make sure we were all in position. 'Now, Maddie,' he said, his voice full of glee, 'this was supposed to be your Christmas present, but Christmas is ten days away, and I don't want you to have to wait another day, so you're getting it early. You and Tommy. So close your eyes – not Tommy, just you Maddie. And Carlotta too, so you'll be surprised at the same time.'

There came a slight creaking sound and a thump as something hit the doorjamb, and I could feel the presence of something large being dragged into the parlor. There was a pause, then the boy said, 'Abracadabra, open your eyes!'

Carlotta and I gasped at the same time. Parked in front of us was a baby buggy, dark blue with metal trim. I was speechless.

'Do you like it? Do you like it?' he demanded, with a note of anxiety in his voice.

'Like it? Are you joking? I *love* it! It's . . . oh, my god, it's wonderful! How did you ever . . .' No, that wasn't polite, to ask how he'd afforded such a thing. I stopped just in time.

'Now you won't have to carry Tommy everywhere. I found one that was big enough for Tommy but small enough that you could fit it on the streetcar. I asked the conductor and he said as long as the car isn't too full, you can do that, and I've seen other mothers do that. And you can take walks in the park.'

'I've wanted one ever since Tommy was born, but I never thought I'd have one so soon. Oh, Freddy, this is marvelous!' I ran my fingers over the navy blue fabric on the side and bonnet.

'Look, the bonnet collapses so you can put it up when it rains or when the sun shines in his face. Put Tommy in it so he can see if he likes it.'

Freddy had lined the bottom with a clean folded towel. Before I could reach for the baby, Freddy picked him up and deposited him inside. Tommy twisted his head to look all around at the strange new surroundings and kicked his feet. 'I can tell that he loves it!' I said.

'Wherever did you find such a treasure, Freddy?' asked Carlotta.

'Mr Jacobson at the hardware store found it for me in the newspaper For Sale section last week. The woman who had it said her children had outgrown it. It was missing its two front wheels, but Mr Jacobson got me two wheels the same size and helped me oil the squeaks. They don't match exactly, but—'

'What do you mean? They're perfect! I never would have noticed a difference if you hadn't pointed it out. This is the best Christmas present I could ever have.' Freddy squirmed with embarrassment when I gave him a fierce hug, but he didn't pull away.

Ideas were swirling in my head. With the buggy, I could take Tommy with me for longer periods of time. Its pockets would hold supplies. He could nap in it. And I thought of something else: another way to protect Tommy from Louis Roth if he should try again to harm him.

'I think we should all go for a walk,' said Carlotta. 'It won't be dark for another hour and the Reynolds boy just finished shoveling the sidewalks. Let's give it a trial run around the block.'

TWENTY-ONE

Two days without word from O'Rourke about the stolen money wore my patience thin as a silver dime. Finally – *finally!* – he showed up at the house to report.

'What happened? What happened?' I asked, my heart pounding with anticipation.

'Do come in, officer,' called Carlotta from behind me.

'Yes, quick,' I added.

But he refused. We stood on the front steps, him in his uniform overcoat, me shivering as a sharp morning wind off the lake cut through my sweater. I knew something had gone wrong when he avoided meeting my eyes.

'Did they arrest Hughes? Is he in jail? Did they get the money? What happened?' I babbled like the village idiot.

The officer gazed up the street of modest row houses and down the other side as he searched for words. The whole block seemed to pause as if frozen in ice. A father holding hands with his two sons waited at intersection; an old woman stopped at a leafless tree to let her cocker spaniel make yellow water; the cross-eyed boy clearing the steps of the house opposite ours leaned on his shovel. No cars passed. I wanted time to stop too, stop right here and now when I still had an expectation of success.

But the father pulled his sons across the street, the dog moved on from the skeletal tree, and the boy gave us a wave of his hand and resumed his rhythmic shoveling. And Officer O'Rourke spoke, his warm breath forming little clouds between us.

'I passed along your information at once. I expected them to go to the Hughes house right away, but they had other priorities. As it turned out, they got there midday the following day, yesterday. By that time, Mr and Mrs Hughes had left.'

'Oh no!' How could the police have wasted their best chance? How could they have failed to catch the crook when I'd all but delivered him into their clutches? Why didn't the world work the way it was supposed to?

'Not knowing exactly when they left or which railroad they—'

'They were heading south to Mexico! They can still intercept them. It would take at least two, probably three days to reach Mexico.'

'Yes, but still, there are so many branches and so many trains. In any case, the officers did wire ahead to several stops on the Atchison, Topeka and Santa Fe line and managed with great good luck to cut them off in Topeka.'

Why didn't he just say so? I gave a huge sigh of relief. The crooks were in custody after all!

But Officer O'Rourke wasn't smiling the triumphant smile of a man who had helped capture an embezzler and possible murderer. 'The Topeka police took them and their luggage off the train and into the local precinct for questioning. I had the report by telephone straight from the mouth of one of our detectives who had it from one of the Topeka officers who was there.'

'And the money? Did they find the banknotes?'

'They found the red leather valise, just as you described it. And the banknotes in it. Five hundred dollars in small bills, an amount easily explained by Hughes as a sum necessary for their lengthy visit to Mexico and subsequent stay in California.'

'But . . . but there must have been the rest of the money somewhere. In another suitcase.'

He shook his head. 'All their luggage and trunks were searched. No other cash was found.'

My thoughts careened around through my brain. He must have hidden it. Where would he hide it? Under Mrs Hughes's petticoats? Large banknotes could be concealed under her voluminous skirts and no policeman would dare think of looking under her dress. Or in hatboxes, under the crowns of the hats? Or had he wired the money directly to a Mexican bank, like he told the estate agent to do with the house money? A smart businessman like Charles Hughes could surely outwit the police.

'But what about the murder? He lied about the drink with Mr Quillen. Did they ask where he was the night Quillen was murdered?'

'Hughes was questioned about that, and you were right. He confessed that he had lied when he told us he hadn't seen Quillen on the day of his death. He said he'd been afraid to mention it because it would have made him the most obvious suspect, as proven by this arrest. He swore they had only one drink after work at the Tree Club in celebration of his retirement and of Quillen's anticipated promotion. He said he left Quillen there at about six and went home to dinner.'

'But his wife's illness, he lied about that too.'

'They asked about that. Mrs Hughes showed them a letter from her doctor recommending a move to a dry warm climate for her emphysema, a disease of the lungs.' He coughed delicately. 'It isn't something visible. You couldn't have known about it.'

'But . . .'

I'd run out of buts.

Like a flower starved of water, I wilted. I'd been a fool. I'd been certain Charles Hughes was guilty of the murder of Herman Quillen. I was sure he had embezzled the North Side Gang's money from Midwest and fled to Mexico. Even now, I clung desperately to the razor-thin chance that he had outfoxed us all. If he didn't do it, who did?

What did I know for sure? That Mr Quillen didn't have a brother, that Louis Roth had come to Carlotta's séance to locate some missing money, that Roth and others had tried unsuccessfully to rob Midwest Savings & Loan, that Roth had threatened my baby, and that someone had broken into Quillen's apartment and Carlotta's house. If Charles Hughes wasn't behind all this, who was? Had Herman Quillen been acting alone? Auditors had found no money missing from Midwest's vault, so where did it come from? Where was it now? If Quillen had acted alone when he stole the North Side Gang's money, had Roth then caught up with him and killed him? That would have been stupid, to kill the only man who knew where the money was. Unless there was another person who knew. I sat on the front steps, too stunned to notice that Officer O'Rourke had taken his leave, too caught up in confusion to feel the icy cement.

Last year, when Tommy was alive, we'd gone to a Sunday afternoon fair with games and prizes for the winners. We paid our nickel and laughed as the shell game beat us at every turn. No matter which cup we chose, the pea was hiding under a different one. It felt like that today, without the laughter. I was no closer to the money, and Louis Roth wasn't known for his patience.

TWENTY-TWO

My determination to ignore Christmas backfired. The holiday was fast approaching and I had nothing to give Freddy or Carlotta. It was my turn for the marketing, so I tucked Tommy into his new baby buggy and set off for Maxwell Street's open-air immigrant market.

Over the years, market stalls and pushcarts had crept beyond

Maxwell and Halstead streets, spilling into alleys and the narrow walkways separating buildings, crowding the sidewalks and choking the streets until no traffic could pass. The noise could reach deafening levels as peddlers hawked their wares, 'pullers' tried to drag customers into their shops, and klezmer music screeched. With only a few days left before Christmas, the crowd was thick with holiday shoppers, Lithuanians and Poles searching for fresh herring, Russians for caviar, and Irish for currants and raisins and plenty of brandy to flame their Christmas pudding. I had promised to make the traditional French *bûche de Noel*, a cake shaped like a yule log that I remember from my Canadian grandmother's kitchen. The recipe called for cocoa powder.

Like-minded stalls often bunched together, so there were some blocks specializing in clothing, shoes, furs, and fedoras; others where live chickens squawked and fish flopped in barrels. I jostled my way through picketing garment workers toward an alley that sheltered women selling homemade wares and secondhand household goods. Squeezed in between the horseradish grinder and the old books, an elderly Greek woman offered her shawls and slippers. Carlotta's slippers, I had noticed, were worn clean through at the toe, so I bought her a new pair in bright crimson – she always favored bold colors. Baby Tommy was old enough for toys now, so at a secondhand stall, I paid a few pennies for some blocks with letters and numbers painted on them. One street down, I bought wooden farm animals from an old Polish man who had carved and painted them himself. At the stall beside his, I purchased a much-loved, life-size baby doll made of composition – no clothes, but Tommy's cast offs would solve that. Freddy was a tougher nut to crack. Next week I planned to stop at a candy store near our house and buy him one of everything, but I needed something more, something special, something that showed him how much I appreciated that baby buggy, and I hadn't landed on it yet.

As I rounded the corner of our street on my way to our house's back door, my buggy narrowly missed a stocky man coming down the rear stairs. Wearing a thick brown coat and a plaid cap that covered most of his silver hair, he touched the brim with two fingers in silent apology as he steadied the buggy and steered himself around us.

My thoughts leaped in the wrong direction – was this the man who had broken into our house? – but of course he was not. He was too clean for the coal delivery man and too late for the milkman. The iceman, maybe? Nonsense. I shook the idea from my head and apologized.

'Excuse me,' I began. 'My fault entirely. The buggy's new, and I'm not used to thinking ahead when rounding corners.'

The man paused just long enough for me to see his face clearly. It was an odd face, one that looked like it had been punched more than once. White hairs sprouted from his nose and ears and bushy gray eyebrows grew together above the crooked nose. 'Sorry, lady,' he said, his cheeks turning red as if he were the culprit and not me. He trudged off toward the corner.

'Carlotta?' I called as I muscled the buggy into the kitchen and hung my coat on the coat tree. No response. A noise from the living room sent me there, where I found her standing beside the window, staring out to the street, so deep into her thoughts that she hadn't heard me calling.

'Carlotta, is everything all right? Who was that man who just left?' A glance around the room told me that nothing had been disturbed, and she didn't look like anyone had harmed her. The mystery man hadn't seemed dangerous, merely embarrassed about something.

She looked at me as if she didn't recognize me, her face a blank slate. Then without warning, she sank into a chair and began to sob.

'What is it? What is it?' I dropped to my knees beside her, taking her cold hands in mine. 'Who was that man? What's wrong? Freddy! Freddy!' I shouted. No answer.

Massaging her hands, I kept talking softly, trying to coax an explanation out of her. 'Everything's fine now . . . We're all safe and sound . . . Don't worry . . . I'll make you a nice cup of tea and you'll feel better.'

I dashed back to the kitchen to put the kettle on and dashed back to the living room, but she couldn't say a word until I had put a cup of hot tea in her hands. 'Here, now, some nice tea with lots of milk and sugar, just the way you like it. Nothing like a cup of tea to wash your troubles away. Take a sip and you'll feel better.'

That did the trick. Swallowing the hot liquid staunched her tears and gave her the strength to talk.

'I'm so ashamed. I'm so ashamed,' she kept repeating.

'Nonsense. What's the problem? There's nothing to be ashamed of, nothing we can't handle.'

'I should have told you last month. You and Freddy. I should have told you then but you were so excited about moving in, I pushed it out of my head like it would go away if I didn't talk about it.'

'Like what would go away? Who was that man?'

'My brother-in-law. Jacob Burkholtzer. My late husband's half-brother.'

So, he was no crook. I hadn't really thought so but it was good to know for sure. 'Yes, I saw him as I was coming in. Why was he here?'

She took a deep breath. 'He owns this house.'

That surprised me. I had always assumed that Carlotta owned the house. I knew she had moved here after her husband passed away and just supposed it was hers.

'I see. And he was visiting? Did he have some family business? Some upsetting news?'

'We have to leave. He's selling the house.'

'I see. Well, that's disappointing for sure, but we can manage. How much time do we have?'

'Until the end of the year.'

Two weeks!

'Carlotta, what's the problem? Have you fallen behind on the rent?'

She shook her head. 'There was no rent. Well, hardly any, just enough to cover city taxes. He inherited the house about the time my husband died and let me move in here rent-free as a family favor.'

'Does he want more money, then? That wouldn't be unreasonable. We could pay a reasonable rent.'

'No, no, no. He needs to sell. He needs the cash. We have to leave. I don't know where to go.'

'Why don't we ask him if he can give us another month or two, until we can scout around and find another place? Surely he'll do that for his brother's widow.'

'He already did. I wasted the month. I hoped he'd change his mind. I hoped the problem would go away. I wanted to stay so badly. I should have told you and Freddy back then. And now it's too late. He's already found a buyer who'll pay $4,600 for the place.'

'If he needs the money, maybe he'd agree to let us buy the house on the installment plan, paying something like two hundred dollars a month until we reached the sale amount.'

'He won't. He needs the whole amount right now. Gambling debts. He owes money to some dangerous men who aren't inclined to wait.'

If Jacob Burkholtzer had been gambling in this part of the city, he was doing it at joints run by the Outfit. And everyone knew what happened to men who didn't pay their debts to the Outfit. They weren't killed, not right away anyway, because a dead man can't pay his debts. It might be his legs were broken or he was beaten half to death or his house was ransacked or his dog's bloody head was left on the front porch. The message usually brought the desired results. As a last resort, the debtor's disappearance into the Chicago River would serve to discourage others. Jacob Burkholtzer needed money now, and no pleas from his sister-in-law could change that.

'Never mind, Carlotta, we'll get right to work finding another place to live. It won't be hard.' I knew nothing about finding rental properties, whether it was hard or easy or how one went about it, but I'd find out. My experience had always been with boarding houses, except for the time Tommy bought us our cozy little house on the South Side.

A noise in the hallway made me look up. Freddy was standing there, still as a statue, his face grim. I hadn't heard him come downstairs. I wasn't sure how much he'd heard, but it seemed to be enough.

'Another place like this will be hard to find,' he contradicted me, 'and an apartment won't work for our business. We've got to have a house we can trick out with special enhancements, which means it has to have a basement, a second floor, and a spirit room on the first floor with side windows above each other.'

He didn't say it but I could read the message in his eyes. Another building laid out like this one would be near impossible to locate quickly. Madame Carlotta would have no séances and no income until we did.

TWENTY-THREE

'Here,' said Freddy as he plopped the *Chicago Daily Tribune* onto the breakfast table. He was still panting a little from his run to the nearest newsie, and removing his cap had caused his carrot-colored hair to spike up like little flames. Carlotta had given him two cents and sent him on the errand while she and I finished our toasted bread and jam. He handed her the front-page section with the international news and me the want ads. 'No time to waste, Maddie. You can start looking for houses right now.'

Not being able to read didn't mean Freddy couldn't enjoy the newspaper. While I surveyed the headings on the narrow columns for Houses to Rent, he turned the pages and studied the pictures, interrupting me or Carlotta when he wanted the accompanying article read. Which he did promptly that morning.

'Whoa Nelly!' He whistled. 'Look who's in the papers again!'

I glanced over his shoulder and grimaced. Was it an omen? Or, as Carlotta would say, a message from the Far Beyond? I'd tossed and turned in bed last night thinking about Al Capone and wrestling with the pros and cons of asking him for help with our house problem. And here he was the next morning, staring at me from the local news pages, almost daring me to try.

Freddy pointed to the caption. 'What's it say?'

I read aloud: '"Albert Capone, businessman, delivering a donation of fifty hams to Miss Jane Addams at Hull House for distribution to the poor for their holiday meal." Well, there's a mistake. It's Alphonse, not Albert. He won't like that.'

Al Capone adored publicity. While his boss Johnny Torrio and other gang leaders like Hymie Weiss avoided reporters like the measles, Capone was happiest when he could find his picture in the newspaper – any newspaper. He usually granted reporters' requests for interviews and never failed to notify them when he was planning to do something benevolent, like this donation to Hull House. I was sure Miss Addams would accept the hams despite their unsavory origins, and Scarface Al could crow about his generosity and 'businessman' status.

I'd sworn to have nothing more to do with Torrio and Capone and their filthy Outfit and I'd meant it at the time. It galled me to go back on that vow, but if there was the smallest chance of staying in our house and keeping our business alive, wasn't it worth the risk? Maybe the photo was a sign. Maybe it meant Capone would be in a generous mood. Maybe it was the right time to ask for a favor. The worst he could do was say no, right?

Seven months had passed since my husband's murder. I'd put aside formal mourning after three months, but my black lace dress had come in handy on many occasions since then, like when I played the shill at one of Carlotta's séances. I brushed it off this morning and twisted my long hair back in a matronly bun, then dressed Baby Tommy in a clean white gown. 'We're going visiting this morning,' I told him, 'in your new buggy.'

Without telling Carlotta or Freddy where I was headed – I hated to raise their expectations when odds were so slim – I bundled Tommy into the buggy and set out, grateful that the morning sleet had stopped falling. My good blue coat and matching hat and gloves kept me warm. The morning rush hour had ended, which meant streetcars were less crowded, so it took only a little effort to pull the buggy up into the car and maneuver it all the way to the back where there was a bit more room. One change took us south to Cermak and from there to a stop near the Hotel Metropole, where Torrio and Capone kept their offices. No one was supposed to know about this location, but in all honesty, all you had to do was drive down Michigan Avenue past the red-brick Metropole to see the thugs in dark coats with bulging pockets hanging about the entrance and the black cars hogging all the curb space in front to figure out that the person called Mr Adams who had offices up on the fifth floor wasn't selling Bibles.

I pushed the buggy into the Metropole lobby and over to the front desk.

'I'd like to see Mr Capone, if he is in his office today,' I said to the nervous wisp of a man at the reception desk. Without answering, he looked past me to a pair of wide-shoulder musclemen in the corner and made a squinty face. They came right over.

'What is it, lady?' one asked, not unkindly.

'I'm Mrs Pastore. Mrs *Tommaso* Pastore,' I added, in case they recognized my husband's name from when he worked there. 'I'm here to see Mr Capone. I have no appointment, but I think he'll not mind seeing me and his godson for a few minutes.'

One of the bodyguards reached into the buggy and pulled back the blanket to see Tommy's face, presumably to make sure there really was a baby in there and not a machinegun. He grunted, then loped away toward the elevator. I waited with the other fella for a few minutes until he returned.

'The big guy'll see you,' he said. 'This way.'

I'd been to the Metropole Hotel once before, a few months ago when I came to ask a favor of Johnny Torrio, so I knew where the offices were and what they looked like. Or thought I did. They had changed. Capone had moved to a different corner on a different floor, the fourth. I wondered if he moved every so often for protection. That other time, I had been shown into Torrio's office so this was my first time in Capone's. A secretary sat in the outer office, a dour-faced woman of about thirty wearing a plum-colored serge suit with a rabbit fur collar. She didn't smile at me or Baby Tommy or respond to my cheerful greeting. Her nod toward a chair indicated that I should sit and wait.

And wait I did for nearly an hour, marking time by bouncing Tommy on my knee and walking him to and from the window overlooking Michigan Avenue. No doubt the delay was my punishment for dropping in without an appointment. No matter, it gave me time to rehearse my speech in my head. Miss Outfit

Secretary didn't seem very busy today. The telephone bell seldom rang. She typed a little and filed a few papers in one of the cabinets against the wall. She didn't speak to me or even look at Baby Tommy, and it's a rare woman who isn't interested in admiring Baby Tommy.

At last the telephone made a buzzing sound. She didn't pick it up; she didn't even look at me when she spoke. 'You may go in now.'

Al Capone sat in his chocolate brown suit at his dark wooden desk. An ivory elephant sat beside the telephone and several others decorated the shelf behind him. The walls were beige; the carpet was the color of dirt. The whole effect made me think of a brown toad squatting in the mud. I sat in the tan leather chair without being invited, holding Tommy on my knees.

Capone's lips twisted into the semblance of a smile as he looked at Tommy. 'A fine boy you have there. Tribute to his father.'

There was no point in wasting time on small talk. He knew I'd come for a favor. I got right to it.

'Mr Capone, thank you for seeing me. Baby Tommy and I have a problem I hope you can help us with. The house we rent is about to be sold out from under us, leaving us homeless in less than two weeks. Of course, there are hotels for temporary arrangements, but finding another house as good as this one is for Madame Carlotta and me and Baby Tommy will be nigh on impossible. The man who owns the house, the brother-in-law of Madame Carlotta, is reluctant to turn us out, but he finds himself in sudden need of a large amount of cash, and the house is his only asset. His problem? Well, you see, he's in debt. Gambling debt. Jacob Burkholtzer is his name, and he owes the money to your Outfit. I don't know exactly how much but your records would . . . well, it's probably about three or four or five thousand dollars. I was hoping that you could, um, forgive the debt so we could keep living in our house.'

There. I'd said it.

He stared at me, incredulous, as if waiting for more clarification.

I rushed to fill the silence. 'I know it's a lot of money and it's asking a lot, and I know this isn't something you would normally do for anyone, but I, well, thought that considering your godson's well-being is at stake, you might make an exception . . .' My voice petered out. I may as well have been talking to the wind.

Capone continued to stare, silent, motionless.

It was hopeless. I'd known that before I came, but I was just desperate enough to try.

Finally, he moved. He reached behind him for one of the smaller carved elephants and came around the desk to hand it to Tommy. I set the boy on the floor so he could play with it.

Capone ambled over to the window and looked out. 'Mrs Pastore,' he began with his back to me. 'You are a woman, not a businessman. I am a businessman. I have a reputation in this town. Some of my product is legal, some isn't, but it's important that people know what to expect when dealing with me or any of my businesses. If I were to forgive a gambling debt, or any kind of debt, every man in the city would take me for a patsy. A chump. I'd get no respect. It would set a bad example for other honest men who are working hard to pay what they owe, wouldn't it? I'd soon have a line in the street of men begging me to cancel their debts, and it wouldn't be fair to do that for some and not others, would it? *Would it?*'

'Ah, no. But you wouldn't have to let anyone know about this. It could be just between us.'

'Word would leak out. It always does.'

That was how Hymie Weiss thought too. Word had leaked out about the one hundred thousand clams stolen from the North Side Gang too, enraging Weiss for the simple reason that someone had bested him. One hundred thousand was a hundred years of salary for me, but it was chicken feed to a gang boss like Weiss. He would never miss it. Heck, he *hadn't* missed it until some bookkeeper brought it to his attention. But he couldn't afford to look weak. He had to get that money back or risk his shot at the top.

I pried the elephant out of Tommy's fingers and set it on the desk. 'I understand, Mr Capone. Thank you for your consideration.'

'Now, now, don't rush off, Mrs Pastore. Maybe there's

something else I can do for you and the kid. You need money? A job? A respectable job, not that spooky stuff you do for the gypsy. We're moving more and more into breweries these days. Turns out there's even bigger money in beer than whiskey. Who knew, eh? But there's a problem: a brewery needs a big factory, big tanks and barrels, lots of workers, and the smell oozes through the air for blocks, so it costs a lot to pay off the cops and prohis. No matter, I'm opening up new breweries all around Chicago, and they all need workers. I could give you a job at one, one close to your home wherever it is. Whatever kind of job you wanted. A regular job, not some Dumb Dora crap, pardon my French. And because I know I can trust you, I'm gonna tell you something, something not many people know. Johnny wants out. He wants to retire, move back to Italy. Next year. He's old. Well, forty-something old. I'm twenty-five and still got ambition. I won't be number two much longer.'

If this news was supposed to cheer me up, it failed miserably. The idea of Capone in complete charge of the Chicago Outfit would have scared the daylights out of any honest cop or politician, of which there were admittedly few. For years, Johnny 'the Fox' Torrio had been the most important crime boss in the city – in America, for that matter. He was murderous, yes, but he didn't kill for fun, like some. He had always tried to avoid killing, preferring compromise to bloody gang wars. It was Torrio who, early on during Prohibition, met with the other, lesser gang leaders like Dean O'Banion to organize the crime business, drawing up territorial boundaries and working out rules about not killing civilians or children or the wives of gang members. 'There's plenty of money for everyone,' he would say. 'No need to kill each other for it.' Now O'Banion was dead – some say by Torrio's orders, others say by Capone's – and a battle was underway to replace him. Were Torrio to quit the scene altogether, the carnage would spike, and it wouldn't be only gangsters whose bodies were left lying in the gutters.

'Thank you for the job offer, Mr Capone, but I am doing very well with my current employment, and I can keep the baby with me while I do that work.'

'Brewery jobs pay good. Three, four times what you make now.'

With a jolt, I realized that was how they snared my husband. That was exactly how they lured him away from Marshall Field's to what was at first a simple liquor delivery job. But once they had him, they owned him. Until the day he was buried.

I shook my head. 'To be honest, Mr Capone, I'd be too afraid. Working for the Outfit is too dangerous. Not for everyone, sure, but for many. For me. I'm my little boy's only parent now. I can't afford to get any closer to violence. I've seen enough blood spilled. I've seen enough murder in the last few months to last my whole life.'

'Murder? Murder, you say? It's not murder, Mrs Pastore. How could you think that? There's killing, sure, too much of it, sure I agree, but not murder. There's nothing personal about it, just business. Like in war. Ask any priest, he'll tell you. He'll tell you that in war, killing is not a sin, not murder. It's for the greater good. And make no mistake about it, Chicago is at war.'

I stood. 'It may be as you say. But I've had enough of this war, with my husband's death and with me being close by when O'Banion was murd— shot. You'll understand if I try to keep my distance.'

'You're a woman, Mrs Pastore. You're forgiven. You should have kept your distance today.'

'You're right. My apologies. Goodbye, Mr Capone.'

That was their world. The Capone brothers, Torrio, O'Banion, the Gennas, Weiss, all good church-going, crucifix-wearing, rosary-toting Catholics, that's how they thought. No matter what their sin, they could always work another deal with God to fix it. White slavery? Shakedowns? Murder? No problem, just confess to the priest, mumble some Hail Marys for penance, make a big donation to the Church, and you're washed clean. A dead gangster need a sendoff? Nothing a hefty gift to the Church won't solve. Drop enough cash in the collection plate and the bishop himself will preside over a lavish funeral complete with incense and fancy robes and then bury the thug in consecrated ground. Nervous about the afterlife? A large contribution will buy enough masses to shoehorn the most degenerate soul into heaven. For the gangsters, God was just another politician with his hand out, eager to cut a deal.

TWENTY-FOUR

No sooner had I returned home, there came a telephone call from Flora Masters. 'Flora *Quillen* Masters, I should have said.'

'Yes, of course! It's good to hear from you, Mrs Masters. How are you and your children doing?'

'Well enough, I suppose. I'm pretending I'm not worried about our future so as not to frighten the little ones but you can't hide things from the big ones. Eleanor wakes up with nightmares, and Julia – my oldest, she's thirteen – cries at the drop of a hat ever since I told her she'd have to quit school. I figure we'll have enough with Herman's coin collection so that Julia can finish eighth grade at least, and then there's a soap factory around the corner that'll hire her. They pay kids seven dollars a week, half what they'd pay an adult, but even that much will help pay the grocer and the landlord. We'll manage.'

'It's hard raising children alone. I know it all too well.' And I had only one to worry about!

'I had word today from the coroner's office that my brother's body has been released. That means I can make arrangements for the funeral. They said I can come pick up his personal effects, the things he had on him when he died, and I . . . well, I've never been to the Deadhouse before and just the thought of it makes my heart pound. I didn't want any of my girls to come with me, and well, I thought, if you weren't too busy . . .'

'Would you like me to come with you? I wouldn't mind. I know this is a difficult time for you.'

She gave a deep sigh. 'Oh, that would be so kind! I don't know how I'd ever thank you, but it would mean a lot to me to have someone by my side for moral support. Someone who knew my brother.' The lie I'd told earlier had circled around and come back to confront my conscience. I didn't know her brother from Illinois' Governor Small. The only time I'd even seen him was in the grainy photo in the newspaper that showed his body in the alley with a policeman standing beside him, and that counted for beans.

'Tell me the day and time and I'll meet you there.'

'I don't need an appointment. They said I could drop in any time. What about . . . would it be possible, I mean, could we meet there now? Or would that be terribly inconvenient for you?'

'Not at all. Do you know where the Deadhouse is?' The Cook County Morgue, or Deadhouse as most people called it, had long been located in a modest building behind the fancy City Hospital on Harrison Street, a mile or so west of Hull House. Everyone knew where City Hospital was. We agreed to meet there at eleven.

I walked out the front door and saw him. Across the street, loitering on the sidewalk, smoking a fat cigar, pacing back and forth as if waiting for someone, there he was, one of Roth's thugs. With that bulky coat and hand-in-the-pocket stance, it couldn't be anyone but a thug. No one I recognized, but never mind that, a child could've figured out it was one of Roth's boys spying on me. I came down the steps and turned left. He gave me a few steps lead, then tossed his stogie into the snow and followed. Because I was alone – Tommy was safe indoors with Carlotta – it wasn't any work at all to lose him when I came to a street with shops. I just popped into a ladies' dress shop and out the back door. But it rattled me, seeing that Roth had put someone there to tail me. How I wanted to believe his threats were just that – threats! But who knew what these brutes were capable of? The only thing that would rid me of him was the damn money. I had to get it back.

Flora Masters and I arrived at the front door of the morgue at the same time. Mrs Masters was wearing a too-large wool coat the color of ripe pumpkin that looked like something from the church rummage sale. She spotted me at once and gave me a wan smile. Her face was creased with strain. My gloved hand squeezed hers and we went through the heavy doors together.

A lady receptionist directed us to the elevator that lowered us into an enormous basement where hundreds of bodies were stored until they could be autopsied and released to their next of kin. A white-haired gentleman with horn-rimmed spectacles perched on the top of his head processed the paperwork, then sent us into the refrigerated area with two young clerks as escorts. A nasty chemical smell made me want to hold my breath, but there was no point. We'd be down here far too long for that. I took out my handkerchief and held it to my nose. Mrs Masters did the same.

'Masters . . . Masters . . .' said the one, running a finger down the column of names on his clipboard.

'No, sir, my brother's last name is Quillen.'

'Number four hundred and eight. This way, then, Mrs Masters.' He led us past columns of bodies stacked on either side of us on narrow pallets six high, each with a number on the edge for easy identification. We shivered in the cold. Mr Quillen was located. The two men pulled out the pallet and drew back the sheet that covered his body far enough to expose the face.

'Is this your brother, Mrs Masters?'

Herman Quillen looked as if he had died yesterday. His hair – what there was of it – had been neatly combed, his mustache looked as if it had been trimmed the day before his death. He had a prominent Roman nose, large ears, and closed eyes. He looked like a banker, not a crook, although he must have been the one who planned the theft and stole the money.

Flora Masters gave a gasp of recognition that choked into a sob. She managed to nod.

The men lifted the mortal remains of Herman Quillen and laid him on a gurney. 'You've chosen the funeral parlor, have you, ma'am?'

'Yes,' she croaked. 'The West Lake. It's only a block away. They'll be by this afternoon to . . .' She blotted her eyes with the handkerchief.

For obvious reasons, several funeral parlors had located their facilities near the morgue. The West Lake morticians would collect the body, dress it, and arrange it in a casket.

'Have you chosen the cemetery?' I asked her.

'All accomplished by telephone, and the funeral is planned for Saturday afternoon.' She didn't invite me, and I didn't offer.

I was feeling bad enough about my pretense of knowing her brother.

'This way, ladies.' One of the clerks led us into a room with hundreds of numbered drawers stacked floor-to-ceiling into the walls like a gigantic post office. He needed a ladder to reach drawer four oh eight. Without comment, he set it on a table and took three large steps backward, hands clasped behind his back, prepared to wait respectfully for the emotional next of kin to examine and claim the deceased's belongings.

Herman Quillen had been carrying very little the night he died, and Mrs Masters fingered the items one-by-one. A pocket handkerchief with an embroidered Q on one corner, a signet ring bearing an unidentified crest, a wallet containing one dollar, a library card, and pictures of Mrs Masters and her children, a gold-wash pocket watch and chain, a ticket stub for a movie theater, four dimes, two nickels, four shiny pennies, two Midwest Bank business cards with his name and job title on them, one business card from something called the Collector's Club that had a telephone number scrawled on the back, a keychain with half a dozen keys and a miniature pocketknife as a fob, and a loose flat key with the number two hundred and sixty-one stamped on it.

'That was just like Herman. Never carried much money on him,' she reminisced fondly. 'Always said he didn't need much, day to day. His expenses were predictable, a bachelor in a rut, I used to call him. Thirty-five cents for lunch at Red Rooster and fifty cents for dinner at Sally's Diner. Weekends he usually ate with me and the girls.'

'Would you like a bag for these things, madam?'

'Oh, yes. Please. Excuse me, jabbering away like that. A bag would be helpful.'

My hand hovered over the loose key. 'May I?' I asked.

'Certainly.'

I examined it closely. Small, flat, brass with a green head, it was clearly not a house key or padlock key. It reminded me of the key to the safe deposit box Tommy and I used to have at the bank, the box where we stored our ten-dollar gold coins – our emergency stash – and yes, *she* got all those too. 'What's this?' I asked Mrs Masters.

She squinted at it. 'A key. I have no idea.'

'It's not on his keychain with the others.'

'I wonder why.'

I wondered too. 'It looks kinda like a safe deposit key. Did your brother have a safe deposit box at Midwest bank?'

'He did. I've already been in it. He kept his important papers there: his birth certificate, his marriage license – he was married briefly, you know, but she died of TB – his high school diploma, that sort of thing. Nothing of monetary value. And the Midwest Bank keys didn't look like this.' She studied it closely, then gave a deep sigh. 'Look, you've probably heard that some people think Herman was involved in a plan to steal money from his bank.'

'I, well, yes, I'd heard.'

'Well, it's impossible. Herman was honest as the day is long. And loyal. I can't believe he would ever steal from the bank.'

'You may be right. Would you mind if I borrowed this key for a day or two? I'll show it around to a few banks and see if anyone recognizes it. I'll let you know if I learn anything.'

'Another safe deposit box, you mean, somewhere else? Sure, go ahead. Can't hurt. Oh, gracious, look at the time! I told Jeannie I'd be home for lunch.'

'Didn't she go to school today?'

'Jeannie doesn't go to school. She's blind. She's my nine-year-old.'

'Blind?'

'Not from birth. She started to lose her sight at six, so even though she can't see, she knows what colors are and remembers how things look. I don't know what I'd do without her. She looks after the two youngest – Frances and Lydia aren't in school yet; they're just five and three. Without Jeannie at home, I couldn't go to work and then where would we be?'

'I thought there were schools for the blind.'

'Sure there are. But not in Chicago. The closest is downstate in Jacksonville and it's a boarding school. Usually they're boarding schools because, well, obviously there aren't enough blind children in the immediate area to provide enough students to make a school worthwhile. Herman said his next promotion would allow him to pay the fees and send her, but, well . . .'

She dabbed her eyes once more and began placing her brother's effects in the cloth bag. There was nothing more to be said.

Flora Masters must have heard my stomach rumbling because she invited me home with her for lunch. I declined. 'I'd better be getting home myself, and I'll stop by a bank or two on the way and ask if anyone recognizes this key. I may be wrong, of course. It may not be a safe deposit key at all, but if it is, someone in the banking world will know.'

And someone did. An hour later, at Chicago Federal, the first bank I tried.

'I found this key in my uncle's nightstand,' I told one of the tellers. 'He's deceased, and we're wondering if it is a key to a safe deposit box.'

The man gave it a glance. 'Looks like it, lady. Not one of ours, but try Harris. Might be theirs.'

'And where would I find them?'

'In the Loop. Big lions on each side of the door.'

It made sense to swing by home first, feed Baby Tommy, and take him with me to Harris Bank. It would be my first trip on the L with the baby buggy, a test of sorts.

The elevated trains weren't crowded at midday so it didn't turn out to be as difficult as I'd feared. Both times, getting on and off, going up and down the stairs, gentlemen sprang to my aid, helping me lift the buggy onto the platform and reminding me how kind Chicagoans could be to strangers.

Tommy and I rolled happily along West Monroe Street toward the headquarters of Harris Trust & Savings, one of Chicago's oldest and biggest banking houses. The streets were crowded with noisy black automobiles and trucks jockeying for position, honking impatiently, bellowing exhaust with every shift of the gears. The sidewalks were only marginally safer, swarming with businessmen, delivery boys, shoppers, and one determined woman battling to steer a baby buggy through the throng.

I'm not sure exactly when I started to feel like I was being followed. Maybe it was the creepy prickling on the back of my neck as I crossed to the other side of Monroe. Maybe it was when I turned the corner and glanced behind me and noticed the same person I'd seen at the previous corner. A man, alone.

He wasn't that far behind me, but I couldn't see his face. He had on a hat, of course, a businessman's fedora, but he also wore sunglasses when we hadn't seen the sun in a week and a scarf that covered the lower half of his face when it wasn't all that cold out. He turned the corner when I did.

Tailing me would have been a snap for the most junior G-man. For one thing, I was the only woman in sight with a cumbersome baby buggy; for another, I couldn't dash down an alley, disappear into a shop, or sprint across the street to lose my shadow. Was it Louis Roth? One of his North Side gangster friends? I couldn't tell. No one would dare do me any harm on a busy sidewalk like this in the middle of the Loop, but a stop at Harris Bank was out of the question for now.

The light at the corner turned red. Pedestrians bunched at the curb, waiting impatiently, but no one budged. The Chicago police didn't look kindly on jaywalking and right across the street, catty-corner to us, a cop was walking his beat.

Suddenly someone pushed up against me from behind, pressing against me in an obscene sort of way. 'You got the dough now, doll, don't you?' he breathed, his mouth inches from my ear. I knew that voice. It was Roth. 'I saw you go in that Chicago Federal bank back there. Is that where it's at? You got it in the buggy here? I'm not waiting any longer.'

The light turned green and the traffic noise stilled for a few seconds as directions changed. There was only one thing to do. I yelled loud enough that the cop across the way could hear.

'Take your hands off me, you brute,' I shouted. 'Help! Help! He's trying to take my purse!' I clutched my purse to my chest to make it look real and let loose my best scream.

A blast from a police whistle came at the same moment that two businessmen grabbed hold of Roth by the arms to hold him until the cop could dodge through the intersection traffic. Panicked, the gangster wrenched away from the two men and hotfooted it down the side street.

'You all right, lady?' asked one of the men who'd come to my aid.

'Everyone OK here?' asked the cop, his forehead creased with genuine concern.

'That man tried to grab her purse,' said a woman, pointing to the figure vanishing down the alley. Another woman backed up her story, ending with: 'I saw it too. Is your baby OK?'

'Yes, yes. We're fine. Just shaken.'

'Of course you are, dear girl! What a fright! And in broad daylight! What is the world coming to?' She looked angrily at the cop as if expecting an answer, but all he could do was motion everyone on their way. The crisis was over. Once the corner cleared, he turned to me.

'You recognize him?'

'I'm afraid not. His face was covered by a scarf and he wore sunglasses.'

'Humph. Clearly up to no good. Where were you heading?'

'To the park.' Grant Park, with its colonnade and statuary, was a few blocks ahead of us, and it made for a logical destination. I didn't dare go to the Harris Bank now. Roth or an accomplice was probably nearby watching me.

'I'll walk along with you, if you don't mind, Mrs . . .?'

'Pastore.'

'Mrs Pastore. Just to make sure that hoodlum doesn't come back to bother you.'

I didn't mind at all.

TWENTY-FIVE

The beat cop left me in Grant Park in front of the Art Institute. The prospect of a warm place to rest and a hot drink in their tearoom sounded better than the long trip home, so I bumped Tommy and his buggy up the stairs and ducked inside. I would pass by Harris Bank on my return, and as long as there was no hint of anyone tailing me, I would drop in then and see if Quillen's key was a match for theirs.

No sooner had I made Tommy comfortable with a clean diaper and myself comfortable with an order of tea and cake than who should walk in but Liam O'Rourke.

'What a coincidence!' I exclaimed. 'I guess I shouldn't be

surprised to see you at the art museum seeing as how you said you come here often.'

'But you told me *you* hadn't been in years. What drew you in today? The paintings? The Egyptian mummies? The Greek sculpture?'

'To be honest, the tea and cake. Sorry.'

'No need to be sorry. Their cakes are famous. May I join you?' I gestured to the vacant chair for a response and he sat. 'I'll have the same as the young lady,' he told the pretty waitress.

'What brings you to the museum today?' I asked.

'The exhibit on Renaissance artists. I've been through it several times, but each time seems like the first, I find so much new. I'd be happy to escort you through it today and provide scintillating commentary for your edification.' He spoke the last words like a snooty professor to make me chuckle. It worked. 'Say yes, Mrs Pastore. It will be good for Master Tommy to absorb some culture.'

'I warn you, I'm a philistine. Tommy probably knows more about art than I do.'

'Philistines are my specialty. When we've finished our cake, we'll head upstairs.'

Thoughts of Harris Bank were no match for the tales O'Rourke spun as we ambled through the near-empty galleries, our footsteps echoing on the polished floor, our whispers magnified by the tall ceilings. Paintings that said nothing to me suddenly spoke volumes when Liam O'Rourke related a bit about the artist and their subject or style. While I knew little of art, I did know something of history and could relate to the history paintings, like Jacques-Louis David's picture of Napoleon. The mythological paintings sprang to life when O'Rourke explained the stories behind them.

'You see, here are the three Greek Fates, the goddesses who work the thread of life. This one spins the thread, this one fixes its length, and that one cuts it at the time of death. Each Fate is symbolized by her tool: the spindle there and the distaff and the shears. The artist is showing his belief that our lives are in the hands of the Fates, not our own.'

There were even some paintings done by women. Any mother

would appreciate Mary Cassatt's beautiful pictures of mothers and children or Berthe Morisot's women. Liam O'Rourke would have made a good teacher.

'Thank you for the tour, Mr O'Rourke, but the sun sets early these days and I doubt I can squeeze this buggy into the L during rush hour.' Plus, I still intended to stop by Harris Bank before it closed, but he didn't need to know that.

'I am going your way. If you will permit, I'd be pleased to escort you home.'

'On foot? Don't you have your automobile?'

'Not today. Repairs. I too must depend on the L and the streetcars.'

'How kind of you to offer. I'd be happy for the company.'

The bank would be there tomorrow. And if Roth was still lurking about, Tommy and I would have male protection.

We set off toward the nearest L station, arriving seconds before the train pulled in. With Liam O'Rourke beside me, I had no trouble navigating the stairs. We stepped off into a busy shopping district where stores were staying open late to accommodate Christmas shoppers. Fancy window displays tempted passersby with elegantly wrapped packages of chocolates, boys' and girls' ice skates, fur muffs and mittens, dolls with golden hair, and books of all sorts.

'Oh!' I gasped, coming to a screeching halt in front of a brightly lit window of a toy store.

'What is it?'

'There! That's what I've been looking for.' Stacked in the corner were various board games and perched on the top was a chess game, open and partially set up.

It wasn't just any chess game. It was the most beautiful chess game I had ever seen. Its board was made of many different colored stones; its chessmen were carved in black ebony and creamy white ivory, each with gold trim.

'You're thinking of a gift?'

'For Freddy. He's the boy who . . .' I remembered in time. 'He's a distant relative who lives with Carlotta and me. I've been trying to think of a present for him, and it came to me just last night that a chess set would be perfect.'

'How old is he?'

'Sixteen.'

'He plays chess?'

'Not yet, but he could learn. I think it would suit him. He's – well, he's different from most boys. He's quiet and solitary, but very bright.'

'Do you play?'

'I did once upon a time, years ago. I've forgotten most of it, but we could learn together and play in the evenings. I think he'd be good at it. But – oh.' My eye fell on a tag that I hadn't noticed. The price.

'What?'

'I should have known. That's way beyond what I can afford.'

'Look, there's another set in that corner. A simpler one and cheaper.'

It was simpler. And a tenth of the cost. The board was cardboard, the men made of some sort of composite, plain black and plain white. A poor man's chess board. Nothing wrong with it, but a sad comedown from the splendid example I'd fallen for. Freddy deserved better.

I sighed. 'I want something special for the boy. He's become like a little brother to me. He sacrificed a lot to give me this baby buggy – it was an early Christmas present. Never mind, let's go. I have several days before Christmas. I'll find something later.'

We hadn't gone ten steps when it was Liam O'Rourke's turn to stop suddenly. 'I just thought of something. I know of a place, a speakeasy of sorts, and it's not far from here. Are you in a hurry to get home?'

'Thank you, Mr O'Rourke, but I don't really have time for a drink now. There's a séance tonight—'

'And you'll be attending?'

'I need to be there to help Carlotta.'

'Help how?'

This was no time for honesty. I liked Liam O'Rourke, but I didn't trust anyone with the truth about my job with Carlotta. There was simply no delicate way of telling him that I helped her trick people into thinking they were contacting their deceased loved ones.

'Oh, by smoothing the séance along. Greeting guests.

Reassuring the nervous ones. Helping people with coats and seating . . .' It sounded pretty lame and I wouldn't have blamed him for being skeptical. I had no idea what Liam O'Rourke thought about mystics and Spiritualism, so I thought it prudent not to travel down that road.

'Hmm. Anyway, I didn't mean to invite you for a drink. I want you to see Carl's place. It's not your typical speakeasy, but you may find what you're looking for there.'

The clients coming to tonight's séance were regulars, so there really wasn't much for me to prepare. I was having an easy few days because Carlotta had decided not to take on any new customers until after Christmas. 'I have too much business over the holidays with our regulars to take on new clients,' she'd explained, but I knew her distress over losing the house was playing a role in her decision. In any case, there had been little in the way of investigating wills and obituaries for the past few days.

'Now you've got me curious,' I said. 'Very well, I can manage a quick visit. "Lead on, MacDuff".'

Within minutes we'd arrived at Carl's place. It wasn't far from Carlotta's house, but I'd never been down that particular street. Even if I had, I wouldn't have recognized it for a speakeasy. No sign, no painted door, no traffic, no music leaking out onto the sidewalk, nothing about it said 'speakeasy'. Whatever sort of joint Carl was running was located four steps down from the sidewalk behind a nondescript door. I parked the buggy and carried Tommy inside.

A high-pitched voice greeted us through a haze of cigarette and cigar smoke. 'O'Rourke, you old son of a – Oh, excuse me. Hello miss. I mean, ma'am.' A person – a small man or a mannish woman, I couldn't say which, was speaking and the harem trousers, blousy shirt, and soft cap offered little clue as to the person's sex. I waited for an introduction to set me straight. O'Rourke merely nodded to the person, took my elbow, and steered me through a maze of tables and chairs toward a bar in the corner.

Carl's was unlike any speakeasy I'd been to, and I'd been to a lot. For one thing, there was no music, not even a Victrola. For another, it was eerily quiet, so quiet I could hear the man across the room clear his throat. And the bar itself was not the main feature, as it was in most speaks. It was small, stuck away in the corner like an afterthought. As my eyes grew accustomed to the dim light, I could make out a dozen or so square tables, each with two straight chairs and a chess board between them.

'Evenin', Carl.' Liam O'Rourke shook the hand of a grizzled old man perched on a high stool in front of the bar, not behind it. His face and hands were covered with liver spots and his long, bushy eyebrows nearly obscured his vision. 'I'd like you to meet some friends of mine, Mrs Maddie Pastore and her son Tommy. Mrs Pastore, may I present Carl Druggit, proprietor of the club and an avid chess player.'

Mr Druggit came stiffly to his feet – or foot, I should say, for he was missing one leg. After making an old-world bow, he greeted me in an accent straight out of the Deep South. 'Evenin', Mrs Pastore. We don't see many women in here, ma'am. You play?'

'She does not at present,' O'Rourke answered for me. 'We're here on a different mission. Mrs Pastore wants a chess board as a Christmas present for a sixteen-year-old boy. I thought you might be able to help her.'

He nodded. 'I might at that. Tell me about the lad.'

'Freddy? Well, gosh, Freddy is . . . he's sixteen, but he's not real big for his age so he could pass for younger. Red hair, lots of freckles. Whip smart but can't read a word of print. I've tried to teach him, honest. He just can't learn his letters, but his memory is amazing. He's good with his hands, good with making things, good with figuring out how to do things. Good with my little boy here too. He's an orphan who lives with the woman I work for. I live there too. He's almost the man of the house.'

Carl's eyes bored into my own as he listened. His thinning hair was snow-white but his overgrown eyebrows were black as soot, giving him an oddly sinister appearance. 'Lemme see what I can do,' he said and, using a crutch, he made his way across the room to a narrow door that opened to a closet.

'Lost his leg during the war,' O'Rourke said in a low voice.

The armistice had come just six years earlier. What on earth had this old man done during the Great War? Acted as a medic? My shocked expression must have made O'Rourke reconsider his words. 'Not that war. The Civil War.'

'Jeez Louise. The Civil War!? I've heard there are a few Civil War veterans left, but I've never met any.'

'Now you have.'

Carl came back with something under his arm. Without a word, he laid it on the bar, a thin tooled-leather suitcase that carried a chess set like nothing I'd ever seen.

It was a lovely piece of woodwork that must have been fashioned by a person with copious amounts of patience and skill. The full-figured kings stood tall, leaning on their swords; the bishops with their mitres and crooks were nearly as tall as their monarch; the rooks were depicted as church steeples with pierced turrets; the knights were mounted on rearing horses. The board alternated dark walnut squares with almost-white holly. No two pieces were alike.

'Jeez Louise, it's gorgeous! But I could never—' This set made the one in the store window look like an actress with too much make-up. That one had cost more than a week's wages. God knows what this one cost.

'How much, Carl?' asked O'Rourke.

He did not hesitate. 'Three dollars.'

I nearly fell over. 'You can't be serious. For this?'

'It was left to me by a man who wanted it to go to someone who would appreciate it. He didn't ask for money, just a good home. Your young friend sounds like a good guardian. There is a requirement – you must bring it back to me if he doesn't show serious interest.'

'Absolutely, I promise! Thank you, Mr Druggit.' O'Rourke took Tommy out of my arms so I could dig the money out of my purse.

'Carl,' he corrected me. 'And there is one more requirement. You send your young man, your Freddy, to us. He can learn here. See that fella over there? Second table from the corner. Name's Stephen. He likes nothing better than to teach the game to young'uns. Send your Freddy here and Stephen will see if he has the makings of a chess player.'

'I will do that, Carl. I promise.'

If I hadn't had the baby buggy to hang onto, I'd have flown out of Carl's and floated home like a hot-air balloon.

I managed to smuggle my prize up to my room without

Freddy or Carlotta noticing. I had to hurry. It was nearing time for the séance. I fed Tommy and sang him to sleep on a folded blanket in Carlotta's bedroom, then changed into my mourning clothes to play the grieving widow. First, I wrestled the kiddie coop down the stairs and into the parlor.

'What in heaven's name are you doing, Maddie?' exclaimed Carlotta as she entered the room. Her gypsy queen attire was in all its glory, and her bangles clanged like wind chimes. 'Putting Tommy in here?'

'He's asleep in your room. I hope you don't mind. I'll move him later.'

'Of course not, but who—'

'What's going on?' asked Freddy. He had finished his supper and was on his way up to the enhancement room to make ready the opening sounds of the séance.

I picked up the baby doll I'd bought the day before. It was dressed in one of Tommy's old outfits, and when I set it in the kiddie coop with a blanket over it, you couldn't tell it wasn't a real sleeping baby. 'I had an idea. In case Louis Roth or one of his thugs comes after Tommy again, I'll have this to confuse him. It won't be so obvious where he is.'

'A decoy!' said Freddy. 'I get it. Good idea! Even a little delay, a little confusion, could make a difference. Anyone breaking in here might go to the wrong place.'

'Exactly. It may not amount to much, but it should confuse anyone bent on trouble. And the doll cost almost nothing.'

'We can move Tommy and the decoy doll around to different spots every day.'

TWENTY-SIX

In the end, I didn't have to decide between taking Tommy with me to the Harris bank or leaving him at the house. My fingers did the work. The next morning, the telephone put me through to the Harris switchboard, where a girl's pert voice answered with one long word: 'Good-morning-Harris-Bank-how-may-I-direct-your-call?'

'I'd like to speak to someone about a safe deposit box, please.' Which after one more connection led me to a Mr Edwards.

'My mother has found a key among her late brother's belongings that we think might be one of your bank's. Are your safe deposit keys brass with a green head? The number is two six one.'

'That sounds like one of ours, miss. You'll find box two six one at the main branch in the Loop.'

Business concluded. Now I had only to drop in and see what Quillen's second box was holding. Since Flora Masters had found nothing of monetary value in his Midwest Bank box, the cash he stole had to be at Harris. With my hand still resting on the telephone, I was debating whether to bring Flora Masters with me when the telephone bell rang again.

Startled, I raised the receiver and answered with our signature greeting, 'Good morning, Madame Carlotta's Spiritual Guidance.'

'Could I speak with Maddie Pastore, please?'

'Speaking.'

'Maddie, it's me, Flora Masters.' She sounded jittery, but then, that seemed to be her natural state.

'Oh my! I was just thinking about you. About the key.'

'That's what I am calling about.' She took a deep breath and plunged into her tale with hardly a pause for breath. 'This morning one of Herman's colleagues from Midwest came by our house with a lovely breakfast pastry for me and the girls, and who do you think it was but that nice Miss Stanley who worked with Herman for years, so thoughtful of her and she said such kind things about Herman and how everyone at the bank misses him, but she was on official business because now that his personal belongings had been returned to me, it was her duty to collect the bank's keys, and you remember Herman's keyring had lots of keys, and well, one opened the bank's back door and another was for an office storage facility and one was to his own desk, and naturally she took all of those, and I told her that there was one other key, a mystery key that I'd given you so you could figure out what it was and well, I described it to her and at first I thought I'd done wrong, she frowned so and seemed upset, but then she said it was one of the bank's keys too and to let you know to return it right away to me or directly to her at the bank, whichever was easiest, so I hope you can do that today, Maddie, OK?'

Over my dead body.

Well, well, well. Wasn't that an interesting development? The mystery – or the first part of it – was solved. Officer O'Rourke once told me that a detective tries to answer six pertinent questions about a crime. Who? What? When? Where? How? and Why? The 'what' we already knew: one hundred thousand bucks belonging to the North Side Gang. The 'when' was the easiest: November twenty-seventh. I had just figured out the 'who': who had stolen the money, besides Quillen. Never mind Flora's confidence in her brother's honesty, it seemed he'd colluded with the saintly Ruby Stanley to embezzle the cash. And now the 'where' was clear: from Midwest Bank to a Harris Bank safe deposit box. The 'why' was the motive – to get rich quick. What I didn't know was the 'how'. How had they done it, given the bank's careful monitoring of cash flow. Nor did I understand what had gone wrong between Quillen and the North Side Gang that cost Herman Quillen his life.

The second part of the mystery was the murder of Herman Quillen. That had its own set of questions. The 'when' and 'where' were givens, the 'how' had been determined by the coroner, but 'why' had he been killed? What had gone amiss? And 'who' had done the dirty deed? Someone with the North Side Gang, probably Roth, but maybe not. I hoped the Harris Bank box would yield some clues.

I calmed Flora Masters, told her not to give the matter another second's thought. 'I'll take care of Miss Stanley,' I said as the beginnings of a plan churned in my head.

Pounding on the front door jerked me out of my thoughts.

'What on earth?' Carlotta murmured from the parlor. 'What's wrong with the bell, I ask you?' But recent circumstances had turned her timid about opening the door, so she peered out the front window to see who had chosen fist over finger. 'Oh dear, Maddie, come quick. It's that awful gangster. Don't answer it!

What shall we do? Call the police? Maybe he'll think we're not home and go away.'

We waited, still as mice, while he pounded again and again. At last, when the sound of his footsteps told us he'd gone, Carlotta dared peek out the window once more. 'Coast is clear,' she announced with relief. For now, I thought. I suspected he wouldn't be going far.

'Don't worry about him. He won't be threatening anyone much longer. I'm going right now to a bank in the Loop to get the money.'

'Will you take the baby?'

'With Roth hanging around here, I think he's better off with me. And I have to take the baby buggy. I'll need it to carry the cash home.' The sooner I got that money to Roth and his North Side Gang, the sooner we'd all be safe.

I pulled the buggy out the back door and was tucking Tommy snug inside when I sensed a presence. I spun around. There was Louis Roth, hands in his deep coat pockets and a sneer on his ugly face.

'Well, well, this is a nice surprise. You going somewhere, doll?'

Keeping my voice calm, I replied, 'As a matter of fact, Mr Roth, I was going to get the money you've been so desperate to collect.'

'I knew you knew where it was.'

'I didn't know until today. And, now that I think of it, I don't need to make the trip at all. You can get it yourself. Here's the key to a safe deposit box at Harris Bank in the Loop. Your money's there.'

He reached for the key, then snatched back his hand like from a burning stove. 'Don't think so, doll. I ain't walking into some trap you've set with the cops. All the banks know my face, see? You get the dough and meet me at the Wrigley Building on Michigan Avenue. Alone. You know it?'

'Of course I do.' The massive new Wrigley Building with its skyscraper clocktower stood where the Michigan Avenue bridge crossed the river.

'On the steps to the walkway that runs along the river. In an hour.'

'I can't get there that fast.'

'Try. Try hard. Oh, and I'll just hold the baby while you're gone, and we can make the switch when you get there.'

I put myself between him and the baby buggy. 'You so much as breathe on my child, I will throw this key into the Chicago River and let your gangster buddies kill you.'

He held up his hands like a man being robbed and gave a phony smile. 'OK, doll, OK, just kidding. No sweat. Just be there. On time. And we'll all be friends again.'

Two larger-than-life lions guarded the entrance to Harris Trust & Savings' headquarters on West Monroe. In the two dozen years since the building was built, time and the weather had conspired to give the original shiny brass bas-relief sculptures a blue-green patina, but whatever their color, the beasts represented strength and power, qualities any depositor would appreciate in the institution that secured his money.

Without knowing the details, I assumed that Herman Quillen had brought the stolen money to Harris because he and Ruby Stanley thought it less likely to be detected there than at Midwest. While I had no idea how they accomplished the theft without leaving any paper trail, I imagined he exchanged the profusion of small bills for larger ones in the vault and carried them out in a briefcase (or perhaps two), then made his way downtown to Harris where he rented a large box. Now that I had seen Quillen's corpse at the Deadhouse, I could picture him alive and imagine how he must have looked returning to work, perhaps winking conspiratorially at Miss Stanley and settling in at his desk without the slightest notion that he would be dead in a matter of hours.

A doorman dressed like a penguin in a top hat swept open the bank's door as I approached. Before I'd advanced four steps into the lobby, another man, this one dressed like an undertaker, stepped up and greeted me in a solemn voice. 'Welcome, madam. How may we assist you this morning?'

I flashed the key and lowered my voice to match theirs. 'Could you show me to the safe deposit boxes, please?'

A snap of his fingers brought yet another man, younger but similarly attired, who offered to lead me to the vault and suggested in hushed tones that I leave the buggy in a corner.

'Oh no, the baby is asleep. I can't take him out now.' And I needed the buggy with me to help me carry out the loot. There was a good deal of room on the platform between the buggy wheels as well as a pocket on the back under the handle. As an added precaution, I'd brought a large fabric bag with straps that I could carry on my back if necessary. I had no idea how much physical space the cash would require or how heavy it would be.

'As you wish, madam. Follow me please.' His leather soles made no sound on the gleaming floor.

Crossing the cavernous lobby reminded me of walking down the aisle of a cathedral. High above loomed a decorated ceiling supported by massive, marble-sheathed columns; under my feet the patterned marble floor shone like a mirror. It sounded like a cathedral too, where even the slightest cough bounced against the cold stone, magnified as it echoed. The implication was unmistakable – this was a rock-solid institution worthy of your money and your trust.

My escort led me to an intricate brass gate, polished to shine like gold, that opened to a room where the walls were lined with hundreds of miniature doors, some as small as a post office box, others as large as a dresser drawer. Each was numbered. On a table in the middle of the room lay a large book. The man flipped through the pages until he arrived at the one for box two six one. 'Sign here, madam,' he said, handing me a gold fountain pen. 'And the date.'

The page had but one entry. Herman Quillen, November the twenty-seventh. Familiar handwriting. I signed my name below his.

The clerk removed the bank's master key from a ring and inserted it into the upper keyhole of the largest size box on the bottom row in the corner. I handed him my key, which he inserted in the lower. He turned both until they clicked, then stood. 'I will leave you to your privacy. I'll wait just outside the gate until you are ready to lock up.'

As soon as he was gone, I knelt beside the drawer. Carefully, I pulled it open. It was heavy, and didn't come easily, but I jiggled it and finally it gave way. I looked inside and blinked with disbelief.

The drawer was empty.

I don't know how long I knelt there, paralyzed with shock. A minute, half an hour? I couldn't think. It made no sense. It was the right key. The right bank. The right drawer. Everything was right. Everything except the money. What in heaven's name had gone wrong? Had someone gotten hold of a duplicate key and beaten me to the safe deposit drawer? Someone from the North Side Gang? The Harris Bank? Miss Ruby Stanley?

Louis Roth was waiting for me at the Wrigley Building quayside, and he wasn't expecting excuses.

TWENTY-SEVEN

The quay at the base of the Wrigley Building gave pedestrians a place to stroll along an attractive esplanade above the river and down curving limestone steps that swept from the avenue to a walkway at water's edge. That's where I was to meet Louis Roth.

I could have run straight home. In fact, that was my first thought. Home was safe. Sort of safe. Until Roth figured out I wasn't coming to meet him and tracked me back there. He would be apoplectic. For him, this was a matter of life and death, which is why he had made it a matter of life and death for me and Tommy. I could call Officer O'Rourke for help again, and he would come again, but no one was going to station a cop on my front steps for the next few years. Roth had proven that he could get inside our house. Even if we managed to thwart him in that, he could always soak the place in gasoline and set it on fire with us in it. Or ambush us coming or going. In my panicked frame of mind, I considered leaving town, packing a suitcase and running to Grand Central Terminal to board the next train to anywhere. But how could I leave Chicago? Chicago was my whole world. I had never traveled outside the city in my life. I knew nothing of other cities, other states, other lands. I knew no one who could shelter me until I got my feet on the ground. I hadn't enough money for a train ticket, let alone a hotel room.

I would have to meet Roth eventually. I would have to explain. Delaying the inevitable only made things worse. Far safer for us to meet in a busy public place like the quay below the Wrigley Building where there would be lots of activity. He wouldn't dare attack me or try to kidnap Tommy while we were surrounded by all those businessmen and office girls. I would tell him the truth and convince him that his best bet was to flee Chicago.

He wasn't among the people on the esplanade by the Michigan Avenue bridge, so I looked over the rail to the walkway below. The wide Chicago River snaked through the city, its turbid waters swollen with winter debris scraped from the streets by snowplows and filth dumped from boats and factories that lined its banks. Barges piled high with coal and ships stuffed with cargo jostled for position at docks that jutted out from warehouses marked Quaker Oats or Pillsbury or Curtiss Baby Ruth. Tugboats nudged their charges toward Lake Michigan or south to the Mississippi River and the Gulf of Mexico. Passenger boats and pleasure craft wove through the thicket of vessels, ducking under bridges that deigned to rise only for the tallest. A few dingy houseboats clung to their moorings against assault from commercial craft that would have bullied them aside without the slightest remorse.

Spying no one I recognized on that side of the bridge, I crossed the crowded street to the Wrigley Building side and repeated the search. And there he was, leaning with his back against the stone newel post at the bottom of the curved staircase, hands in his pockets, looking out at the river traffic, a lone man obviously waiting for someone. Two dozen people were nearby, strolling, sitting on the stairs, chatting with co-workers during their lunch break, eating sandwiches, enjoying the brief splurge of midday sun before the clouds returned. The scene was very public, quite safe. A kind gentleman helped me bump the buggy down to the walkway.

'Thank you, sir,' I said to the gentleman. He tipped his hat.

Roth took a last drag of his cigarette and threw the butt on the ground. He didn't even attempt a smile. 'Where's my money?'

'I went to Harris Bank, Mr Roth. I had the key.' I held it out to him. He ignored my hand. 'There was nothing in the safe deposit box. Someone must have gotten there before me. It was empty. Completely empty. Not a nickel.'

Those cruel eyes narrowed to slits. With a malevolent twist of his mouth, he spat on the pavement near my foot. I held my ground.

'I don't believe you,' he said.

Determined to show him I was not afraid, I looked him straight in the eye. 'I can't help that. What I've said is gospel truth. I thought the money would be there. I was sure Quillen had stashed it there. If he did, it's not there now. I've tried my best for you, Mr Roth. I tried to find the money and return it. I have no more ideas as to where it could be. If you're in danger because of that, I'm sorry, but I can't help you. You should leave town if you are afraid of the consequences. New York, Detroit, Baltimore, I'm sure you could find work in any city.'

Clearly, our conversation was not a friendly one. People nearby shot us curious looks, which served to reassure me. Their close proximity would restrain violence. In a moment, I would go back up to street level and wave down a taxi. Once home, I'd telephone Officer O'Rourke for help.

But at this moment, I was still waiting for Roth's reaction. I expected an argument, more threats, surely an eruption of foul curses. I did not expect him to snatch the baby buggy handle out of my hands and push it with five quick steps toward the river. Nearing the edge, he gave it one mighty shove and watched it sail into the dark water below.

I screamed. Or maybe I shouted. I think I ran to the edge of the water. Or maybe he dragged me there. Right in front of scores of people in broad daylight, Roth grabbed me by one arm and flung me, arms flailing away like a windmill, into the river after the buggy.

I hit the water on my back, my fine blue coat that Tommy bought me at Marshall Field's absorbing none of the smack of the hard water. The fall knocked the breath clean out of me. Icy fingers pulled me and my sodden clothing down as fast as if I'd had been made of lead. Freezing water burned my flesh.

The world went black.

The next thing I knew, I was lying on my stomach on the pavement surrounded by dozens of shoes. Someone was pounding me on the back until, gagging and choking, I threw up. People were dithering about in helpless confusion. Voices called out, 'Get a blanket!' 'Get back!' 'Get the police!' 'Get a doctor!'

Strong hands turned me on my back and held my head up. A familiar face. River water dripped from his hair down his cheeks, or maybe it was tears. My anxious eyes must have asked the question.

'God, Maddie, I tried. I couldn't . . . I couldn't reach—'

My lips shivered so hard I couldn't form the words. The buggy. The baby. I tried to explain.

'I couldn't see in the water. It was all too dark. It's too late. I'm sorry,' his voice broke. He looked so young. And scared. 'I'm so sorry. I couldn't reach him.'

My icy fingers reached up and gently touched Liam O'Rourke's chin. 'Doll,' I managed to croak. 'Doll.'

TWENTY-EIGHT

'Maddie, dear, you have a visitor,' Carlotta whispered as she ushered Liam O'Rourke into my room later that afternoon. He glanced at Freddy who was sitting on the rag rug playing peek-a-boo with a happy little Tommy, and sat on the edge of my bed. Carlotta raised her eyebrows at this familiarity but swallowed her objections.

I managed a weak smile. 'I can't thank you enough . . .' It hurt to talk. My voice was hoarse, maybe from the river water I swallowed or the vomiting it back up.

'Hush,' he said, taking one of my hands in his. 'You can repay me by getting better quickly.'

Liam O'Rourke looked different somehow. Dry, sure, but something else I couldn't put my finger on. My brain was moving at the speed of a slug.

'She's doing very well, Mr O'Rourke. We can never thank

you enough for your bravery. Such a miracle you were there at just the right moment to save her! As soon as you brought her inside, just after you left, I gave her a slug of brandy – medicinal, of course – and put her right quick in a tub of hot water to warm her up and wash away all that river filth. She won't eat, but I'm insisting on tea with lots of sugar. Perhaps some buttered toast later.'

O'Rourke squeezed my hand. 'I can't tell you how relieved I was to know that the baby wasn't in that buggy! You were carrying a doll?'

I opened my mouth to explain but nothing came out. I waved my fingers in Freddy's direction. He got the message.

'This morning, a gangster named Roth came by and pounded on our door, scaring the crap out of all of us. He thinks Maddie knows where some money is, but she doesn't. Maddie decided to take Tommy with her to the bank because it looked like Roth was going to hang around here. We have this doll the same size as a newborn baby – well, we *had* the doll – Maddie figured to use it to confuse anyone who was trying to find Tommy. But Roth came around to the back as she was leaving and threatened them both. He thought the money was in a bank box and he ordered her to get it and meet him by the Wrigley Building. Soon as he was out of sight, she brought Tommy back inside and put the doll in his place. She needed the buggy to carry the money if it was there.'

The whole time Freddy was talking, Liam O'Rourke's eyes never left mine. 'And then the money wasn't there?'

I shook my head. Freddy kept telling my story. 'The safe deposit box was empty. Maddie can't figure out what happened to it. Maybe the money was never there. Maybe someone got there first.'

'I saw the policeman out front,' said O'Rourke.

Carlotta spoke up. 'Your brother arranged that. We're very thankful. It feels safe having him here now. We're hoping Roth'll leave town for good now that he can't return the money to the gang. Seems they think he stole it in the first place. Maddie doesn't think that's true, but what can she do?'

'Hymie Weiss isn't one to cross,' said O'Rourke. 'Word on the street has it he suspects Roth was working with someone at the bank, that Quillen clerk, and the two of them filched it from the deposit. Which reminds me, Maddie, we made the evening papers, you and me. Page three.' And he took a folded newspaper out from under his arm and began to read aloud.

> In a dramatic rescue this noon, an unknown man pulled a woman from the Chicago River near the Michigan Avenue Bridge but failed to save a child.
>
> The quay below the Wrigley Building was busy with pedestrians shocked as they watched an argument between a man and a young mother escalate into violence. According to several witnesses, the man pushed the baby carriage into the river, then turned on the woman, throwing her in the water after the child. An alert man standing on the stairs rushed to the river's edge, threw off his coat, and without hesitation plunged into the forty-two-degree water after the woman.
>
> 'We couldn't believe our eyes,' said Marie Zokolski, a Girl Friday on her lunch hour. 'Jumping into that freezing water! He got to the woman and grabbed her by the coat and pulled her to the edge. Two or three other men rushed to help him pull her up. They wanted to pull him up too, but he dived and dived until he couldn't dive any more, trying to find the baby.'
>
> In the dark frigid water, that proved impossible, and after several minutes, the rescuer allowed himself to be pulled up to the quayside. Tragically, the child and buggy were lost. In the confusion, the attacker disappeared. Someone summoned a taxi and the anonymous rescuer bustled the woman into the car and left with her just as the police arrived on the scene. Anyone having further information about the victims' or perpetrator's identities should contact the police at once.
>
> The police ceased dragging for the body at sunset. As the current in the river is flowing at the rate of six miles an hour toward the drainage canal, it is expected that the body will be found in the canal within a few days.
>
> This is the seventeenth fatality from drowning in the Chicago River this year.

'You're not going to tell the police, are you?' I croaked. 'Your brother said he'd keep it under wraps. I don't want Roth to know he failed to kill Tommy, or he might try again.'

'The secret's safe with me.' He squeezed my hand again.

Carlotta cleared her throat. 'Now, Mr O'Rourke, I think that's long enough for a visit. You can come back tomorrow if you like, but Maddie needs her rest. And more tea, right, dear? I'll make another pot after I show Mr O'Rourke out.'

As I lay warm in bed with Freddy murmuring nonsense to Tommy on the floor beside my bed, something was knocking at my consciousness. Something was odd. Something wasn't right. I wanted to think but thinking hurt. The fog descended like a curtain at the end of the flickers and I slept.

TWENTY-NINE

The strangest thing happened after my swim in the Chicago River. My milk dried up. Whether it was from the fall or the shock or the freezing cold, no one could say, but from that day on, I had nothing to give Tommy. He was eating mushy foods by now, but he still needed milk, so Freddy ran to the shops where he bought some evaporated milk to mix with corn syrup and heated a batch of substitute. The look on Tommy's face when he took his first suck was priceless, but he got the hang of it. 'In a day or two, he'll be slurping down a full bottle,' said Freddy, sounding more like a proud papa than a sixteen-year-old orphan. It made me wonder if anyone had loved him when he was growing up.

Lying in a warm bed with only the cracks in the ceiling for entertainment can really free the mind. As I listened to city noises in the street that afternoon, my thoughts kept returning to Quillen's last day.

November twenty-seventh. Herman Quillen arrives at Midwest Savings & Loan as he has for years. At some point during the day, perhaps that morning, he sneaks off to Harris Bank and opens a safe deposit box, as his dated signature confirms. At another point, he sees Roth and his bodyguards enter Midwest Bank with the gang's regular deposit. He relieves one of the tellers and takes over the transaction. He counts the money – mostly small bills as one would expect with cash coming from petty gamblers, prostitutes, and backroom liquor purchases. This takes a while. The total comes to several hundred thousand dollars. Nothing unusual about that. Somehow he and Ruby Stanley manage to bypass the bank's rigorous accounting controls that were designed to thwart embezzlers – that much I couldn't figure out. Somehow they also manage to fool Roth. Or was Roth part of the scheme too? Roth is a courier. Maybe he doesn't know how much money he's carrying, so if he even looks at the receipt slip, the number won't mean anything. But the North Side Gang's bookkeepers would notice the discrepancy eventually. Word on the street had it the gang was in complete disarray after O'Banion's murder. Did the chaos extend to the men minding the books? Wasn't it possible – even likely – that more than one person was seizing the opportunity to drain a little from the till? What was that old saying? 'In confusion there is profit.'

However they accomplished the actual theft, Quillen deposits the money according to regular procedure and takes 'his' hundred thou to the vault where he exchanges small bills for larger ones, hence the unusual number of small bills and shortage of larger ones that one of the tellers noticed. Miss Stanley might have helped him with that. They put the large bills in a valise or briefcase or nondescript satchel to carry to Harris. But the biggest question remains: at some point during this caper, Quillen changes his mind and doesn't go back to Harris Bank. Why, I couldn't guess, but something spooked him. He stashes the cash somewhere else and returns to Midwest to resume work. Was he afraid the gangsters were watching him? Was he trying to cut Miss Stanley out and keep all the money for himself? How could he do that without causing her to turn him in and claim her own innocence?

Anyway, back to the story. At five o'clock, the bank closes. Retiring President Charles Hughes invites Quillen to the Tree Club for a farewell drink. They have only one – Hughes isn't much for socializing with employees and Quillen isn't much of a drinker. Hughes leaves a big tip and walks out of the club. Quillen leaves shortly after. A few hours later, he consumes something poisonous and collapses in an alley.

All of a sudden, a gaping hole appeared in Quillen's day, the hours between the speakeasy and his death. How had I not focused on that before now? What happened during those hours? Where did he go after drinks at the speakeasy?

The answer was so obvious, I wondered where my brain had been all along. What would any bachelor do after having a cocktail at a speakeasy? *He'd go to dinner*. And where did Quillen's sister say he regularly dined? Sally's Diner.

I knew Sally's. I'd not eaten there but I'd seen it. It was a modest establishment located two blocks west of Midwest Bank in the direction of Quillen's home. According to his sister, he ate there most nights except weekends when he dined with her and her kids. I wanted to leap out of bed in my eagerness to run over to talk with the waitresses who would surely remember a regular like Quillen. I bolted upright and was rewarded with a pounding in my temples like someone had taken a hammer to my head. Just then, Carlotta came into the room and tsk-tsked me back onto the pillows. It was Friday night, our busiest, and we had back-to-back séances scheduled. Sally's Diner would have to wait until tomorrow. I was needed downstairs.

'Nonsense, Maddie,' she protested when I tried to get up. 'You stay in bed. Freddy and I can handle everything for tonight's gatherings.'

No, they couldn't. 'Most nights, sure, but you know tonight's different. Our new slate enhancement depends on me. Freddy and I've rehearsed it to death, and if we aren't both there, you'll have to cancel Miss Semple which wouldn't be good for her. Don't fret, Carlotta. I'm up to it, honestly. Tell Freddy I'll be all set at seven thirty for the first session.'

The first session was the largest and easiest. No newcomers, just six regulars I'd investigated weeks ago. Carlotta knew their stories and their idiosyncrasies. Freddy knew the enhancement protocol. Toughing it out through my splitting headache, I contributed an Undark symbol painted on my palm that spoke meaningfully to Mrs Blair, an 1850 Liberty head penny I'd mined from our collection of pennies to represent the birth year of Mr Whittaker's father, and a spray of rose cologne to remind the Trask sisters of their dearly departed friend, Rose. When the séance concluded and the grateful clients had gone, Carlotta pocketed the forty-five dollars they'd left in the basket and slipped away to her bedroom for a rest. Communing with the spirits took a heavy toll on her constitution. Mine too.

A knock at the door less than an hour later sent me scooting out the back and around to the front, where I could enter on the heels of elderly Miss Semple, a spinster who had outlived most of her relatives and friends but enjoyed communicating with them through Carlotta every Friday night. Usually she could be merged at a table with two or three others, but last week she had told Carlotta that a friend of hers had experienced slate messaging with another medium, and she wanted to see if that would work for her. Not willing to disoblige a good customer, we set about learning the slate trick.

Harry Houdini's book, *A Magician Among the Spirits*, saved our bacon. He mentioned three or four tricks by which fake mystics used slate writing to communicate with the Great Beyond, and all I had to do was adapt one of those techniques to our own abilities. The most impressive involved a shill hidden below the séance room floor, listening to the conversation through a portal cut in the floor beneath the table and writing answers on a slate which would then be sneaked into the medium's hand under the table. That wouldn't work for us because Freddy couldn't read or write and Carlotta was miserable at sleight of hand. We'd have to make do with second best. Freddy and I practiced the move until it was smooth as silk.

Freddy had moved the large séance table to the far end of the room and arranged a small one near the corner beside the thick velvet curtains that hung ceiling-to-floor across the windows. He put three chairs at the table. Miss Semple would sit with her back to the curtain. I would sit directly across from Miss Semple. Carlotta would sit between us.

Miss Semple rapped on the door precisely at nine o'clock. She was removing her fur coat and gloves when I, in my role as a client who shared her interest in slate writing, came up the front steps. Carlotta offered tea. 'You two are my only spiritual travelers this evening,' she said. I could tell Miss Semple was tickled with the attention.

Poor Carlotta was wrung out from her first séance and I was still shaky from my near drowning, but, as they say in the theater world, the show must go on.

'Miss Semple, Miss Duval, you have two slates in front of you. Please examine them to make sure they are blank on both sides.'

The slates were small, like ones used by schoolchildren learning their letters, with thin slate boards and wooden frames. When we had verified that they were blank, Carlotta lit a small candle in the center of the table and turned off all electric lights.

'Now we will join hands and gaze deeply into the spiritual flame as we begin.'

Carlotta started as she always did with a prayer and, lowering her tone, continued with Latin gibberish for several minutes. Then she lapsed into a soothing hum interrupted by the occasional plea to the spirits to come speak with us. We waited. And waited. Her hum grew so soft, I was afraid she'd gone to sleep.

Finally she roused herself enough to say, 'Miss Duval, your slate please. The spirits are ready. Hold it over Miss Semple's head.'

This was not the plan. I was supposed to go first, but as Freddy and I well knew, Carlotta was difficult to manage when she was in one of her trances. I raised my slate above Miss Semple's head, right as Freddy reached out from behind the velvet curtain and in one second flat, exchanged my blank slate for one that had a message written on it. Because the switch occurred above Miss Semple, she could see nothing of it, she only felt Freddy's slate as it came to rest gently on her head. An electric fan on the floor beside our table – ostensibly there to circulate the air – provided a soft vibration sufficient to cover up any of those infinitesimal sounds a human being makes by breathing or moving the air.

'You hold it,' I whispered, handing it off to Miss Semple.

Carlotta continued her chants and humming for a few minutes before opening her eyes and pronouncing the departure of Miss Semple's friend. 'Have we communicated?' she asked innocently.

Miss Semple held the slate to the candlelight. 'Why yes! Yes, lordy mercy, child, I see some writing! I can just make it out. "Difficult times belong in the past, my friend," it says. "Follow your heart into new realms that bring happiness. We shall be together again in eternity." Oh, how delightful! Oh, my goodness, what joy! Can you imagine it, my dear friend Isabel coming to me like that! I loved her so. And it sounds just like her.' She heaved a sigh. 'We will be together again one day, as she says. I'm certain.'

We weren't finished. It was my turn. Carlotta reprised her chants until she felt the spirits descend, at which point she directed Miss Semple to hold her blank slate over my head. Miss Semple knew just what to do. She reached across the table with the slate and when it touched my head, I gently took it from her hands. We waited. After a few minutes, Carlotta motioned to examine the slate. Naturally there was no writing on it.

'Oh, such a disappointment!' cried Miss Semple. 'I feel so bad for you, my dear. After having such good fortune myself, it's a pity you couldn't share my success.'

I assured her I was not discouraged. 'I am well aware that every attempt to contact the spirits does not end happily, Miss Semple. Madame Carlotta works wonders most of the time, and I hope for a better outcome on my next visit.'

We donned our coats and hats and left at the same time, saying goodbye on the front porch. 'Oh, look,' she cried happily, 'the moon!' It was overcast but the wind blew the clouds away for some minutes, revealing a pale half-moon glowing directly above us. Suddenly her mood fell and she whispered, 'Did you read about that madman in the newspaper this evening? The one who threw a woman and her baby in the river today?'

'Mm-hm.' I shivered.

'Such evil in the world! Who could imagine it? But I heard they caught him.'

'They did?' I glanced up and down the dark street. The policeman who had been assigned there was nowhere to be seen. Maybe it was true!

'I heard it from my neighbor whose son's wife's best friend works for the alderman's office. She said he's going to hang.' And tut-tutting her way down the steps, she bade me good night and made her way to her Dodge touring car. The chauffeur saw her coming and leaped out to assist her. I headed in the other direction for half a block before doubling back to the house. They'd caught Roth. We'd all sleep better tonight.

THIRTY

'Here's another one,' said Carlotta, holding Saturday's classified section in one hand while she sipped her morning coffee with the other. '"Three-bedroom house with bathroom and basement, one hundred seventy dollars a month." That's outrageous! These rents are twice what they were before the war. How can they charge such amounts? Anyway, never mind about that one. Elmhurst is too far west for my clients anyway. Freddy, your plate is empty. Are you finished? What about another of Maddie's pancakes? The pan's still hot.'

Instead of Carlotta's usual weekend breakfast of pancakes, I'd made the thin sort so popular in Quebec where my family came from. The French call them crêpes and sprinkle them with sugar or douse them with preserves and roll them up. Freddy was an easy convert.

'Sure, but stay where you are. I'm gonna try to make one myself.'

'Good for you!' I said. 'A modern man should know how to cook. Put a pat of butter in the pan first, then pour a little batter. Give it two minutes and flip. Nothing to it.'

'Here's another,' continued Carlotta. '"Four bedrooms, three stories. Modern kitchen. Two hundred a month." Sounds nice and good location but honestly, I don't see how we can afford that much.'

The search process was proving disheartening. 'How much do you think we can afford? I'll give up half my weekly salary.'

'I'll give up all of mine,' added Freddy. 'I don't need any money, just food and a place to sleep.' Poor kid was scared about ending up on the streets again. To tell the truth, so was I.

'Well, we can afford one hundred for sure. Maybe a little more.' She gave a sigh that sounded like she'd given up. It was our third day of looking for house rentals, and we'd yet to come across anything worth checking out in person. Time was ticking. Sure, we could fall back on cheap hotels, but two rooms would gobble up our money faster than Freddy could swallow crêpes, and we'd be unable to hold séances to earn more.

'I'm going to put Tommy down for his morning nap and go out for a bit. Is that all right?'

'Of course, dear,' said Carlotta. 'If he wakes up, I'll just give him a bottle.'

'Where are you going?' asked Freddy.

The boy wasn't being nosy; he was concerned for me. 'Sally's Diner. Not far, and it's broad daylight. I want to see if any of the waitresses remember Mr Quillen. He used to eat there pretty regularly.'

'You still looking for that money?'

'More like looking for the person who killed Quillen. I really hate murderers getting off scot-free.'

'I'll come with you.'

'I'd rather you stay here. If anyone needs protection, it's Tommy.'

'But Miss Semple said they'd caught him.'

'I know, but there was nothing in the morning paper about an arrest, was there? So we can't be sure he's behind bars.'

Freddy nodded. 'I'll double-check the doors and windows after you leave, just in case.'

Long a Chicago institution, Sally's Diner advertised itself as the next best thing to Mom, dishing out hearty homestyle meals to a largely male clientele that had yet to secure a wife to take over cooking chores. Inside, it even looked like home, with friendly checked tablecloths and mismatched wooden chairs that could have come straight out of any American dining room. Small vases with a few sprigs of fresh holly and swags of greenery over the windows gave the place a Christmassy touch.

I stepped through the vestibule past a basket of miniature candy canes and into a room warm as toast. The lunch hour crowd had not arrived. The place was quiet. Most tables were empty. A skinny, rosy-cheeked girl who couldn't have been more than fourteen greeted me.

'Good day to you, ma'am, and Merry Christmas! Are you alone or will someone be joining you?'

'Actually, Sarah,' I said, noting her nametag, 'I'm here for some information. I hope you can help me. I need to know which waitresses were working on the November twenty-seventh dinner shift. I want to ask them about a customer who dined here that evening.'

'Gosh, let me think. The boss makes up a schedule for each month. I'll run back to the office and see if November's has been thrown away. I'll just be a minute.'

She returned in less than a minute with a man wearing a scowl so fierce that his eyebrows almost met. The boss? Her father? The owner? Before he could speak, I introduced myself as Madeleine Duval of the *Chicago Tribune*.

'And what is it you want to know about our schedule, Miss Duval?' he demanded, without mentioning his own name.

'I'd like to speak to any of the waitresses who were working on November twenty-seventh. I'm doing some legwork for Lloyd Prescott. He's working on an article about the murder of Herman Quillen, a banker who, if you remember, died that night from alcohol poisoning.'

'I remember.'

'At first, the police thought it was accidental death or suicide, but now they are considering murder.'

'Murder?'

'It's been three weeks, but Mr Prescott believes Quillen ate dinner here that night, then left and met his fate some hours later.'

'He didn't get no Mickey Finn here, lady.'

'Of course not. That happened later in the evening. And that is why we need your help. We are hoping that one of your waitresses will remember him and be able to give us some information that would tell us where he went after he left Sally's.'

'We don't have any information. Now, excuse—'

'Mr Prescott would be very grateful and promised to include a nice mention of you and your restaurant in his article as having helped with the investigation. It would be good publicity. He would use your name, if you permit.'

The boss rubbed his chin as he considered my offer. 'The *Chicago Tribune*, you say?'

'Yes. Do you have a copy here? I can show you Mr Prescott's byline if you want proof of what I'm saying.'

'I seen his name in the paper.'

I held my breath. The girl shifted her weight from foot to foot. She held a piece of paper, the November roster no doubt, as she waited for the boss's decision.

'OK, that seems fair. What's the schedule say, Sarah?'

'Alice and Joanne were on duty that evening. And they're both due in at noon.'

Fifteen minutes. 'I'll be happy to wait. And my questions won't take more than a couple of minutes, I promise.'

'The name's Paul Czajkowski. Spelled C-Z-A-J-K-O-W-S-K-I. And it better be a nice comment or someone'll be hearing from my fist.'

I took my notepad from my purse and wrote his name down carefully. Before I'd finished, he strode back to the office.

'You can wait here,' said Sarah. 'Would you like some coffee or something to eat while you wait?'

'A cup of coffee would be lovely, thank you.'

Not five minutes later, a plump older woman approached. She was wearing a plain black dress covered by a festive red-and-green bib apron. 'Good day to you, dear, and Merry Christmas! I'm Alice. Mr Czajkowski said you wanted to ask me a question?'

'Yes. I came in early so I wouldn't interrupt your busy lunch hour. I need to talk with any waitresses who might remember one of your regulars, a man who dined here most nights until last month.'

'I work almost every day. So does Joanne over there.' She nodded toward another woman, middle-aged, with a big beak-like nose and sharp dark eyes that put me in mind of a hawk. Joanne, also dressed in black, was donning her own red-and-green apron. I wondered if management tried to hire women who looked motherly, or was this just a coincidence. Alice beckoned to Joanne who joined us.

'I wonder if either of you remembers a man named Herman Quillen. He used to come in quite often, according to his sister, but he was—'

'The man who died!' Joanne said breathlessly. 'Of course I remember Mr Quillen. You remember him too, don't you, Alice? I waited on him a lot. So did you.'

Alice nodded vehemently. 'Always ordered the daily special except when it was liver. Liked his coffee black, one sugar. Always left a dime tip. Always said please and thank you. A real gentleman.'

'We were shocked to read in the paper that he'd died. Suicide some said.'

'So he did eat here on the twenty-seventh?'

The two women nodded.

'I thought as much. Who waited on his table?'

'I did,' said Joanne. 'I was working the front tables where he liked to sit.'

'But I spoke to him too,' said Alice. 'I got him his coffee.'

'Did he seem anxious or worried about anything that night?'

'No,' said Joanne 'He was always so calm and polite and untroubled. Not the type of personality who'd be thinking about suicide, I'd say.'

'The coroner ruled his death was caused by methyl alcohol poisoning. Wood alcohol. Now, no one thinks for a minute that he got that here. It must have been after he left. But I'm wondering whether you remember that particular night, whether he mentioned where he was going after dinner.'

The two women exchanged glances and shook their heads.

'It was just like every other night, then?'

They nodded. Then Alice spoke, 'Well, except for the woman he ate with.'

'What!'

'An older woman had dinner with him that night. You remember her, don't you, Joanne? He paid for hers too. That was unusual. He usually ate alone while he read the evening paper. They ordered drinks that night.'

'I think she was his mother,' said Joanne. 'Or maybe an auntie. The family resemblance was there if you looked for it.'

'Was she thin? White hair in a bun on the top of her head? In her fifties maybe?' I asked, hardly daring to believe my luck.

'That sounds about right. Maybe sixties.'

'Did you happen to hear any of their conversation?'

'I'm afraid not. I wasn't trying to eavesdrop.'

'Of course you weren't. I was just wondering . . . hoping you might have overheard something that would give us a clue as to where they went afterwards. What kind of drinks did they order?' Any restaurant that didn't keep a discrete supply of liquor in the back had gone out of business long ago.

'I don't remember,' said Alice. 'He didn't often order a drink, though. After dinner, they left together. I saw them go. He held the door for her, just like the gentleman he was.' She sighed. 'I miss him.'

THIRTY-ONE

'Maddie, telephone for you,' Freddy shouted up the stairs.

'Man or woman?' I shouted back.

'Woman.'

The call I'd been waiting for. I was ready.

Setting Tommy in his kiddie coop with a rattle of tin measuring spoons, I took a deep breath and headed downstairs. Approaching the witness stand for cross-examination at a murder trial would feel like this, I thought, and I wondered if I would actually have to do that at some point in the near future.

'Hello?'

'Hello, Mrs Pastore. This is Midwest Bank with a message from Midwest's new president, Mr Randolph Abercrombie. You have in your possession one of our bank's keys that belonged to our late employee, Herman Quillen, a key that Mr Abercrombie would like returned at your earliest convenience.'

'Hello, Miss Stanley.'

There was an awkward pause, then she continued as if there

had been no interruption. 'Mr Abercrombie understands that you were lent the key by Mrs Flora Masters, who did not realize it was Midwest property. She has properly returned all of her brother's bank keys save this one. May I send someone from the bank to your home to pick it up at two today?'

'This is a surprise, Miss Stanley. I didn't realize the bank was open on Saturdays.'

'For important matters of security, like this, Midwest is open twenty-four hours a day, every day. Do you have our key?'

'I have a key. It is not, however, a Midwest key. As you well know.'

'It is most certainly—'

'Nor is it a Harris Bank safe deposit box key, as you expect,' I lied. 'Mr Quillen seems to have executed a change in plans shortly before you executed him. Your mistake.'

'I have no idea what you're talking about.'

'Well then, let me explain. I have the key. After some sleuthing, I have figured out what it unlocks. I know what's inside. And I'm going to get what's inside very soon.'

'I warn you, Mrs Pastore, when I hang up, I am going to call the police and report the theft of the Midwest key.'

'That would be another mistake, Miss Stanley, because I would then be forced to report to the police everything I know about what you and Mr Quillen did.'

'No one will believe your lies.'

'They will when they see my evidence, namely the key that opens the door to the hiding place where Mr Quillen stashed the hundred thousand dollars you and he stole. They will when they talk to the Midwest tellers who were working on November twenty-seventh and the waitresses at Sally's Diner who served you and Mr Quillen the night he was murdered. They already suspect his death wasn't accidental. They're already looking at murder. My evidence will give them a good direction to look. Oh – and the result of all this is that you will not get your hands on any of the money.'

'There's nothing to connect me to any embezzled money.'

'Me either. So why don't we behave like two sensible women and discuss calmly and quietly how to recover all this cash from its hiding place. After all, if I am forced to turn it over to the police, it will just disappear into that cesspool of corruption called a precinct station, and who benefits from that? Certainly not us. If neither of us blabs, we can both profit.'

'I don't know what you're talking about.'

'Sure you do. You and Mr Quillen were planning to share the spoils. What was the cut, fifty/fifty?'

There was a long silence during which I nearly despaired of her coming around. If she was too smart to bite, I would be the loser. I was out of options, betting on greed to overcome caution.

'It was to have been two thirds/one third,' she admitted, validating my gut.

'Let me guess, one third for Mr Quillen, right?' Actually, I bet it *was* fifty/fifty, and Miss Stanley was merely starting off the negotiation with a bid in her favor. 'I ask you, Miss Stanley, does that seem fair when he did all the work and took all the risks?'

'Nothing would have happened if not for me.'

'Hm, maybe so. But the tables have turned, haven't they? I have the key and I know where the cash is. You have nothing without me. No, that's not quite true. You have the threat to turn me into the cops, but I can use that against you too, right? So we have a standoff. Here's my proposal: I will pay you Mr Quillen's share, one-third of the contents of my box, to counter that threat. What do you say, Miss Stanley? Will thirty-three thousand buy your cooperation? I'll wager that's more money than you could make if you worked the rest of your life.'

For a moment it seemed as if the telephone wires had frozen. I waited with mounting impatience. At last the wires thawed.

'Half or I talk.'

'Deal.'

'I'll meet you this afternoon. Where and when?'

Oh, no. I wasn't going to tip my hand like that. 'I'm afraid my calendar is full this afternoon. And Sunday is, of course, the Lord's day of rest. But Monday morning, yes, Monday would be a good time to divide the spoils. The money is quite safe where it is. You'll be working at the bank on Monday. I'll call you about the time and place. Goodbye, Miss Stanley. And, might I add, you've made the right decision for once. For perhaps the first time.'

THIRTY-TWO

Standing in the middle of the frenetic Dearborn Street Station, I made a slow circle, scanning the crowd for Ruby Stanley. I was ten minutes late for our ten o'clock meeting, late on purpose, hoping the delay would crack her rock-hard self-control even a little. Behind me was the information desk, strung with Christmas garlands and ably manned by a quartet of uniformed clerks in pillbox caps. Above them, hung two huge timetables, one for arrivals, another for departures, their letters and numbers making a soft slapping sound as they flipped over every time a train puffed in or out of the terminal. From the platform came the squeal of engine brakes and the crack of couplers as the rail cars joined.

The terminal teemed with travelers eager to reach family and friends before the big day. Everywhere I looked, they were standing in lines, sitting on hard oak benches, hauling luggage toward the platforms, or running to catch their train as it pulled out. Shouts of 'Red cap!' and 'Bon Voyage!' and 'Yoo-hoo! Over here!' rang out above the hum of conversation. Dearborn was one of Chicago's busiest rail terminals. It served the Atchison, Topeka, & Santa Fe trains heading west, C&O and Chicago Eastern lines going southeast, Erie trains heading to New York, Grand Trunk lines going to Canada, and a dozen other smaller railroads branching out every which way like spokes from the hub of a great wheel. It would be hard to spot one small older woman in such a noisy throng.

On one side of the immense hall, a lone policeman paced aimlessly past the entrance to a Fred Harvey restaurant, a railroad joint that dished up everything from Blue Plate Specials to a simple cup of coffee. Occasionally someone stopped him to ask a question, and his arm pointed in one direction or another, but for the most part, his was a humdrum beat. Next to the Fred Harvey were ticket counters, waiting rooms, and, until yesterday, two shoe-shine stands which we had moved, just for today, to the opposite side of the terminal near the row of small shops – a candy store, a gift shop, a tobacconist, a news stand, and a flower shop (the only place in the building that didn't reek of smoke from the coal-fired steam engines). More to the point, on this side were the luggage lockers, arranged in three banks jutting out from the back wall like a capital E. That's where we positioned the shoe-shine stand, beside the lockers in a spot that gave the occupants of the two chairs a clear sight line to locker number forty-two.

Where was she? Had she changed her mind? Was she playing the same game I was, arriving late to throw me off balance? If so, it was working. I picked at a cuticle and paced the floor in small circles.

Then I saw her.

She had seen me first. By the time I caught a glimpse of her, she was heading purposefully toward the information desk, a large leather satchel under her arm. Her snow-caked galoshes left a slippery trail in her wake, and her dark eyes fixed on me with a ferocity that called to mind the phrase 'if looks could kill'.

I tried to give as good as I got with my cold greeting. 'Good morning, Miss Stanley.'

She wasn't wasting breath on pleasantries. 'Where is the key?'

I took a gloved hand out of my pocket and dangled the key to locker number forty-two.

She gave it a glance, then looked toward the lockers. Without making a move, she studied the people milling around the locker area, then scanned the shops, and finally turned toward the ticket counters and restaurant, probing for a trap. The cop on the far side of the station caught her eye. I watched her watch him for a full minute before his desultory patrolling seemed to calm her suspicions. He must have looked like a bored cop on routine duty, which is what we intended. No policeman on duty at all, Officer O'Rourke had said, would seem suspicious.

I followed her gaze as she overlooked the crowd. Suddenly, in the distance, I thought I saw a familiar figure coming through one of the doors. One I didn't expect. I squinted to get a clearer look, but he disappeared into the surging sea of travelers. My mistake. I brushed away the thought and dangled the locker key to recapture Miss Stanley's attention.

'Satisfied? It's just me here,' I said. 'And the money. There's safety in a crowd, don't you think? Shall we?'

She gave a curt nod.

I led the way through the throng toward the lockers, careful not to look at the two gentlemen sitting in the shoe-shine chairs. One of them – a good-looking, sandy-haired man in his early thirties – had draped his full-length racoon fur on the coat-tree beside him. A colored boy knelt at the stool, buffing the leather uppers of his brown Oxfords, while the man stared into the bank of lockers, evidently lost in thought as he waited for his train. That was Officer O'Rourke.

In the chair beside him waiting for service was another gentleman, this one with his nose buried in a newspaper so you could barely see his round, red face with skin badly marked by acne or smallpox scars. He was perhaps a decade older than O'Rourke, and he wore a gray Derby that matched his business-man's suit. His suitcase lay on the floor beside him and an old-fashioned, navy blue Chesterfield coat with velvet collar had been thrown over it. This was Detective Kelly, a man I'd met yesterday. He was the detective who had been assigned to the Quillen case once it became a suspected murder. Although originally reluctant to work with me, Officer O'Rourke had persuaded the detective that my plan was the only one likely to snare Miss Stanley. Of course, O'Rourke didn't call it my plan. He presented it as his idea. I didn't mind him taking the credit. Detective Kelly would never have involved himself in this trap if he thought the idea came from a mystic's assistant, and a female one at that.

The colored boy gave a professional slap of his rag to indicate he had finished with O'Rourke's shoe. 'Other shoe, please, sir,' he said.

Detective Kelly rustled his newspaper as we walked past, turning the thin pages and tapping the crease. O'Rourke switched feet. Neither man gave us a glance.

The Dearborn Station lockers were organized from small to large, top to bottom. The smallest would have held a woman's hatbox or her purchases from a day's shopping at Marshall

Field's or Carson Pirie & Scott; the lower ones were large enough for two or three suitcases or even a steamer trunk. I had chosen number forty-two, next to the bottom, because it seemed like the right size for two satchels or briefcases, which is what I imagined Mr Quillen used to carry the stolen cash.

'Carrying more than two cases would have looked very odd,' I told O'Rourke yesterday when we debated about locker selection. 'And I've measured the amount of space that a stack of large denomination bills would take. That amount could have fit into one valise. Certainly into two.' O'Rourke agreed, so we chose the second to bottom row. Number forty-two was on the end of that row nearest the shoe-shine stand. Anyone sitting in those chairs could see locker forty-two quite clearly and, more importantly, hear any conversation that went on between the people standing there. I was reminded of something I'd read the other day in the *Chicago Tribune*'s real estate column. 'All that matters here: location, location, location.'

At the locker bank opposite number forty-two, a man knelt on the floor beside the row of largest lockers, busily repacking clothing from two smaller suitcases into one large one. Lloyd Prescott's back was toward us so Miss Stanley couldn't see his face – she would undoubtedly remember him from his interviews at the bank – but he was positioned so he too could hear every word we spoke. He wore a hat with a wide brim pulled low over his eyes and his coat collar was turned up to hide his jaw. O'Rourke and Kelly hadn't wanted him there, but I'd insisted. 'He took me with him on those interviews with Miss Stanley. If he hadn't done that, I wouldn't have become suspicious about her to begin with. I owe him the return favor. Besides, he'll mention you both by name in his article.'

As Miss Stanley and I wove our way through the crowd toward the lockers, I launched the conversation.

'So, tell me. I'm curious. I think I understand the whole plot, but there's one part I can't figure out. You were counting on the power struggle and confusion from O'Banion's murder to disrupt the North Side Gang's regular bookkeeping practices and leave them in such disarray they would never notice the missing money, and you were partly right. The gang's deliverymen handed over the bags of cash to Mr Quillen, who stepped to the window to accept the deposit in place of the regular teller. He finagled it somehow so that the theft of a hundred thou wasn't picked up by the bank's controls which, as you so often told us, are foolproof. So how did he do it?'

We had arrived at the edge of the locker bank. Her hostile stare remained fastened on my face. She didn't spare a glance for the shoe-shine boy or the man repacking his suitcases or the people walking past us to get to their lockers, nor did she deign to respond to my question. I continued.

'Mr Quillen exchanged the small bills for larger ones – out of sight in the vault, right? And he left the bank with the cash in a couple of pouches or briefcases. His plan was working perfectly so far but—'

'*His* plan? Quillen's plan? How dare you! It was *my* plan – entirely mine! I'm the only one with any brains in that entire bank. That imbecile Quillen couldn't plan his way out of a broom closet. None of them could, but I chose him because he was docile and I thought I could count on him to follow simple instructions. The moron couldn't even do that!'

'He was supposed to take the cash to Harris Bank in the Loop, wasn't he? But something made him change his mind. He brought it here to the Dearborn Station lockers instead. Why was that, do you think? I think he had a change of heart and decided his one-third cut wasn't enough. Maybe he decided that one hundred percent was justified since he was taking all the risk. Maybe he didn't trust you to live up to your agreement.'

'I could sense his betrayal. He was always so easy to read. He should have trusted me. He should have been loyal to me. I'd've kept my side of the bargain if he had been loyal.'

'He should have been loyal to the bank! *You* should have been loyal to the bank. After all those years of employment, how could you and Quillen steal from your employer?'

'How dare you lecture me about loyalty!' she hissed, the venom in her voice cutting through the din. 'For thirty years, I've trained them all, tellers, clerks, accountants, even the presidents. They gave the young men to me and I groomed them for their positions. I taught them everything they needed to know, every damn one of them. They went on to promotions, raises, fat salaries, and respected reputations in the community, and when I dared apply for a higher position, what did they say? "Oh, Miss Stanley, you're too valuable where you are!" "Oh, Miss Stanley, you must understand, none of our clients will deal with a female loan officer." "Oh, Miss Stanley, surely you know that male tellers are a banking tradition." "Oh, Miss Stanley, you must realize, it's just not good for Midwest's professional image to have a woman at that desk." At Midwest, loyalty went one way. I thought Quillen was different.'

'So when you suspected he wasn't sufficiently loyal to you, you killed him.'

'It was his own fault. If he hadn't made me suspicious, he'd be alive today. As you can see, I was right – he did betray me. He didn't follow my plan. Enough of this drivel. Open the door.'

I held up the key, dangling it out of her reach. 'Certainly, Miss Stanley. But you haven't answered my question. How did you bypass the bank's supposed foolproof accounting controls?'

The look she sent me could have curdled cream. 'You think you're so smart because you stumbled onto some information. You think you know it all. You're as stupid as the rest of them. I didn't have to bypass anything. That money never entered the banking system. Quillen counted off the amount we wanted and set it aside. The he made out a deposit slip for the exact amount, less one hundred thousand dollars. One small digit's difference. I have a friend in the North Side Gang who told me their office has been bedlam ever since O'Banion was gunned down. Money was running out the door. Those pencil pushers would never notice the one-digit mistake, or if one of them did, they'd throw the blame onto the bag men.'

'Which they did. Louis Roth. Or if they suspected someone at the bank, you'd have handed them Quillen, I suppose.'

'I didn't need to. I planned his death to look like a gangster's revenge. Or an accident. So shut up and open the damn door and give me my half,' she ordered tersely.

'It was clever of you, slipping him the poison alcohol. It must have been tricky doing it without anyone seeing you. The waitresses said you ate dinner together that night and that you left together afterwards. He died a few hours later. How did you do it? Pour methyl alcohol in his coffee when he wasn't looking?'

'Stupid girl. Anyone would taste that. The simplest solution is always the best. I bought him a drink, a celebratory Tom Collins for each of us. Sally's makes excellent cocktails in the back room. It was easy slipping it in when he stepped away from the table.'

'And he wouldn't taste it in a Tom Collins?'

She regarded me with undisguised scorn. 'You don't know much for a grown woman, do you? Methyl alcohol tastes like regular. That's why it's so dangerous. People don't know they've consumed it until it's too late.'

'One more thing—'

'No, I'm through humoring you. Open the door.' So fast it was a blur, she snatched the key from my hand and leaned over to fit it in the lock. In two seconds there was a resounding click and the door swung open.

Miss Stanley stared into the empty locker.

In the blink of an eye, she plunged her gloved right hand into her coat pocket and pulled out a pistol so small it looked like a toy. Holding it behind the satchel where no one but I could see it, she said, 'I expected no less. You got here first. Where is it? And don't think I won't shoot. No one will hear the sound in here.'

She was probably right about that. No one could see the pistol either, it was so tiny in her hand, and any retort from such a weapon from way over in the locker corner wouldn't stand a chance against the hubbub from the terminal. Thankfully, O'Rourke was tuned in to the sound of her voice. Moving so fast I didn't have time to panic, he came up behind her back and lifted the weapon from her hand with a simple, 'I'll take that.'

Right then, at the worst possible moment, along comes a Mom loaded with Christmas packages, with her kid, a boy dressed in plaid knickers and a matching cap that she must've had to beat him bloody to get him to wear, just as Miss Stanley was reacting to the collapse of her hopes and dreams. They say a cornered animal is the always the most dangerous and Miss Stanley proved the rule. Quicker to react than O'Rourke or Kelly, she charged the mother, who dropped her packages in a crashing mess, and grabbed the youngster, circling his neck with her arm.

'I'll break his neck if you make a move.'

Mom gave a weak cry and sank toward the ground in a graceful faint. Officer O'Rourke, closest to her, instinctively reached out, catching her before she cracked her head on the floor. Detective Kelly wavered. Miss Stanley's ability to break the boy's neck with her bare hands might be highly suspect, but there was always the chance that she could do him serious harm.

The boy didn't wait. In the second it took for the two policemen to weigh their options, he struck out, kicking and flailing and landing a solid blow to her shin with his sturdy shoes. He had almost succeeded in twisting away when Miss Stanley backed into the solid chest of the uniformed cop who had rushed over from the other side of the terminal when he realized what was going on. With little fanfare, he took the gun from her hand and clamped her wrists together with a pair of handcuffs. The lad gave her another kick for good measure before dropping to his knees at his mother's side.

'Ma! Ma!' he cried, shaking her shoulders.

O'Rourke handed the tiny gun to the detective. 'Colt .22 pocket pistol,' he said. 'Wouldn't do much damage normally, but at that range, it could certainly have killed her.'

Meaning me.

As Detective Kelly and the uniformed cop led Miss Stanley off to the paddy wagon, Officer O'Rourke raised Mom up to the nearest shoe-shine chair. There was a small commotion as several people noticed the lady in distress and offered smelling salts and a paper fan. One dashed into the florist shop for a glass of water.

'Billy? Where's my Billy?' she muttered, her eyelids fluttering.

'Right here, Ma. Don't worry, they got that old lady but good.'

'How old are you, Billy?' asked O'Rourke, fanning the mother's face with a printed timetable.

'Ten.'

'You're a brave lad. A good fighter.'

'He has four brothers,' sighed his mother by way of explanation.

O'Rourke took a pencil out of his pocket. 'Let me get your names and address in case we need to call on you later for help.' Billy's face lit up at the prospect.

Meanwhile, on the other side of the bank of lockers, Lloyd Prescott was practically dancing with glee. 'What a scoop! This is the greatest! Come over here, Maddie, and help me get these clothes packed up. I did pretty good, huh? She never noticed me with all my props. What a story this is gonna make! Can't wait to start tapping those typewriter keys. Hey, look over there. Isn't that . . .? Wonder what he's doing here . . .'

THIRTY-THREE

'Who? Where?'

I followed his pointed finger and there, near the information desk, was the man I thought I'd glimpsed earlier, standing stock still, staring at us. When he saw that we had noticed him, he gave a two-fingered salute and melted into the crowd. 'You mean that man in the gray topcoat? That was Liam O'Rourke.'

'What did you say his name was?'

'Liam O'Rourke. William, properly.' I glanced at the shoe-shine stand where O'Rourke was talking quietly to Ma and Billy, wondering if I should be divulging any more information to the reporter. I couldn't see the harm. 'He's Officer O'Rourke's twin brother, although they're not identical.'

'You don't say!' I could see the gears grinding inside his head, and then the lightbulb lit up. 'I get it now! He's here to make sure the locker really was empty.'

'What do you mean?'

A funny feeling crept over me. Once again, Liam O'Rourke was nearby at a critical moment. Another coincidence? Like the time he just happened to run into me on the sidewalk and invited me to his studio. Like the time he just happened along at the Art Institute right after Roth had accosted me on the street – and it just occurred to me, perhaps he had been there to scare off Roth. Like the time he just happened to be on the steps below the Wrigley Building to jump into the river and save my life. How dumb could a girl be? How many coincidences had to happen before I realized I was being shadowed? Had Officer O'Rourke appointed his brother as my secret bodyguard? Were there other times when he had followed me that I hadn't noticed?

'The money, sister. Follow the money. He's making sure the plan to trap the Stanley woman was on the up-and-up. That there really wasn't anything in that locker.'

'Why would he care?' I asked, sensing an answer was coming that I didn't want to hear.

'Because he's part of the North Side Gang.'

'That's not true.'

'Sure it is. He's a torpedo.'

'A what?'

'An enforcer. A hitman. A gunslinger. The only name I've ever heard for him is the Artist. I always wondered if that meant he was artistic in his style of killing or if he liked to sketch posies. Now I know his real name. Thanks, hon.'

'This can't be right. His brother is . . .' I looked around for Officer O'Rourke who had gathered up all Ma's packages and was escorting her and Billy toward their platform. 'His brother's a cop, for Pete's sake.'

Prescott shrugged. 'So what? There's a lot of that in the gangs. One brother's a priest, one's a mobster. One sells cars, the other steals 'em. One's a prohi, the other smuggles booze across the lake. Scratch any gangster and you'll find law-abiding relations. But this Artist fella, you know him?'

'I, uh, well, yes, I've met him.'

'Word on the street has it the Artist bopped that gangster Roth. You know, the one who robbed the bank last week.'

'Roth is dead?'

'As a doornail, sister.'

'I didn't see anything about it in the papers.'

'You will tomorrow. They found his body a couple nights ago with a bullet through his skull, but he was only identified this morning. 'Course no one will ever know for sure who planted the slug, but word is, it was revenge for throwing that woman and her baby in the river. Tried to kill 'em both. Didn't kill the mother, of course, someone fished her out, but the baby's body was never found. No one at the scene identified Roth, or the woman for that matter, but inside the gang they must've known who did it. And gangsters don't take kindly to men who target women and children. They're all a bad bunch, sure, but they have their own code and it forbids killing women and children. Word has it that this Roth fella strayed from the path and paid the price. I'm not crying in my soup.'

Liam O'Rourke was an assassin for the North Side Gang? So he'd been tailing me ever since we'd met, not to protect me as I so briefly fancied, but to follow me to the missing money, just like Roth. He must have assumed I knew where Quillen had hidden it. Or that I would find out.

The betrayal stung. I had liked him. I thought he was my friend. And all along, he was using me. Now I knew the real reason he'd jumped into the river after me – he needed me alive so I could lead him to the money. And all the while, I'd thought . . .

Prescott snapped his suitcases shut with a mighty click. 'Here, you grab this one. I can get the other two and we can get to my car. I'll give you a ride home or wherever you want to go.'

'Sure. Thanks.' It looked like Officer O'Rourke wasn't coming back for me. 'What do you think will happen to Miss Stanley?'

'Sounded like she was the robbery mastermind and Quillen's murderer to boot, but unless I'm missing something, the cops don't have much in the way of hard evidence against her. The four of us can testify to what she said here, but there's no proof that she poisoned Quillen's drink or planned the heist. She could change her story and say that Quillen had done everything. Paint herself as his victim and accuse Roth of killing him. I've seen it done before. Of course, she pulled a gun on you and tried to snatch Billy the Kid, and that won't look good to a jury, but all in all, I'm afraid a shrewd lawyer could beat a murder rap. My money says she'll get off with a prison sentence.'

I shuddered. Miss Stanley seemed like the type to hold a grudge and plan for revenge. 'I hope it's a long one.'

'The mystery of the missing money is still unsolved,' said Prescott. 'Sounds like a case for Sherlock Holmes.' But he looked at me when he said it.

THIRTY-FOUR

It was five o'clock when the doorbell chimed. Carlotta had just retired to her room for her gypsy-queen transformation. I'd finished feeding Tommy his supper of oatmeal and apple-sauce. Freddy was out. I answered it.

Flora Masters smiled at me.

'Do come in,' I said, surprised to see her so early. 'You're welcome to wait in the parlor until our other guest arrives. Can I bring you some tea?'

'Oh dear, am I early? I thought Madame Carlotta said come at five.'

'The séance is at six, but you—'

'I'm so sorry. I'll come back.'

'Nonsense. Come in out of the cold. We can visit while we wait.'

It was to be a small séance with Flora, who wanted to contact her brother's spirit, and Miss Sylvia Greene, a regular who enjoyed communicating with her grandmother. I would fill in if necessary with my tried-and-true widow's routine, but it was seldom required now that Carlotta had become more adept at manipulating clients' expectations.

Flora settled onto the sofa, twisting her gold wedding ring and looking hesitantly about the room. It was clear to me that this was her first séance.

'You needn't be nervous,' I said, holding Baby Tommy on my lap while he sucked his fingers. 'It may be that nothing at all happens. Madame Carlotta may not be able to reach Herman tonight.' Carlotta had tried without success to get Flora to reveal exactly why she wanted to contact her brother. Without knowing what she wanted from him, we couldn't very well make plans.

'Oh, I know. I'm hoping . . . that is, I just want to ask him about his coin collection.'

'What about it?'

'It was so very precious to him, his only real interest in life besides his job and us, his family. I hate to sell it, but I'm not a collector and, well . . .'

They needed the money. 'I'm sure he understands, Flora.'

'But I don't know how to go about it. I mean, who can I trust? If I take it to another collector, what's to prevent him from saying it isn't worth much and short-changing me? I don't want to be cheated. It would be like cheating Herman and he doesn't deserve that. What did you do with your husband's collection when he died?'

That caught me off guard. 'Oh, well, I, uh, I didn't really have the chance to sell any of our belongings because another person – a relative of sorts – claimed everything we owned.'

'You don't say!'

'I'm afraid so. And the law was on her side. It's an unpleasant story . . . But I understand your problem.' And now that I knew her purpose, I could nose around and find the name of a reputable coin dealer and make sure the buyer wasn't in cahoots with the appraiser. Carlotta could reveal that helpful information at Flora's second séance.

Tommy made a gurgling noise that Flora chose to consider conversation. 'Yes, I see you there, little one. You are such a good boy, aren't you?' she said in that falsetto people use when they talk to babies and puppies. 'Didn't you tell me he was born after your husband had passed away?'

'I'm afraid so. Tommy never had the chance to see him, never knew if I was carrying a boy or a girl.'

'That's the same with my youngest. She was born after Edward died. Did you know there's a name for children like that? Posthumous. They're called posthumous children. I think that's sad. I mean, if there's a name for them, it must be something that happens quite often, don't you think?'

Flora's youngest was three, which meant her husband must have passed away about four years ago. 'If you don't mind me asking, how did your husband die?'

'An infected cut. I mean, knife cuts are practically a daily occurrence at the slaughterhouse where he worked, but this one got infected and, well, there wasn't much the doctor could do. We were doing well enough until then. Nothing high on the hog, mind you, but we managed. Herman came to our rescue. He was like a father to the kids.' She gave a great sigh. Defeat had dulled her eyes. 'Sometimes I think I've reached the end of my rope.' In truth, she looked as if she might collapse from exhaustion right there on the sofa. Her face was pale as paper, and her skin was wrinkled like a woman's twenty years older. 'And then, just when I thought things couldn't get worse, I nearly lost my job today. The supervisor warned me I'd taken off as much time as he could permit. He was sorry for my loss but said I needed to get back to work fulltime tomorrow or else. And with Christmas just two days away and with the funeral and the apartment clean out and everything to sell, well, I haven't had the chance to bake anything special or get anything for the little ones from Santa Claus and . . .' She dropped her head in her hands as if to hold back the tears.

I crossed the room to our crooked Christmas tree and picked up the box of candy I'd assembled for Freddy. 'Here, Flora, take this back with you. It's just candy, but it's special candy from a candy store. It's not much, but it's something the kids will like.'

'Oh, I couldn't.'

'Of course you can. I'll get more tomorrow.'

'Well, thank you. You're such a good friend, Maddie. I only met you a couple of weeks ago yet I feel I've known you for years.'

'These are tough times, Flora, but you'll get through them. As soon as you sell Herman's collection, you'll have money to last you a while. What about your sister? In Nebraska, isn't she? Is there anything she can do to help?'

'Becky has a husband and six children, and they don't have much to spare. She's done what she could by giving me her half of Herman's estate. His will left everything to the two of us equally, but she's not taking her half as long as I pay for his funeral. I can't expect her to do more than that.'

I squeezed her hand. 'You're doing a good job, Flora. You're stronger than you think. Now, tell me more about your children. I must meet them one day.'

'Oh, yes, you must!' And soon I knew all about Julia, the little scholar who decorated their apartment with colored paper daisy chains, and Eleanor, who had helped nurse the twin boys through the measles last month, on down the stair-steps to the baby who could count to ten and knew her colors. Like any proud mother, Flora needed little prompting to extol the qualities of her remarkable offspring. We continued in this vein for some time until the doorbell chimed again. I glanced at the clock. Five thirty.

'It must be Miss Greene.' But before I could rise from the sofa, Carlotta swanned down the stairs and into the hall, her shawl trailing dramatically behind her like a monarch's train.

'Stay where you are, Maddie, I'll get the door.'

I heard men's voices, although their words were unintelligible, so I knew it wasn't Miss Greene. 'Excuse me, Flora, would you mind holding Tommy for a moment?'

I deposited him in her eager arms and joined Carlotta in the hall. There were two men, both about my own age, wearing identical bulky overcoats. The shorter man had big ears that stuck out from the closely shaved sides of his head. His hair on top was thick and shiny like he'd brushed it straight up and held it stiff with Vaseline to add a couple of inches to his height. His companion could probably claim average status, but with his pop eyes and wide mouth, he made me think of a frog. Carlotta gestured first to the shorter fella and introduced us. 'This is Mr Henry Earl Weiss and his friend, Mr John Doyle. Mrs Pastore here is one of my regular clients, gentlemen. Now, as I was saying, I'm afraid I can't manage drop-ins tonight. My table is full. But if you'd like to make an appointment for after Christmas, I can suggest—'

The short man interrupted. 'Are you the fortune teller that saw Al Capone last month?'

At that, I grasped who he was. I should have recognized him by his last name and the way both men kept their hands hidden deep inside their pockets. His Christian name may well have been Henry Earl, but all Chicago knew him as Hymie. Hymie Weiss, the sworn enemy of the Capones and the Outfit.

Hymie Weiss of the North Side Gang who had pledged to kill Capone in revenge for the Outfit's murder of his best friend, Dean O'Banion. Hymie Weiss, probably one of the gang who shot my husband over a truckload of booze and left him lying in the gutter to die.

Carlotta raised her chin in haughty protest at the use of the word. 'I'm no fortune teller, Mr Weiss. I am a spiritual medium. As the word suggests, I am the mediation between the living and the dead. I connect people to the spirits of their loved ones.'

'Did you "connect" Capone to somebody last month?'

'I regret to say I cannot discuss my clients' private interactions with their—'

Without another word, Weiss backhanded her across the face. Instinctively I reached out to prevent her from falling to the floor. Neither man so much as glanced at me.

'That didn't answer my question, lady. Try again.'

'Capone was here last month,' I said, answering for her.

Now Weiss gave me the slow once over, head to toe and back up again, as if evaluating my role in this little scene. The mourning dress would have told him I was a widow, but unless he remembered that Pastore was the last name of one of the Outfit drivers his men had shot last spring, I should have looked like nothing more than an insignificant client of Carlotta's.

'When's he coming back?'

'He isn't. The séance didn't go well.'

'You were there?'

'Yes. He left suddenly, very upset.'

Weiss and Doyle exchanged glances. 'Good to know. Now listen up.' He turned back to Carlotta who was dabbing her bleeding lip with a handkerchief. 'You, Gypsy Woman, you get Capone another appointment. Soon. Then you call this number and tell us the day and time. Got it?'

It was a simple plan. As soon as Weiss knew where Capone would be at a certain time, he and his men would lay an ambush. Probably try to gun him down as he came up the steps or hide behind the curtain in the séance room and shoot him during the séance itself. Probably kill everyone else in the room at the same time to eliminate witnesses.

'He won't come,' Carlotta stammered. 'The archangel Michael couldn't find his brother.'

'He was trying to reach that sonovabitch Frank, was he? Well, well, well. So your job is to tell old Scarface that Frank is ready to talk now and get here quick before he flies away on a cloud. Got it?'

She had no chance to respond for at that moment, tires squealed and a volley of gunshots exploded in the pitch-dark street outside. Shouts erupted. Boots pounded the pavement.

Weiss and Doyle pulled guns from their pockets and moved as one into the parlor where Flora was sitting with Baby Tommy on her lap. Dismissing them with a glance, the two men crouched below the windows and carefully peered out.

Carlotta and I dropped to the floor. I was about to shout to Flora to do the same, but she didn't need any orders. With Tommy under one arm, she slid to the floor just as the two gangsters smashed the window glass with their gun butts and began firing wildly into the inky night. Almost as if it had been timed, all the lights in the houses across the street went out. Our neighbors knew enough to bar their doors and hunker down in the dark, hoping the fury would play out fast.

Flora scooted behind the sofa, out of the line of incoming fire. The commotion riled Tommy who began wailing his protests at this rough treatment. I followed on my hands and knees, motioning for Carlotta to come along behind me, but she had disappeared, perhaps down the basement stairs. Before I could reach my baby, more gunfire erupted from behind the house. I lunged the rest of the way.

'Are you all right?' I gasped.

Too terrified to speak, Flora gave a shaky nod. I knew she had no idea what was going on, but this was hardly the time to explain.

'There must be men stationed at the back entrance as well as the front. I hope it's the police shooting at them instead of thugs from the Outfit.' Or the Gennas or any of the other smaller gangs that terrorized the city. If so, how soon could the police arrive?

I could hear bullets striking the house, thankful it was built of brick. An explosion of glass shards told me one had penetrated the parlor window. A shower of plaster dust rained on my head from where it buried itself in the wall. A long minute passed before the gunfire out front stopped; then the back yard went quiet. I thought I heard Doyle say something that sounded like 'Joe's down'.

The next thing I knew, Hymie Weiss was standing over me with his gun. Without a word, he grabbed me by the hair and dragged me up from behind the sofa. I shrieked in pain. He only pulled harder.

'Game's over, Weiss,' called a voice from the street. 'You're surrounded. Come out with your hands up and nobody else gets hurt.'

Doyle snatched Tommy out of Flora's arms. 'Don't hurt the baby!' I begged, but as far as Doyle was concerned, I didn't exist. In any case, he didn't want the bother of a baby, he wanted someone larger for a human shield. He wanted Flora. Throwing my wailing boy on the sofa like a sack of flour, he grabbed Flora just as Weiss flattened himself at the edge of the broken window and shouted back to the gunmen outside.

'Don't shoot! We're coming out. We got a coupla dames with us who gonna get plugged if you don't let us by. Got it?'

No response.

He dragged me to the front door. With his right hand holding the gun, he let go of my hair long enough to fling the door wide and shove me into the doorway, in full view of every armed man out there, just like Roth had done days before at the bank. If anyone was going to shoot, I was a perfect target framed by the door jamb, lit from behind. Time seemed to stop as I waited for a barrage of bullets to tear into my flesh.

'Hold your fire!' called a male voice.

'Let's go, Doyle,' snapped Weiss. 'You drive.'

Down the stairs the two men went, with Flora and me pressed tight against their chests. Weiss, with his arm around my waist and his mouth by my head, smelled like a filthy cigar. He dragged me to one of their sedans parked along the curb in front of our house. A body lay beside it on the sidewalk. I made out several other black Fords with the telltale yellow star on the door and a dozen cops crouching behind them. Chicago police, thank God, not the Outfit. Outfit boys would've shot through me in a second to get at Weiss.

Without warning, Hymie Weiss shoved me to the gutter and climbed into the motorcar. I scrambled to the sidewalk before its wheels could flatten me. With an ear-splitting screech from its rubber tires, the motorcar tore off. I lay on the sidewalk, my right leg throbbing, shaking too hard from fear and cold to move.

Within seconds, friendly hands were helping me up. After one hesitant step, my knee buckled and I collapsed with a cry.

'I've got her,' said a familiar voice, and Officer O'Rourke scooped me up and headed toward the house.

'My baby . . .' I gasped. He'd been screaming to beat the band moments earlier and now I heard nothing but an eerie silence coming from the house.

'Boy's fine. Everybody's fine,' he said, stepping over the dead body on the sidewalk. Over his shoulder he spoke to a pair of medics approaching with a stretcher. 'When you're done with that body, one of you come have a look at this lady's leg.'

Everybody was fine. Everybody who mattered to me, that is. Carlotta was holding a smiling Baby Tommy who watched, fascinated, as uniformed officers milled about asking questions, taking notes, examining the damage, digging slugs out of the back wall. He came to my arms with a happy smile. I squeezed him tight and kissed his peach-fuzz head over and over like I'd never let him go. Flora had been discarded by Weiss's bodyguard at the same time Weiss had thrown me into the gutter; she was sitting on the steps rubbing a bruised shoulder. Over in the corner, Freddy was talking to a cop, saying something about how he was suspicious when he saw the cars pull up and the men get out. Evidently he was the one who had called the precinct station from a neighbor's house.

O'Rourke wasn't the highest-ranking officer on the scene, but he seemed to take charge. 'I'll get some cardboard and cover up those windows tonight, Mrs Pastore. It won't keep the cold out entirely but it'll help. And tomorrow morning someone will come replace the glass.'

'Weiss got away?'

'Yep. No sense in chasing after him. If we'd arrested the guy, his lawyer woulda sprung him in an hour. He shouldn't have left his own territory. North Side cops protect him.' I could hear the disgust in his voice. He didn't like it, but that's the way the gangs worked. Buy off the cops, elect friendly judges, terrorize the juries. Throw the occasional bone to honest law enforcement by turning over any gangster who stepped out of line. The gangs controlled the city, no two ways about it.

THIRTY-FIVE

If the Ghost of Christmas Yet to Come had paid me a visit last year and shown me a picture of my future Christmas – seated in the parlor with the mother of an old schoolfriend reading chess rules to a street orphan – I'd have politely suggested that he was haunting the wrong person. Yet here I was, Christmas morning, with Carlotta rattling pans in the kitchen while Freddy and I puzzled over all the ways you could move a pawn. After our presents were opened and admired and our breakfast consumed, Carlotta took herself off to church.

'I know what we should do, Freddy,' I began. 'Get your coat. It's time for the rest of your chess present.'

'There's more?'

'Someone wants to meet you, and I promised to make the introduction. You'll need to bring your chess board. Come on.'

I was feeling pretty good. It was Christmas. Roth was dead. Definitely dead. Had he been shot by someone from his own gang? Was his murder meant to put the fear of god in anyone thinking about stealing money from the gang's coffers? Or was it meant to demonstrate what happens to killers who kill innocent women and children? What didn't feel too good was the thought that Liam O'Rourke had done the deed.

In ten minutes, we set out on the short walk to Carl's speakeasy, Freddy carrying his board, me carrying Tommy. My sore leg slowed us down, but I was lucky to have suffered nothing worse than a bad bruise, so no complaints from my mouth. Not until we reached Carl's did it occur to me that the place might not be open on Christmas morning.

Fortunately, it was. And there was Carl, presiding from his usual place in front of the bar. He gave me a nod of recognition as we entered and raised himself from his stool to greet us.

'Merry Christmas, Mrs Pastore. So good to see you again, so soon.'

'Maddie. Please call me Maddie. This is Freddy, the young man I was telling you about. I gave him the chess set this morning and we've been reading through the rules book together.' Carl shook hands solemnly with the boy. 'I'm doing my best but I think he would learn faster from a player who knew what he was doing.'

Christmas Day was a holiday for some and, as with any day off, a lot of people flocked to their neighborhood watering hole for fellowship, beverages, music, and games of chance or skill. Freddy gazed about the room with a confused expression creasing his brows, trying to make sense of this peculiar sort of speakeasy where the main attraction was not booze. Carl signaled to a muscular fella with the crooked nose and cauliflower ears of a boxer, who left his table by the fireplace to join us at the bar.

'This is Stephen,' Carl said. 'Freddy here has a Christmas present he wants to learn.'

'I'm your man,' said Stephen, holding out a hand big enough to crush both of Freddy's. 'You got an hour or two to spend, I'll get you started. Send me over a whiskey, Carl, and some Christmas cheer for the boy. What'll you have, kid?'

'Uh, gin rickey, please.' Looking a bit dazed, Freddy followed the man to his table where they began setting up the board. I had nowhere else to be, so I settled into a chair with Tommy on my lap and ordered a gin rickey for myself.

'Care to have an old man for company, Maddie?'

'Delighted.'

Carl poured himself a cup of coffee and joined me at the table.

'I see you got a gimpy leg today.'

'Mmm. A little accident Tuesday.'

'So I heard.'

'It's getting better.'

'I take it the boy liked his chess set?'

'I think so. We'll see if he takes to the game.'

'Nobody better than Stephen to get him started.'

'Thank you for that. We were struggling over the directions in the booklet. Turns out I don't remember much from my childhood.'

'Don't you wanna be over there with him, learnin' too?'

'I think I'll let Freddy teach me after he gets the hang of it. He needs to feel good about himself and teaching somebody something would be a start. Besides, my little man here would distract me from learning anything right now.' He nodded approvingly. 'This is a good place you have here, Carl. I never knew such things as chess speakeasies existed. Is it unique?'

'Hell, no. And we call it a chess club, not a speakeasy or bar. We've been here since before Prohibition. Since 1901. The only difference is that nowadays the drinks are illegal.' And he gave a dry laugh. 'Funny thing, that. How one day these here drinks were legal and after the stroke of a pen, they weren't.'

'I know what you mean. Like when wine's illegal in one place but a not across the street, because it's inside a church.'

'There's other chess clubs in Chicago. Couple I know of on the North Side, one on South Side. It's not as popular as gambling – which is something I don't tolerate in here, by the way, so you needn't fret about young Freddy – but there are other gaming clubs scattered around the city where you can play bridge or mah-jongg all the live-long day if you choose. And collectors' clubs. All of 'em serve liquor or at least beer to pay the bills.'

Something buzzed in my brain. 'Collectors' clubs?'

'Folks who collect things like gettin' together in clubs too.'

'What do they do? Besides drink.'

'Share knowledge, argue, buy and sell. Or just gab with people who like the same things. There's comfort in that.'

'Collect what, for example?'

'Oh, I reckon there's collectors for jest about anything. The most popular are coins and stamps. Like chess, it's something that appeals mostly to men, but there are collectors' clubs for women too. Now the ladies, they mostly collect dolls or silver do-dads and such like. Rich men like to collect antiques, old maps, hell, even automobiles. You name it, there's a collectors' club for it in Chicago somewhere. I gather you're not a collector?'

'I don't have the money. But tell me something. I saw a business card for a place that's called the Collectors' Club. Do you know it?'

'Know of it, sure. Over on the Near North Side. Never been there, but I believe it's for stamp and coin men.'

Herman Quillen was carrying a business card from the Collectors' Club when he died. There was a telephone number on the back. I hadn't thought anything of it at the time, but suddenly, it seemed crucial that I get to that club, the sooner the better. Who did the telephone number reach? Did the business card in his pocket mean he had gone there the day he died? Wouldn't a man empty his pockets of such things at the end of the day? My Tommy always did. Regardless, this was a clue that should have been pursued days ago.

In no time I'd learned the street address for the club, paid Carl for the drinks, waved goodbye to Freddy, and hurried home, where I fed Tommy mashed pears and cream of wheat and set him down for a nap. Then I changed into my most professional looking outfit, a wine-red suit and jacket that hadn't been new for several years, and gathered up my professional-looking accessories. As soon as Carlotta came back from church, the *Tribune*'s unofficial girl reporter hopped a northbound streetcar.

THIRTY-SIX

Chicago's streets were pretty quiet that Christmas Day. The holiday meant streetcars and busses ran less often, but still, I made it to the Collectors' Club in well under an hour in a streetcar I had almost to myself.

You could tell from the outside of the building that once upon a time, the Collectors' Club had been a rich man's house. The huge four-story, white-stone building took up half a city block. Its columned porte cochère, originally meant to shelter guests arriving in their horse-drawn carriages, now welcomed automobiles and taxis. The sidewalks out front had been scraped clean down to the pavement and sprinkled with sand. Each window on each floor had been dressed with a boxwood wreath and the front door was outlined in della Robbia swags. I pulled the cord that made a bell chime deep inside the house, and a prissy butler-type fella creaked open the door to reveal a forest of burning candles behind him, set out on tables and candle-stands and mantelpieces. The strong scent of bayberry seeped into the afternoon air.

'Merry Christmas, madam. May I be of service?'

Unsure of my welcome – did they admit only members? Only men? – I peered into the dimly lit entrance hall with some hesitation.

'Yes, please. I'm Madeleine Duval from the *Chicago Tribune*, doing some legwork for Lloyd Prescott for an article about a man who was murdered a few weeks ago. We're trying to find out where he went the day he died, before he met up with his killer. The man was an avid coin collector, and Mr Prescott thinks he might have been here that day. He was carrying a Collectors' Club business card in his pocket. Is there any way I can find out if he was a member?'

'Certainly, miss,' he said, without indicating the slightest suspicion of my story. 'I have a membership roster at the desk, if you'll follow me.'

He led me through the candles and past a row of Chinese urns on pedestals. White marble busts in niches and portraits of stern men gazed down on me, not unkindly, but I fancied they were wondering why this young woman had invaded their mansion. We stopped at an antique desk where the man pulled a thin morocco volume from a drawer.

'The name?'

'Quillen. Herman Quillen.'

He turned a page and ran his eyes down the alphabetized list. 'Ah yes. Here he is. Herman C. Quillen, member since 1916.' He snapped the book shut. 'Does that help?'

'Very much, sir,' I said, rather surprised. My track record in persuading people to answer my questions hadn't been the best of late. This man's eagerness was refreshing. I chalked it up to my girl reporter ploy. 'Thank you. And now, is there any way to tell if he was here on November twenty-seventh?'

Without speaking, he set the morocco book down and pulled out a leather volume so heavy he had to lay it on the desk to open it. 'This ledger is our record of who visited the club each day. Members sign in when they arrive. November twenty-seventh you said?' And flipping back several pages, he arrived at the right place. Peering over his shoulder, I watched as his finger traveled along the list of names until it stopped at the second from the bottom. I recognized the handwriting.

'There. Herman Quillen. What does that tell you?'

That I'd found the money.

My excitement rose. Quillen had visited the Collectors' Club on his last day alive. What if, instead of returning to Harris Bank with the cash as planned, he'd brought it here to hide instead? What if he'd sensed Ruby Stanley was going to double-cross him and decided to double-cross her first by hiding the money where she wouldn't find it? If he left it here, where would it be? I needed to find a reason to have a look around.

'Excuse my poor manners, sir. I didn't get your name for Prescott's article.'

'Abbott. Allen Abbott with two Ls, two Bs, and two Ts. I've been working here for ten years as the official receptionist.'

'You must know everyone, then. Did you know Mr Quillen personally? A man of average build, middle-age, spectacles, toothbrush mustache, with hair combed over the bald spot?'

He gave it serious consideration, then shook his head. 'We have six hundred and forty-two members as of today. Some come in often, every few days or every week. Some of those I know by name, but some don't come in at all or maybe just once a year. Tell me about this Mr Quillen.' Ah, a man interested in crime solving. I could use that.

I gave him an abridged version of the story: how the police found the banker's body in an alley, how the coroner ruled he'd died from drinking wood alcohol, how the police believed the mob was involved. 'Probably the North Side Gang,' I said. His eyes lit up as I continued. 'Lloyd Prescott is trying to reconstruct Quillen's movements on his last day to see if that gives us some clue to his killer. I wonder, Mr Abbott, I see you have a telephone at your desk. I wonder, could I make a quick call? I want to call Mr Quillen's sister, who might have something to add here.'

'Allow me, miss.' He reached for the candlestick telephone. 'What number shall I dial?'

'Calumet 5-6969, please.'

He completed the dial and handed me the receiver. Flora Masters answered on the second ring. Of course she was home – it was Christmas Day.

'Hello Flora. Maddie here.'

'What a lovely surprise! Merry Christmas, Maddie.'

'And a very Merry Christmas to you and the children. Listen, I was wondering, do you still have your brother's personal effects from the coroner's office? You haven't thrown them away, have you?'

'Heavens, no! I'd never do that.'

'Good. Well, can you find that business card from the Collectors' Club?'

'Wait a sec. I'll be right back . . . Yes, Maddie, I have it here.'

'There was a telephone number on the back, wasn't there? Would you read it to me?'

'Two, eight, two, seven, three, five.'

'Read it again, please. There's something missing.'

'No, that's all there is.'

'Are you sure?'

'Quite sure. Six numbers.'

A telephone number had seven digits and the first two were letters that stood for the exchange name, as in CA for Calumet or SU for Superior. Something was amiss. It must not be a telephone number after all. Why had I jumped to that conclusion in the first place? I'd glanced at the back of the card, seen a string of numbers, and supposed it to be a telephone number. Obviously a hasty assumption.

'Something's wrong, Flora. I don't think it's a telephone number after all.' What could it be? Perhaps nothing related to the Collectors' Club, perhaps the card was simply a handy place to jot down a few numbers Quillen needed to remember. But he was here on his last day and he must have picked up the card then, so the number *had* to relate to the club.

'What else could it be, Maddie?'

'I don't know, but I'll call you back as soon as I have any ideas.'

Mr Abbott could tell I was disturbed from the scowl on my face. 'What can I do to help? Would you like to look around the club? I can leave my post for a few minutes. Would that help?'

'It might. I'm looking for something that relates to a string of six numbers. Can you think of anything, like files or membership numbers or something? Two, eight, two, seven, three, five.'

'Or maybe twenty-eight, twenty-seven, thirty-five.'

'For that matter, it could be two hundred eighty-two and seven hundred thirty-five. And so forth.'

As we mused over the arrangement of the numbers, Abbott led me on a tour of the old mansion that had been turned into a swank club some thirty years earlier. 'The main bar is through here,' he said, holding open the door to a darkened room where mahogany paneling and polished brass put me in mind of a fancy ocean liner. A score of businessmen lounged on leather chairs, the low hum of their conversation blending with the gentle music from a player piano in the corner. Behind the bar were glass shelves stocked with expensive liquor, mostly imports from Ireland, Scotland, and Canada. No bathtub gin for this crowd! We peeked into several empty rooms where Abbott said the American Numismatic Society and the American Philatelic Society held their weekly meetings, then headed up the grand staircase to the second floor.

'This is the main library, the reason most people join the club. It's the finest library of its kind in the country,' he said proudly. That was something I could believe, seeing the hundreds – no, thousands – of books and journals on shelves reaching so high you had to climb a narrow ladder to reach the top.

It was quieter in here than in the bar, as most men – and two women, I noticed – were reading or conversing in whispers as they pored over their own coin albums or glycine pages of stamps, bartering for new acquisitions or admiring what others had. Magnifying glasses were never more than an arm's length away, and a microscope sat on a table by the window where the light was good. Any one of the cupboards and drawers built into the exterior wall would have been large enough to hold Quillen's stash of banknotes, but I couldn't imagine someone could hide anything in those places, not with so many people around and no visible locks or security. To be certain, I opened the doors of a few cupboards only to find stacks of magazines or newspapers or boxes of extra lightbulbs.

'That side of the library contains the publications about coins; this side is all about stamps. Everyone specializes.'

'Specializes how?'

'Some people collect only Roman coins, for instance, or even just Roman coins of one particular emperor. Others collect stamps from Brazil or stamps from the last century or stamps with animal themes. And it's here that they learn and trade and buy and sell.' I could feel the energy percolate through the room as collectors negotiated back and forth over what would perhaps become a prized Christmas gift. Several heads turned as we walked through, but no one seemed overly curious about my presence. As long as I was with Mr Abbott, I was acceptable.

'Mr Quillen was a coin collector,' I said. 'I never saw his collection, so I don't know his specialty. I can ask his sister. She wants to sell his collection now that he's gone. I suppose this is the best place for her to do that?'

'Most definitely. I can give you a few names of members who appraise collections. Then we can introduce her to the Marketplace service. Now this way, up here on the third floor is our ballroom. A New Year's Eve gala is scheduled for next week. We expect five hundred people.' I tried to visualize five hundred people in this cavernous space, dancing, chattering, listening to the band play from the stage. With a kitchen and some storage rooms on one side and rest rooms in the corners, there was nothing I could see that could possibly be connected to six-digit numbers.

'The top floor is just offices, lockers, and storage. Do you want to go up there too?'

Lockers?

'You have lockers? By all means, let's have a look. Are they numbered?'

'Naturally, but there aren't two-hundred-and-eighty-two-whatever-thousand of them.'

And I had no key. All the keys Herman Quillen possessed had been accounted for.

'Still, let's go.'

THIRTY-SEVEN

Never mind the offices and storage rooms, I made straight for the bank of lockers covering the entire north wall. Large, identical gray-metal lockers, forty across and five down, had been bolted into the wall decades ago. They numbered from one on the top left to two hundred on the bottom right. Almost every one of them had a padlock dangling from its latch. And every one of those was a combination padlock.

Eureka!

But where to start?

'Do you have a list of who is using each locker?' I asked Allen Abbott.

'I'm afraid not.'

'You don't know which member is using which locker?'

'We don't keep a record of that. On purpose. For security reasons. Some of our members store their most precious collections here.'

'I think Mr Quillen put something in one of these lockers. I think that six-digit number is his combination. Is there a master key or master combination that opens them all?'

The man shook his head sadly. 'You've got to understand, these lockers are for members who want to store their valuable collections in utmost security, in a place outside their own homes. They are safe here, safer than in any bank vault. Everyone supplies his own lock so there can be no other way to get in.'

'Is there a telephone on this floor?' I asked, hardly able to contain my excitement. He led me to an office with a new style dial telephone on the desk, and I dialed Flora Masters again, direct.

'Flora? Maddie again. The Collectors' Club card, is there nothing else on it? Another number somewhere? On the front side, maybe?'

'No, Maddie, nothing else. Just the numbers two, eight, two, seven, three, five. What is it? What have you found?'

'Another set of lockers, this time at the Collectors' Club on the Near North Side. They're combination locks, however, which means that the numbers your brother wrote on the back of that card are almost certainly the combination to one of them. Trouble is, there are two hundred lockers in front of me and no way to know which was his. I'll have to work through them all, one by one. Can you come?'

'Holy moly. I'll get there as soon as I can.'

I turned my back on Allen Abbott and spoke to Flora more softly. 'Bring your brother's collection. At least some part of it. Take a cab.' She didn't waste time asking why.

After I'd cradled the receiver, I turned back to Abbott. 'Mr Quillen's sister will arrive shortly. Could you show her up here as soon as she comes? I'm going to get started testing these locks.'

'Sure thing, miss. When she gets here, I'll bring her up. Maybe I can stay a while to help.'

That's exactly what I didn't want. If we should find the money, I didn't need anyone else around to blab about it. What was it Al Capone told me once? 'Three can keep a secret if two of 'em are dead.' Allen Abbott seemed like a nice man, but if he knew about the money, even if he was completely honest, word could leak out and spread to someone in the North Side Gang. The slightest hint of found money would bring Hymie Weiss and Bugs Moran with guns blazing. Baby Tommy's godfather would be no protection at all.

I'd think of a plan to sideline Allen Abbott later, after Flora arrived. For now, I sat on the floor, my injured leg stretched inelegantly out to one side, and started at the bottom row, left-hand lock. Combination: twenty-eight twenty-seven thirty-five.

I was thirty-one lockers along when Flora showed up, dressed in trousers and a large sweater I took for one of her brother's. I made no comment – at least she'd be comfortable crouched on the floor or up on a step stool. Allen Abbott escorted her to the top floor, then he excused himself.

'Wish I could help you, ladies,' he said with a crestfallen expression, 'but I can't leave my post right now. Let me know if you need me for something. I'll be by the front door, like always. Good luck!'

I watched him go with considerable relief. As long as he thought we were looking for a coin collection, he posed no threat.

Flora fished a case of her brother's antique coins out of her large handbag. 'Why did you want these?'

'If we open a locker and find any cash, we'll want to leave something else in here that we can say we've found. Something that isn't cash. The last thing we need is for Hymie Weiss to hear about you or me finding any missing money.'

'I sure as heck don't wanna see him again. Well, look. Here's Herman's card. See? There are only six numbers, like I said.'

'I didn't doubt you for a minute, Flora. But look, you said this was a seven.' I pointed to the fourth numeral. 'It looks like it might be a one. My Canadian father made his ones like this, like they do in France. Europeans make their sevens with a slash through the stem. Do bankers write their sevens like that?'

She peered at the numbers. 'No, I'm sure Herman was making a seven here.'

But it made me nervous. 'I think it's best when we test the combinations to also test that as a one. It'll take a little longer, but no one's pushing us out of here.'

'Whatever you say, Maddie. You're in charge.'

'Each lock needs to be tested twice, just to make sure we don't accidentally miss a number by one click. And then a third time with a one in place of the seven. You'll notice that a few of the padlocks have rotating discs with four numbers – we can skip those. Why don't you start on the third row up with number forty-one?'

And so we worked our way along our respective rows,

growing ever more discouraged as the combination failed, one after another, to open a single door.

'This *has* to be right!' I muttered. 'It just has to be one of these! There simply aren't any other possibilities.'

And it was right, for finally, at locker number fifty-six, Flora gave a squeal as the padlock fell open in her hand. Inside were bundles and bundles of banknotes, one hundred thousand dollars in all, I presumed. Spiders and mice didn't give me vapors and I had never swooned in my life . . . nonetheless, an attack of lightheadedness left me feeling woozy. I sank to the floor.

Flora's jaw dropped at the sight. 'Oh my god,' she breathed. 'So Herman did steal the money. I never really believed he would do such a thing. I thought . . . He wasn't a bad man, Maddie. Not at all.'

'He and Ruby Stanley concocted a plan to siphon off this money from the North Side Gang's deposit before it ever reached the bank's books. He probably didn't think of it as stealing since it was gang money taken from illegal gambling and bootleg liquor and such. Just like most people don't think drinking is bad. They were going to split the dough but Miss Stanley wanted it all, and she poisoned your brother without realizing that he hadn't stashed it at Harris Bank as they'd planned. He must have suspected she was going to double-cross him and brought it to the club locker instead.'

'Oh, poor Herman. Oh, dear, whatever will I do now? We must take this to the police.'

'Listen, Flora, your brother wanted you to have this money. He wanted to help you and the kids. If you turn it over to the police, it will disappear from the evidence room, I guarantee it. And do you really want to give it back to the North Side Gang? You think Hymie Weiss would thank you for it? I don't want your brother to have died for nothing. This is your money. But you can't keep it and stay here in Chicago.'

'What are you saying?'

'I've been thinking . . .' I had given it some thought, in case this very thing should happen, and I believed I had come up with a surefire plan. 'Take some of this money with you today. As much as you can stuff in your handbag. Let people know that you and the kids are leaving Chicago and moving to

Milwaukee. Pack up and go – tomorrow if you can. When you get to the train station, buy tickets for your sister's town, Lincoln, Nebraska, wasn't it?' She nodded. 'Don't tell a soul. Not even the kids, not until you get on the train, and then when you get to Lincoln, check into a hotel for a few days while you find a house to buy. A nice house. A big house. Pay cash. Open accounts in two different banks for a few thousand dollars but leave most of it in a safe deposit box, so no one knows you have as much money as you do.'

'But how will I explain to my sister about buying a house?'

'You say the money came from your late husband's father who died last month and left you a modest legacy. Like five thousand or some number that won't arouse suspicion. Come back here in a month or so and get the rest. And sell Herman's coin collection when you come, so they think that was what he had stored in his locker. Abbott will help you get in touch with some appraisers and buyers. You can tell your sister the coin collection brought a lot of money and buy her family a house too. How does that sound? Can you do that? For Herman.'

Flora squared her shoulders. 'I can. But, oh, Maddie, carrying so much money around scares me.'

I knew the feeling. It had happened to me right after Tommy's death, when I carried almost a thousand dollars in my purse to the bank to deposit in our account, only to see it snatched up later by *her*. 'I know. It seems like everyone is looking at you, like they all know you're carrying a fortune, unprotected and alone. But no one knows. You just have to tough it out, Flora. You need to be tough for your children. This will give them the life your brother wanted them to have. Julia can go to high school, college even. Jeannie can go to blind school. You won't have to work a lousy switchboard job. You can help your sister's family. Don't lose courage.'

Without another word, she straightened her back and began stuffing packets of bills into her purse until it bulged. Then she looked at me. 'Here, take some. You've earned it. I wouldn't have this without you.'

A nobler person might have refused. I put several packets into my purse and dropped one more down the front of my blouse. I could buy a house too.

Really, what else could I have done? Return the money to Weiss? Give it to the crooked cops? Flora Masters would tell no one, and neither would I. Two people could keep a secret if both of them were smart. Lloyd Prescott's Mystery of the Missing Money would have to remain unsolved.

In spite of my bold words, the thought of carrying that much cash made me nervous too. Instead of taking the bus or streetcar home, I had Abbott call each of us a taxi. When I got back to Carlotta's, I came in the back door and found her sitting in the parlor with Freddy, drinking tea and eating some of the bûche de Noël I'd baked the day before. To their chorus of 'Where have you been?' I answered, 'Earning some money.'

Before I could reveal my windfall, Freddy leaped up off the floor. 'Wait 'til you see what came while you were gone. Quick! Look! It's in the hall.'

There by the front door was a shiny new baby buggy. 'What . . .? How did you . . .? Where . . .?' I sputtered. How had they ever found the money?

'It's from Officer O'Rourke and his brother. To replace the one you lost.'

Such unexpected generosity (and from such an unexpected source) temporarily knocked me speechless. When I could assemble my thoughts, I managed to say, 'It's lovely. How kind of them.' As I stroked the gleaming metal handle and raised and lowered the bonnet, I realized the implications for Freddy. 'I'm very grateful for this, but nothing could replace the one you gave me, Freddy. I'd swap this one for yours any day of the week. That was the best gift I could have had.'

The lump of banknotes inside my blouse brought me back to earth. I took the packets out of my purse and laid them in Carlotta's lap.

'Here's another Christmas present. I think this will be enough to pay your brother-in-law for the house.' I explained with as few details as possible the origins of the money. With trembling fingers, Carlotta counted the bills.

'Is it enough?' I asked anxiously.

'More than enough. But this isn't right, Maddie. It's your money. The house should be in your name.'

'I can't buy the house. Capone knows I don't have any money.

It wouldn't take much imagination on his part to figure out that I found the missing North Side Gang money.'

'Then . . .' Her gaze drifted to Freddy. 'Then it could be in Freddy's name.'

Freddy's eyes grew round as saucers, and I know I saw him flinch. Home ownership was not something he wanted to tangle with.

I shook my head. 'Good idea but he's too young. You have to be eighteen to own property. No, Carlotta, you're the only one.'

'Where should I say the money came from?'

I'd given this some thought on the way home. 'Your daughter in California. She and her husband have become quite rich and she sent you the money as soon as she learned you needed it.'

Carlotta looked thoughtful for several moments as she assessed the believability of this story. At last, unable to find any flaws, she nodded. 'That sounds possible. I'll telephone my brother-in-law at once.'

The mention of the telephone brought to her mind another call. 'Oh, and Maddie,' she said. 'I had a ring just an hour ago from a Mrs Frank Baylor who wants to bring her cousin to contact the spirit of their late grandfather. General Ramsey Templeton, his name was. A Civil War general. I scheduled them for January the third.'

'I thought you weren't taking any reservations for after January first? You didn't know we could stay in this house until this very minute.'

'But I did, dear. The archangel Michael told me all would work out, so I began taking reservations again yesterday. He's never wrong.'

AUTHOR'S NOTE

So how did a historian specializing in colonial Virginia wind up in the Roaring Twenties? Easy. The 1920s is the most fascinating and innovative decade in American history, offering a mystery writer infinite possibilities for murder and mayhem plus access to the weirdest people and most incredible events imaginable. People living in that decade experienced amazing highs (women's rights, silent movies, vaudeville, jazz, and the spread of wondrous new inventions like radio, electric appliances, and motorcars) and depressing lows, notably the misery of Prohibition with its corruption, gangsters, bootleggers, and the Ku Klux Klan. Beats the Articles of Confederation of 1777, right?

I have to admit, historians are compulsive about getting details right, which explains why I feel compelled to let you know where my facts stray into fiction. My main characters – Madeleine Duval Pastore, Madame Carlotta Romany, Freddy, and the O'Rourke brothers – are fiction, but the bad guys – Johnny Torrio, Al Capone, Dean O'Banion, Bugs Moran, and Hymie Weiss – were very real and if anything, more deadly than this story makes out. Only Torrio managed to 'retire' from the mob and die of old age; the others were gunned down in the proverbial barrage of bullets while in their twenties or thirties, save for Capone who died of syphilis after serving a long prison sentence. It's not hard to understand the motivation for such violence when you understand that the Torrio/Capone Outfit *alone* grossed about seventy million dollars each year – the equivalent of around one billion in today's money. Each year.

The Roaring Twenties also brought interest in the occult to its highest level. Mystics, fortune tellers, mind readers, hypnotists, Tarot readers, astrologers, ESP practitioners, Ouija board players, and spiritualists flourished. Spiritualism, a quasi-religious movement that began in the 1840s and peaked in the 1920s, had millions of followers. Many (all?) of the practitioners were frauds, and the great magician Harry Houdini set out to prove it by offering ten thousand dollars ($150,000 today) to any genuine spiritualist who could contact the dead. As a magician, he was always able to expose their fakery, so no one ever claimed the reward. His book, *A Magician Among the Spirits*, published in 1924, reveals many of their tricks. As you can imagine, this was a great help to me in describing Madam Carlotta's séances. Houdini's book is still available if you want to read about his success in exposing the frauds.

Don't think Maddie was a bad mother – one hundred years ago baby care standards were different. Things she does, like putting little Tommy on his stomach to sleep or leaving him propped up on the sofa where he might roll off are discouraged today. But the most surprising thing she does is use a kiddie coop. This is a wood-framed, six-sided cage, each side with wire screens, about the size of a steamer trunk. These were popular with mothers through the 1950s. I clearly remember the light blue one my grandmother used for my father back in the 1920s – for all I know, they used it for me too. You can see a picture of a kiddie coop and other pictures of the people and places in this story if you look on my Pinterest page. https://www.pinterest.com/mmtheobald/the-mystics-accomplice/

Writing books is a collaborative endeavor. I would like to thank Jeff Lacker, former president of the Federal Reserve Bank of Richmond, for steering me to some historical sources for banking practices in the 1920s. *Standard Banking* (1924) and *The Businessman and his Bank* (1920) proved helpful, although I can't recommend them for entertaining reading. I would also like to thank Margaret Miley and Marilyn Mattys for their valuable help in plotting and critiquing the first draft. Do let me hear from you; I'm on Facebook and can be reached most easily by email: mmtheobald@gmail.com.